HYPOCRITE'S ROW

HYPOCRITE'S ROW

THE ADVENTURES OF NATE MORAN

ELIOT KLEINBERG

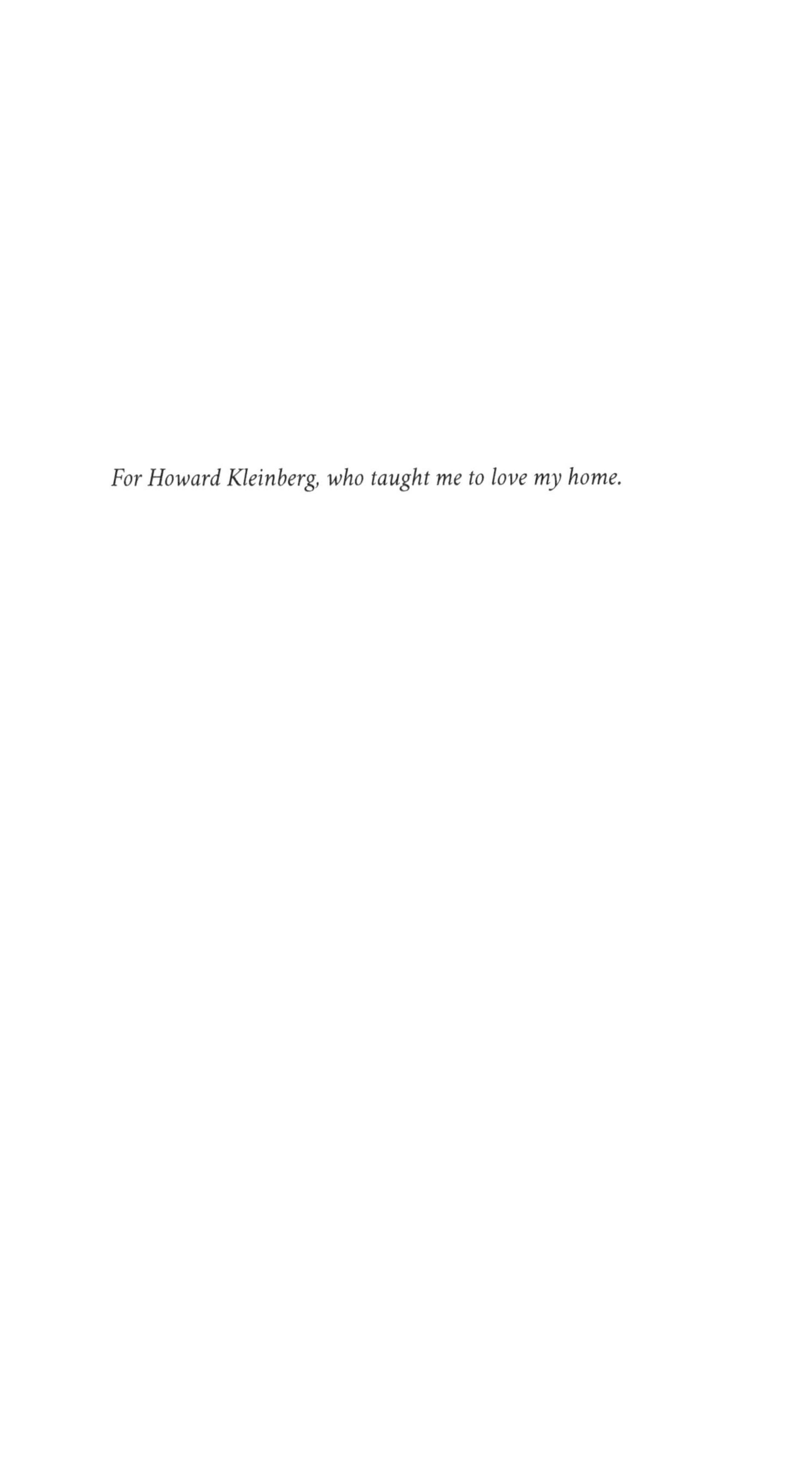

For Howard Kleinberg, who taught me to love my home.

"South Florida probably flouted Prohibition more than any other part of the country. We were called the leakiest place in the country."

— Miami historian Paul George

Contents

Praise for Hypocrite's Row

"Overall, this is an accomplished, well-written period crime novel with strong characters, authentic detail, and an engaging plot. This will be an excellent addition to the historical mystery genre. The moral complexity, especially regarding Prohibition enforcement and police conduct, gives the book depth beyond typical procedurals."—**The publisher**

Chapter One: A Search Warrant

The roadster lurched to the corner. Kicked-up gravel on the unpaved street shot up dust that swirled like fog, then settled.

Bailey Monk opened the driver's door. On the other side, Fred Paxton stretched a Florsheim and stood.

Monk was a six-foot-three, two hundred and sixty-five-pound bull. His partner: A beanpole. Both men's suits were wrinkled from the car seats and the July heat.

The neighborhood looked like a checkerboard. A house, a lot, a house being built, a lot, a house. It being a Saturday evening, streets were empty. Most folks were trying to stay cool by drinking lemonade in their backyards. Some were out looking for hooch.

That's why all Monk heard was the gravel crunching under his sole and the hiss of his engine cooling.

His piece was holstered on his hip. The Prohibition agent had just one thing in his hand: A piece of paper. He silently motioned Paxton to the back of the house. He stepped on the porch and stood at a wire screen door. Behind it: A wooden door with a glass pane at around eye level.

He was out of the sun. But the back of his neck was dotted with sweat. He pulled a hanky from his back pocket. He felt like he was under water. It had rained. Heck. In South Florida, in the summer, it rains every afternoon. Pours for about forty-five minutes. Then stops, like a closed faucet. Then it's a steam bath.

He brought the hanky around his neck and wiped his face. Then he banged on the wooden front door.

Noises inside.

Mark Gregg pushed open the screen door and stepped onto the porch. From behind him. stifling, hot, stale air drifted out and hit Monk's nose.

A hairy pot belly pushed out the bottom of Gregg's white undershirt. Black circles darkened it under the armpits.

The two men eyed each other.

The agent held out the document. His thick, damp fingertips stuck to a corner.

"Gregg, I have a federal search warrant."

Gregg just said, "Nope." He stepped back and slammed the wooden door.

Monk's wide face turned as red as a tomato. Enough of this baloney. He jerked the screen door open.

The wooden front door shattered just below the glass pane.

Out back, Paxton heard the blast. He pushed through the rear door and smelled gunpowder and hot metal. And gore. Up ahead, he saw Gregg in the living room, looking out the front. Haze hung at the man's head.

"Look out, Mark! Back of the house. He's going to shoot you!" It was Gregg's wife.

Gregg wheeled and saw the profile of Paxton in the kitchen, a hand reaching for a sidearm. Gregg swung the shotgun up and fired. Paxton dropped.

Shelley Gregg's eyes rolled and her thin body crumpled. Mildred, just behind her, bent and pulled her up a staircase, bumping her limp body at each step. Gregg helped his daughter half-carry, half-drag Shelley.

Dead silence.

Gregg heard Shelley breathe steadily. Heard Mildred sob. Heard his chest thump. He could swear he heard dust settle.

A dim whine. It grew louder and ended in a squeal of brakes. Through the walls, Gregg would have seen a Ferguson ambulance out front. And behind it, a Miami Springs police car.

Chief Mark Franks, on the porch, knelt beside Monk. He saw the warrant lying in his friend's blood. He stood and stared through the jagged hole in the door.

"Mark Gregg."

Nothing.

Then, muffled, from inside: "Come upstairs, Chief."

Franks pushed open the shattered door. He stepped over shards of wood and glass. The inside heat washed over him. Paxton was back in the kitchen. Not moving.

Each step was silent. But the chief's ears roared.

He came to the stairs and slowly climbed. Above, in the shadows, Gregg kneeled behind a rail. With each of the chief's steps, more of Gregg came into view. The man held a shotgun, muzzle up.

"Gimme, Gregg."

"Nope."

"C'mon, Gregg."

"Chief, people I didn't know were breaking into my home. I was defendin' it."

"Gregg, you come down, everything's jake, and you get your day in court. You don't come down, we gotta do what we gotta do, and there's more of us. You know how that'll end up. And in front of your wife and kid."

In the kitchen, Fred Paxton half-sat, half-leaned, his .45-caliber pistol beside him. A patrol officer had slipped in through the back door. He dropped to a knee. He pressed against the door jamb and shouted out to the backyard, "He's still alive!" He grabbed Paxton under the arms and dragged him out. Other cops helped carry him to the ambulance. Its doors slammed, and it raced off.

At the stairs, Gregg and the chief never had broken their locked eyes.

Out front, neighbors stood in yards, their lemonades losing chill. They pointed at the stiff on the porch. They didn't know it was a cop. A lot of 'em didn't know who lived in the house. People moving here too fast.

Someone pointed.

Chief Franks came out from around back. He had hold of Mark Gregg's elbow. Franks led him to a patrol car. An officer held the top of Gregg's head and pushed him inside. The door slammed. The car made a U-turn. Franks watched it race off and turn a corner. The dust it had picked up on the gravel road swirled like fog. Then it settled.

Franks looked up at the sky. His right hand balled into a fist. He slammed it on the hood of his roadster. Again. And again.

"Damn! Damn! Damn! Damn!"

The patrol cop who'd pulled out Paxton looked at Franks, the toughest guy he'd ever known, except for his own father. The chief sniffled and wiped the corners of his eyes. He motioned at the porch, where his old friend lay on his back on bloody slats.

"Monk."

The patrol cop knew Monk. He waited.

The chief let out a big breath.

"What a mess. I knew it would come to this. I knew it!"

The cop could see the chief's fists still were clenched.

Franks looked down the street, like magically Bailey Monk would pull up and step out, wearing a big grin. He took another big breath.

"Who's gonna tell Sandra?"

That would be me. I'm Nate Moran.

Chapter Two: Monk

I've worked for Miami police since I was fresh out of Miami High. The usual crimes are bad enough. But in the past few years, we had people pouring in to buy every inch of the place. When that kind of money flies around, crime comes with it. And messy crime.

And that's nothing compared to the booze people. Down here, Prohibition is just a suggestion. Things get wild. And people get killed. Sometimes cops.

Shadows stretched across the porch of Bailey Monk's home. Wood frame. White. Like most of the houses here.

The sun was below the horizon, and the sky was more than gray. Miami still was hot as Hades. Inside my suit, sweat rolled down my back.

I heard Sandra Monk walking around inside.

I hate this. I hate this. I hate this.

Bailey Monk and his wife and twelve-year-old kid lived close to us. They'd been in Miami since a year after Prohibition started.

Florida's next to a big ocean. A boat can get to the Bahamas in a few hours. And there are plenty of places in the Everglades to build a still. And plenty of eateries have big oak doors to hide speakeasies. And plenty of hotels have secret party rooms where tourists and high rollers will pay whatever it takes to have a snort. All Prohi has done down here is benefit the crooks.

And it's hell for the enforcers. I wouldn't have Bailey Monk's job for all the moolah in Miami. A lot of goons would be happy to see him in the morgue.

Damn. They got their wish. My friend.

I took off my fedora and gripped its brim hard, which rubbed sweat into it.

I sure could use a cig. Every time this happens, I have to remind myself that I quit.

I used my right hand to knock. The door flew open. Sandra looked at my grimly set mouth. A second passed. She knew. Her eyes rolled. Her knees went soft, and she sat. Hard.

I went to one knee. Sandra buried her face in my shoulder. The sobs went on for a while. She hiccupped. She wiped her nose on my sleeve. I didn't care.

I barely heard her. Her voice came out as a croak.

"How? When?"

I crouched awkwardly, and the back of my right leg had cramped. I could handle it. This lady just lost her husband.

I heard a noise. Nancy. From across the room, the girl saw her mom, then me. She clapped her hand to her mouth. She screamed so loud my ears rang. She ran to us and dropped and threw herself around her mother.

Screaming. Sobbing. Moaning. I held both of them for a long time. My cramped leg hurt like hell. I didn't move.

After a few minutes, I was able to extricate myself and stand. I rubbed the cramp. Sandra and Nancy stayed on the floor, still clutching each other. Still sobbing.

A shadow caught my eye. The open doorway. I tensed. But it was a middle-aged woman in a plain olive house dress, her graying hair in a bun. She'd raised her white apron to her mouth and wept silently into it.

I slid out my badge. I said, nearly in a whisper, "I'm Nate Moran. Miami PD."

The woman wiped her runny nose with the apron and let it drop. She said quietly, "I'm Mrs. Grimsby. I live next door. I—I heard the scream."

I motioned, and we stepped onto the porch.

"Monk's bosses knew I knew the family, and they asked if I'd...let them know."

The woman had steeled. Her voice was steady. "I'll stay with them."

"They're shook up."

She wiped her nose. Took a deep breath.

"When…when…when the Spanish Flu came, it took my Timmy. Just fourteen year old. And me already a widow. I thought a house had fell on my head. Sandra was there. I prayed I'd never be in a place to pay her back. But I knew the kind of job Bailey did."

She looked down at the mother and daughter, still sobbing, still clutching. Then back at me. Her eyes were clear.

"I'll stay. You go get the animal who done this."

The two of us gently helped up mother and daughter and led them to their sofa. They wouldn't let go of each other.

"Sandra, Mrs. Grimsby will stay with you for a while."

Sandra gasped and hiccupped and lifted a sleeve to wipe snot from one nostril. Her red eyes were swollen nearly shut. I handed her my hanky. She blew her nose. She asked again.

"How? When?"

There was no way around it.

"Miami Springs. He was serving a search warrant."

Sandra Monk looked into my face, questioning. I said, "The guy's in jail."

I saw in her face a loss that might soften in time. But it never goes away. Ever. I barely heard her. She spoke not at me, not even at herself. Just to the ether.

"How can I go on living? How can I go on living?"

She hiccupped and gulped again.

"Other women lose their husbands. But not such a husband."

I leaned and hugged mom and daughter around their necks. I stood and mouthed to Mrs. Grimsby, "Thank you."

I walked the few blocks home. I met the Missus at the door. The two of us had a good cry.

"How's she doing?"

"She's a wreck, Hon. The kid, too. A neighbor's with them. A real angel."

Charlotte Harper's green eyes filled again. "I am such a heel. All I can think of right now is myself." She looked me in the eye. "I ever lose you…."

Down the hall, three little faces stared. All white as sheets. Matt had a look no ten-year-old boy ever should have. Anna clutched her big brother's arm. Zach squeezed his toy bear.

Matt said, "Mr. Monk?"

I nodded.

Tears filled the boy's eyes. He pushed his wet face against my white shirt. Anna and Zach just stood, wearing that same confused look. The one kids get when they have to deal with grownup things. Things like death. That's a big one.

Matt took a deep breath. My belly muffled his voice.

"Pa, I get so scared, you being a cop and all. Cantcha—cantcha do somethin' else?"

I looked over at the Missus. Her face said the same thing.

Neither of us felt like dinner. The night was too hot anyway. She fed the kids, and we all went to sleep early. At least, I tried.

I looked over to the Missus, breathing steadily. I loved my job. But it was tough for her. Of course, she's the toughest dame I know.

Funny thing is, I never met the Missus when we both were at Miami High. Big place. It had started in 1896 in a downtown storeroom. By the time I got there, around the time of the Great War, the school had a couple hundred kids in a three-story building. Now it's a sprawl, with about eighty classrooms and room for more than two thousand students. That's how much my little hometown has grown just in my young life.

My dad's father came down from Chicago around the time of the Civil War and married him a Cuban-born beauty. My dear mother told me she named me as a nod to that Cuban beauty's mom, Natalia, back in Hay-vana. We never let go of that Latin blood. Gave my skin a bit of a tint, made darker by a life in the Florida sun. That and my black hair, and more than one person's taken me for a Cuban or other such islander. Actually comes in handy sometimes.

My grandpa had taken over his uncle's cattle ranch near Fort Myers. Back then, all of Florida had only about as many people as Dade County does now.

Dad grew up around cows, but he decided it wasn't for him. He came across to Miami just before the Spanish-American War. A fellow he knew had set up a general store along the Miami River.

That's where he met my mom. She came in for peaches. Her dad had brought his family down from New Jersey. He had grown tired of ice and decided Henry Flagler was the pied piper. Got a clerk's job in the back office at Flagler's new Royal Palm Hotel.

I grew up skinny, but by the time I got to high school, I looked like most boys. I played all the sports, but not good enough for a varsity letter in anything. Mostly, it was baseball and football after class. It was just me. No brothers or sisters. But I had a knack for making friends.

I especially liked history. I blame that on my teacher, Mr. Richter. He's only about a dozen years older than me, but of course a lot more grown up. Friends of mine told me they hated history because the teacher made it boring. Mr. Richter made it, well, come alive.

When I started my senior year, everyone was asking each other, "What you wanna do?" I didn't have a good answer. But I figured I had time to sort it out. Some of my pals hadn't waited. They'd dropped out and signed up for the Great War. I was too young. A couple of guys I knew would stay in Europe. In the ground.

In the early spring of that senior year, the school had a "career day." We heard from plumbers, truck drivers, lawyers, doctors. Near the end, it was a tall man in a dark uniform and a shiny badge. Dirk Monroe. He said Miami police couldn't keep up with how fast the city was growing, and they needed smart young men.

"One thing I don't do is lie. When you're a policeman, things go from jake to grim in a heartbeat. There's guys put a hole in you and won't blink an eye. They don't care about your momma or your girl. Just so you know that goin' in. But you'll be serving and protecting your friends and family and your city. I'm proud to wear this badge. Maybe some of you will be, too."

That night at dinner, Pop said, "He's right. This town's young and wild. Lots of bad actors. And folk pourin' in every day. And money gettin' thrown around. It's only gonna get worse."

Mom put down her fork. She gave me that look every momma gives her teenager when he starts talking about the rest of his life.

"Well, Nathan,"—she was the only person on the globe who called me by my full name——"we like to think we raised you right. That you learned respect for the rules. Some cops get sick with the diseases of greed and contempt. My daddy saw a lot of it back in Jersey City. First, it's the grocer slips you some money, make sure you give a little extra attention, or maybe if he don't pay, he gets no attention. Or a fire. Or maybe you hit a fellow a little too hard when you're arresting him, but you know you won't get in no trouble."

She stared me down.

"But that's not the boy I raised."

My jaw set.

"Momma, if I'm gonna do this, I do it right, even if it means other fellows get farther along than me. You know the part about getting a fortune and losing your soul."

None of our family is very religious, but we have many friends who are. The particulars are different, but the important stuff sounds the same.

I still wasn't decided. The next day, between classes, I went to see Mr. Richter.

From the door, his desk was so piled with books I couldn't see him. I had to step over stacked books. I'd always loved this room. It was like a doorway to another world.

Richter leaned back, and he almost vanished behind books. He rubbed his beard.

"I'll tell you true, Nate. I love what I do. I love watching kids——like you——get all lit up in the face when I tell them stuff that happened and how it shapes where we are now. But being a cop. Well. That's also a public service. And, well, a lot more exciting than standing at a chalkboard and grading papers."

I slept on it.

The next day, after class, I walked to police headquarters.

Patrol guys ran in and out like bees buzzing a hive. Kids younger than me walked papers between desks.

At the front, in a cushioned chair behind a long counter, sat a man with stringy brown hair over a pink dome and a gut pressing on his police-issue belt buckle. A table lamp stood to his right, and a giant ledger lay to his left. His badge said just "Leo."

His chair creaked. "Help you, son?" He tried to sound official, but his eyes twinkled.

"Umm, here to see Mr. Dirk Monroe."

I walked past rows of desks. Lots of uniform guys. But some in plainclothes. They must be the detectives.

Dirk had a big desk. A big desk for a big man.

The department's senior detective wasn't at all fat. Just solid. He wore a nice suit. Not fancy. Just nice. And it fit him perfectly. He's about fifteen years older than me. He's a handsome man—don't think other guys don't notice——who married his high school sweetheart, also a handsome woman. (Sorry, Hon. Not as beautiful as you, of course.) They have two young daughters you just can tell will grow up gorgeous and break hearts. I've seen him be as gentle as a lamb to one of his little girls. But he could cold-cock a bad guy with one punch.

"Son, with the war over, this town is growing so fast they can't hammer a nail fast enough, someone already standing out front with a steamer trunk, ready to move in. Why we need men." He leaned forward. "Good men."

He asked why did I want to do this. Did I listen when he said the bad parts. Did I have a gal. I didn't yet. He asked all sorts of stuff, and I asked all sorts of stuff.

A few weeks later, I walked the stage and got my diploma. And took a week in the Keys.

On a Monday morning, I walked past City Hall and into Miami PD. I wore a dark police uniform and a shiny badge.

The same guy sat in his big chair at the big counter, between the lamp and the ledger. Leo. He wrestled his way out of the chair and to his feet. He held out his hand. Big grin. And there was that twinkle again.

"Moran, right? Welcome to the Miami Police Department, kid. Best job you'll ever have."

* * *

"Let him go?" I was shouting.

Chief Theo Burke practically growled. "These rumrunners have good lawyers. The sumbitch bonded out." He leaned forward, and his usually red Irishman's face and bald head were lobster pink.

"Don't worry, Nate. I'll be damned if Mark Gregg gets away with this."

Burkie pointed a finger. "Chief Franks up in Miami Springs is as hard-boiled as they get. He was a hell of an assistant chief for us before the Springs got him. I'm gonna do him a favor." He paused. "I'm loaning you out to him."

I would help nail the man who made Sandra Monk a widow.

"Thank you. Thank you, Chief."

Then, "Chief, I don't even know for sure where Miami Springs is. Never been there."

"Give you a map."

He looked down his eyeglasses. "Messy stuff. Nate, I don't have to tell you these guys are getting more and more brazen, especially down here. Just ask Sandra Monk. They're also moving too much inventory, and pocketing too much dough. And getting too powerful. It's all connected. Miami goons are working Palm Beach and Tampa and the Keys and so on. And having turf wars with the guys in those places. With innocent people in the way. It don't matter how you feel about hooch. We can't let these thugs be more powerful than us."

Then, "Go to Miami Springs right after the funeral."

I said, "The Missus and I are going over to the Monk house this morning for the visitation."

"Tell Sandra I'll be over to the house directly."

I stood.

"One more thing, Nate."

I turned back.

"Paxton died this morning."

My shoulders dropped.

* * *

Sometimes our detective bureau would hold weekend backyard gatherings at Chief Burke's place in Coral Gables. We'd bring the kiddies. Burkie's were grown up and had kids of their own. The chief'd never taken down the playsets.

At one of these gatherings about a year back, a bunch of us guys stood around a table loaded down with hot dogs and salads and brownies. The brownies called to me like the sirens luring Ulysses. Monk was putting away a sausage on a bun. A drop of mustard plopped onto his shirt. Even for this party, he wore a white dress shirt.

I said, "You know, Monk"—we all called him "Monk" instead of Bailey—"there's plenty of street trash who might take a shot at a city copper now and again. But you're federal. And Prohibition. You're in even more danger."

South Florida's the center of the universe for bootleggers, moonshiners, and gin mill owners. It's their land of milk and honey. Feds like Monk are in the way. The bad guys would just as soon gun him down as they would a mutt. Or they can afford hatchet men.

"Nate, you're not gonna believe this. I don't like the Prohi. It's costing us more to try to stop it than it's worth. We might as well be pissing into Biscayne Bay. But when the Feds came to our city department in Baltimore and asked me to serve my country, I did it. During the Great War, friends of mine went to Europe and got shot and gassed. I figgered I can come to Miami and chase rumrunners."

Monk was too humble to make a big deal about it, but he'd gone to Europe too. Never saw battle. But he didn't miss it by much. He was a sailor and a merchant marine. Pulled more than one mother's son out of the drink, dead and wrinkled and discolored and rotting. And he roughed those freezing seas. Where the wind tears your face off. And those rolling waves. I'd be puking three times a day. No thanks.

Monk had come home from the war and tried farming in Maryland. But police work drew him. When Prohi kicked in, Monk, being near Baltimore, and right next to Washington, caught the eye of the Feds. Plus, his dad was a judge and was an old college pal of the guy who was heading up a new federal outfit set up just to enforce the dry law.

Monk reached for another sausage sandwich. I told you he was a big guy.

"It hasn't been fun, I gotta admit. I had a cousin—my dad's cousin—move over to the Prohis after twenty-five years at Annapolis PD. One night, he did a raid with the Baltimore PD, and he caught a bullet." Monk looked down at his sandwich. "Nicest guy you ever knew."

Then he reached down and lifted his pants cuff. His left shin was a mass of knotted pink skin. I grimaced.

"Did a raid at a still out to Hialeah. One of the goons pushed over a vat of boiling mash. I didn't walk for about three weeks."

He picked up his sandwich.

I said, "But no one ever went after you directly."

He smiled. "They haven't tried to kill me. But they've gone after me."

He pointed his sandwich hand toward a car parked at the curb. He talked and chewed at the same time.

"See that clunker? It's on its last legs. I'm holdin' it together with epoxy and moxie. Sure could go for a new car."

Another bite.

"A few months ago, fellow come up to me up in Miami Springs. He—"

"That's cow country."

"Pretty much, Nate. Lots of open space to break the law without no one looking. I was up there visiting the chief. You know the guy. Mark Franks. Used to be your deputy chief."

I said, "Great guy."

A voice behind me. "One of the best."

It was Dirk Monroe. One hand held a soda pop. The other stroked the hair of a daughter. He said, "Franks was my mentor when I was coming up."

I never thought about it, but of course, my mentor had mentors.

Dirk Monroe has been that since I started as a detective, and even when I walked a beat.

Dirk's family came from New England to Coconut Grove. Back then, it was a jungle. You couldn't drive, bicycle, or even walk from there to downtown Miami. You had to come around on Biscayne Bay in a boat. And Dirk's dad had a beauty.

It was thirty feet. Huge sails. Put together up in a place called Essex, near Boston. Where they made big boats that fishermen sail into those northern gales, and they limp back with their holds groaning with cod. Or they sink. Or no one knows what happens to them.

Dirk's pop brought that boat all the way down the East Coast. Dirk's mom had TB, and the doctors said the warm air could help. The old man hacked out a clearing along the bay. Packed in supplies and built a house by hand. Took years. Kept going even when the wife died.

Dirk remembered as a kid dropping a line off the porch in the afternoon, bringing up something and eating it a half hour later. Nothing like it.

As a teen, he'd go with his pop around the bay to downtown to get supplies. Miami was just a little fishing village. But it was growing fast. Dirk's brain was like a sponge. He jawed with the merchants, the restaurant operators, the guys coming in with the day's catch. Mostly, he liked to talk to the cops. They'd fill him with stories.

Dirk finished school and became a cop. Then a detective. Now he was in his thirties, but already an old hand.

Dirk said to Monk, "Miami Springs. A lot of open space to cover."

Monk said, "Right. Lots of places way out there to put hooch so it's under nobody's eye. Naturally, that made it not just Chief Franks' business, but ours, too. The Feds, I mean.

"After I met that day with Franks, I decided to take a walk up the main street. It ain't very long. Ends in just gravel and grass. I turned around to walk back to my car. There's a guy standin' there. Just standing. Work jeans, denim work shirt, farmer's cap. Lots of farmer sunburn on the back of his neck. Calmly smoking a cig.

"Being a good lawman, I already got a hand on my piece. The man waved his hand. He said, 'No need to be so dramatic, Monk.'

"I wanted to say, 'How do you know my name? Were you laying for me?' Before I could say somethin', he said, 'How I know you? Well, that don't make no never mind. Thing is, I got a offer for you. You say no, it's all jake.

It ends here. I'll swear on a stack of King John bibles I never said it. But if you say okay, we're both happy.'

"I waited him out. He said, 'What I'm thinking is, on a particular night, you make sure you're chasing some hot lead way down south in Coconut Grove. Take some Miami PD with you. Only it turns out to be a bum tip. And all this time, no one is anywhere near Baker's Haulover. You make sure of that.'"

Baker's Haulover is an inlet at the north end of Miami Beach. Before they cut it a few years back, you had to drag your boat from the Atlantic Ocean to the top of Biscayne Bay. How it got its name. It's become a real popular place for rumrunners to come in loaded from the docks in the Bahamas. Turn left and you come right down the bay to wherever you want.

Monk dipped his sausage in a splotch of mustard on his plate.

"The fella says, 'And then, a few days later, a shiny new Packard shows up in your driveway.' I didn't even count to three. I said, 'Get out of my way, sir.' The fella took another puff. Cool as a block a' ice. He says, 'Just think about it.'"

Now Monk was pointing with the sausage.

"I said, 'I don't have to think about it. I'd never be able to drive that car without looking in the rear-view mirror.'"

Chewing.

"The fella said, 'Suit yuself.' He ground out his smoke with a heel and tipped his farmer's cap. And walked off."

Monk shoved the last of the sausage down his gullet. On the other side of the yard, kids laughed and screamed. I heard a car drive by a block over. Our gaggle of cops was silent as housecats.

Dirk spoke up.

"Did you know the guy, Monk?"

"We'd never met before that." Monk spat pieces of sausage while he talked. "But I knew him. He's one of the biggest smugglers in town. Lives right up there in Miami Springs, so the chief up there knows all about him, too. Name's Mark Gregg."

* * *

On the way to Bailey Monk's wake, I stopped at my house. The Missus had dolled herself up as only she could, but in a respectful way.

Matt sat on the couch, itching in that suit the Missus had picked up in Sears. He must be eighty pounds now. Amazing how fast kids turn into boys. I'd sent Anna and Zach to stay with my mother-in-law. Too little. Maybe shoulda sent Matt too. No. He should go.

I whispered to the Missus, "Not a word about Mark Gregg getting out. Sandra'll find out soon enough. She don't need that today."

My wife nodded. Amid this sadness, I loved her even more. If that was possible.

Charlotte Harper was a young teen when her family moved to Miami. Her dad had started a peach farm near Macon, but a freak winter snap wiped him out. He decided he was done with cold, even by Georgia standards. Set up a mango grove west of downtown Miami. A little after the Missus and I got married, speculators gave her dad top dollar for the farm. Now it's a long block of houses full of New York transplants. I liked it better as mangos.

I told you I never met Charlotte in high school. Like I said, Miami High was a big place.

One day, not long after I'd started with the PD, the hotel dick at the Royal Palm nabbed some mope who'd lifted a wallet from a Manhattan high hat who was in town for the week. Caught the palooka nearly in the act, so the bigwig whose billfold had been nicked was ever so grateful to the hotel.

I'd been over to the Royal Palm a few times on patrol. The manager, Ted Forman, was a good egg. In the lobby, he waved me over.

"Hiya Nate. Good to see ya. We've got the kid in the back room."

The pickpocket looked like a schoolboy. When he saw a man in uniform, he looked like he'd pee his pants.

I said, "What's your name, son?"

"Uhh…uhh…Willie."

This could take a while.

"Keep going, kid."

"Umm…umm. Willie Collins."

"Good. Willie. How old are you?"

A long pause.

"C'mon, Willie. Save me the trouble of looking it up."

"Umm, sixteen."

He's lucky. He'll go to the Juvenile Home. If he keeps his nose clean, he'll be out in no time with a clean record and the fear of God in him.

"Okay, Willie. I gotta cuff you. Can't help that."

He said, "Can I get a drink of water? I feel like I'm gonna throw up."

Forman's face turned almost as white as Willie's. The manager didn't want a cleanup in his business office. He called, "Hey, Charlotte."

"Yes?" A young female voice from a back room.

"Could you bring this kid a glass of water?"

A minute later, the girl walked out. I don't have to tell you the rest. We got married about a year later.

In that year, we had a lot of talks. Mostly about my job.

"Why you gotta be a flatfoot?" she'd say. "You'll get yourself knocked off. Leave me a widow. Maybe with a little mouth to feed."

"Hey. The department has good death benefits."

"That ain't funny, Nate. Ain't funny at all."

"Look. I'm in good with Dirk Monroe. He already told me I'm on a track for the detective bureau."

"What. Detectives never get it?"

Yes, I allowed. Sometimes detectives get it. But I could get hit by a car crossing Flagler Street on my day off. I told her not to worry her blond curls. She said good luck with that. Then we got married anyway. And had three kids. And now here we were in the middle of just what she feared. We were paying our respects to the widow of a lawman.

I stopped with Matt at the front door so the Missus could walk in and give mother and daughter long hugs.

The summer heat and the crowd of people in the room had made things toasty. Everyone put up with it. A few folks mingled at a card table that held cookies and a pitcher of lemonade. Off in a corner, I saw Mrs. Grimsby, the neighbor. We traded smiles. That lady was my hero.

I walked with my son to the sofa. "Matt, you remember Mrs. Monk."

Sandra squeezed the kid so hard I thought she'd suffocate him. She let him go, and I motioned he could go over to the cookies. The Missus moved to a side chair.

Sandra was, well, how I guessed the Missus would look in ten years. Still beautiful. Nancy was thirteen now, I think. She had her mom's brown hair and hazel eyes. Sandra's eye stuff had run and sent a line down her cheek. She and her daughter didn't look very pretty right now.

I always told the Missus the only time she wasn't pretty was when she was crying, so I had to make sure that never, ever happened. Nothing I could do about Sandra and her kid. Tore me up.

People see a cop killer in court, in a nice suit, with a fast-talking lawyer alongside, and his boo-hooing relatives in the back row, like he's a Boy Scout who loves his mom and apple pie. People don't see a cop's widow and children with broken hearts.

I dropped to a knee and took Sandra's hands. We didn't say anything for a while. Then, out of nowhere, looking into the center of the room, she said in a clear voice, all matter-of-fact, "We'll bury him in Arlington. He earned it. And he'll be close to his family in Baltimore."

"What about you, Sandra? And Nancy?"

She sighed. "I—I—I don't know. I might change my mind later. But seems to me this is our home now."

She looked at me. "Last week was our anniversary. Fourteen years. And Bailey and me knew each other three years before that."

Then she said, "I know the man is out of jail." I didn't ask how she knew. Or try to explain to her how that happened.

Sandra turned to the Missus. "Charlotte, I want to ask you a favor." She reached to a side table and pulled out a piece of stationery, folded in half. "Will you read this over tonight, please, and look it over for my grammar. I'd like to send it to the newspaper. I'm not much of a writer, but"—her voice caught—"but I owe it to him."

She said, "It's not just about Bailey." And looked at me.

That night, after we'd put the kids to bed, the Missus read Sandra's letter out loud, with shaking hands and shaking voice.

"My daughter has lost a kind, wise, indulgent father. Her country has lost a conscientious, courageous, and tireless fighter. Parents have lost a son, tender, affectionate, and generous. I have lost—"

The Missus stopped and took a deep breath.

"Oh, what have I not lost? A protector. A pal for the past seventeen years. Yet, if the eyes of this so blind country could be opened, if the dry-voting, wet-living congressmen could be made to realize the conditions as they are, if the corrupt judges who encourage these men, by taking advantage of every technicality available to release them, could be impeached, I would face my broken home and my joyless future with calm resignation and feel my ruined life a small price to pay."

The Missus looked up.

"But, my fellow citizens, I mostly blame you. You make these monsters your heroes, as long as you can get your drink. The real killer is the man at the small end of the bottle."

I spent another night eying the ceiling. The next morning, I rode to the chapel in a department jalopy with three patrol guys. Wore my dress uniform. We pulled up to a long line of cars and walked about a block. The room was full. We stood just outside the open door. Matt had said maybe he should go, but the Missus and I agreed he already had done enough for a boy. Plus, I hadn't wanted to take him out of school. The Missus had come with Mrs. Grimsby. I just could make them out in one of the front rows. The place was stifling. No one complained.

Afterward, I walked outside and stood with the other officers in the heat and bright sunlight. As the casket rolled past me, I saluted. Our line of cops saluted as one, following the casket with their eyes to the back of the truck. It drove off for the train station.

I turned to one of the patrol guys who'd rode over with me. Young kid. About the age I was when I started.

"Rawlings, right?" He nodded.

"Do yourself a favor. Every once in a while, you're going to watch someone you care about get buried. You should pray to whatever you believe in that such moments are few. And at the right time. Not like this."

Not like this.

* * *

It was a solid twenty miles up River Drive to Miami Springs. A lot of it unpaved. I had the windows open to fight the heat, and gravel dust swirled. The humidity smothered me. I'd laid my coat on the car seat, and I wiped the back of my neck with my hanky. Even wiped my fingertips with it so they didn't slip on the steering wheel.

And all that bouncing. My tailbone was sore.

I heard a noise. Like a jalopy engine. But not exactly. And I could swear it came from over my head.

What was that? A shadow raced unnaturally across the road in front of me. I slammed the brakes and pulled to the side. I leaned out and stared up into the sun. And saw the thing.

It was as long as a truck, and its two wings were wider. I saw it dip and disappear in the glare as it soared over the pastures.

It took me a while to calm down. I unfolded the map Chief Burke had given me. I followed a line with my finger. Didn't have to make any turns. This was the only road. I put the jalopy back in gear.

Dust drifted into the window and stuck to my sweaty face. Soon, my hanky was black and gritty.

Pastures gave way to a small cluster of buildings, and I pulled up to the whitewashed town hall. I pulled on my jacket over my sweat-drenched white shirt and fitted my fedora.

A big floor fan in the lobby cooled me a little. In less than a minute, Mark Franks came out. He didn't look like a cop. More like a shop owner. But he had a face and bearing that instantly made you want him to be in charge.

The chief gave me a strong handshake and a half-hug.

I said, "Monk."

"Yep." His face was tight. "And on my watch."

I said, "You know Monk was my neighbor. Sandra and the daughter are wrecks."

"Talked to her on the phone the next day."

In Franks' office, he opened an icebox and pulled out a pitcher of ice water. It hit the spot. He reached for a pack on his desk and held it out to me. I put out a hand. "I'm off the stuff."

Instead, I chew on candy cigarettes. Go figure.

When the Missus and I dated, I put away half a pack a day. One day, after we'd been married about a month, I was at breakfast. I'd already had a smoke and was working on my second cup of joe. She'd come into the kitchen in her bathrobe. I didn't like the look on her face.

"Nate, I'm gonna give it to you straight. You stink."

"Pardon?"

"I know you already had one this morning. I know everyone smokes, especially down at headquarters. I didn't like 'em when my pop stunk up our house. And I don't like 'em stinking up this house. We're already talkin' about startin' a family, and I don't want 'em growing up in a stunk-up home. I shoulda said something when we were goin' out, and I'm sorry for that. But I'm saying it now."

Out of nowhere, I could taste the stale tobacco inside my mouth.

Then she said, "When you smoke, it makes me, well…" She looked away.

Charlotte Harper's a proper lady, but she's no wallflower.

"When you smoke, it makes me…makes me…umm…not attracted to you."

I stood. I dropped the pack in the kitchen trash. That was the last cig I ever had. I know my priorities.

After I told Chief Franks no thanks for the smoke, I said, "Tell me about Gregg." He shrugged. "He got out."

"You're tailing him?"

"Gingerly." Nice word. "Gregg's been around the block. Can spot a dick from a mile away."

Franks dropped into a big chair behind a big desk. I plopped down in front of him. The padded chair partly soothed my sore tailbone.

I heard grunts from the open window. Franks leaned across and separated a cotton curtain. About fifty feet away and across a fence, about a dozen cows stood in the oppressive afternoon heat, chewing and switching their tails. They stared at nothing, with that stupid walking steak look. Little white birds stood on their backs, one now and again dipping a beak.

"Cattle egret," Franks said. "Cows supply the bugs, the birds supply the relief. It's a great partnership."

"Not for the bugs."

"Right, Nate. Like Gregg. He thinks he's the bird, and he's just scratching an itch for the cows. Doesn't care that sometimes there's victims. To him, they're insects, too."

Some of the cows had dropped to that strange position: bellies to the ground, legs folded under them. Behind them, the sky had gone from white to gray to black. Out in the Everglades, a whopper was brewing.

Franks let go of the curtains, and they fell together.

"Cows are king out here. Mostly dairy. Some beef." He sighed. "But the builders already are here. Like weeds. Stinkweeds."

"C'mon, Chief. Say what you really mean."

He smiled back at me. It was a sad smile.

"When I got hired out here, Nate, I brought the family with me. My folks had brought us down to Miami at the turn of the century, when I was little. I don't remember much of South Carolina, but I find myself liking small-town life. It's why I didn't mind coming out here. I just worry this place won't be small-town for long."

Sometimes the concrete of downtown Miami gets to be a little much. But I do like my work. And the Missus likes the conveniences. But I saw Franks' point, too.

Outside, a low rumble of thunder.

I turned at a sound. A slender, pretty girl of about twenty stepped in and wordlessly handed Franks some papers. He said, "Thanks, Marian." She silently vanished.

I said, "I knew a little about Gregg from Monk and my chief."

Franks leaned back. "He's a headache. Worse than that. He's the devil, you ask me. Come down from Jacksonville. Feeds hooch to hotels from Coral

Gables up to Palm Beach. Maybe more. Funny thing, he doesn't touch the stuff. Says he doesn't believe in breaking into his inventory. But he'd just as soon cut your throat as look at you."

"C'mon, Chief. Say what you really mean."

Franks smiled back. "You just used that line a couple minutes ago."

Dang. The Missus always tells me I repeat myself.

"Three times, Prohibition agents raided Gregg's haunts, and one time they nabbed a hundred eight cases right at his home. Each time, he beat the rap on a technicality. Gregg also warned the Feds about what might happen if they came to his house. Warned them more than once.

"A couple weeks ago, a snitch told the Feds he'd bought thirteen quarts of whiskey from Gregg. Good stuff from the Bahamas. Said Gregg's guys got it right off the dock at Freeport. That was enough for a warrant." He sighed. "That's what I pulled out of Monk's hand."

We sat for a minute. Another distant, low rumble.

"Nate, we'll keep an eye on Gregg. But I suspect he'll mostly lie low while these charges are around his neck."

I said, "I'm not sure." Franks said, "Me neither."

"Even if he does, Chief, the world ain't a vacuum. Some big players will just pick up the slack. Monk knew 'em all."

"Right, Nate." Then, "Chief Burke told me you're the best guy he could loan us. He's got a good track record on these things. Not to put no pressure on you."

I smiled. I said, "I saw a funny thing on the way in, Chief. An aeroplane. Went right over my jalopy."

"Yep. Fellow named Glenn Curtiss started an airfield out at the edge of town. Well, it's the edge of town for now."

Another roll of thunder. This one louder. Closer.

"Curtiss owns a service spreading fertilizer and bug killer and weed killer onto crops from the air. Also, a flying school. But the main thing is the airfield. He makes a nice dime on fuel and storage and maintenance and repair."

"I seen those flying machines just a few times, Chief. No way you'd get me up in one. Too scary. Don't think they'll catch on."

Franks stood. "How about some barbecue?"

"Don't have to ask me twice, Chief."

We walked down the row of businesses. I eyeballed the darkening sky.

We stopped at a place called the Old South. I have a favorite barbecue place in downtown Miami, but this was dang good. I was starting to realize there's different kinds of barbecue.

"The Missus says I define my travels by grub," I said.

"Me too, Nate."

Then the chief wasn't looking at me anymore. He was looking past me.

Mark Gregg stood three feet away.

I'd never met the man. Don't ask me how I knew it was him. It was like he sent out vibrations. Work jeans, denim work shirt, farmer's cap. Lot of farmer sunburn on his neck. Calmly smoking a cig. Just as Monk had described him.

"Howdy, Chief."

Franks looked like he'd swallowed turpentine. "What do you want, Gregg?"

The man had this smile that made me want to put my fist into his face. A lot. Which I already had wanted to do before I ever met him.

"Chief, you need to train your tails a little better. Though I don't know why you bother. Wasting tax money harassing a law-abiding citizen like me."

Gregg's north Florida accent was a soft drawl. Like a pitcher of lemonade.

He looked over to me like he was noticing me for the first time. He gave a sort of half nod. My face was set in stone.

"I'd say you a lawman too, sir. Didn't catch your name."

I didn't feel like giving it.

He shrugged. "Suit yuself." Same thing he'd said to Monk. Then he was out the door.

I reached for my sandwich, but my hands shook. Not with fear. With rage. I locked eyes with Mark Franks.

"I feel the same way, Moran. Exactly the same way."

Chapter Three: The Storm

Miami doesn't get blizzards. Or ice storms. We don't get earthquakes or tidal waves. And we get a twister about once in a lifetime. What we do get is hurricanes. And how.

There's people won't move to Florida because they might get a hurricane, but they still live where it's guaranteed to freeze every year, and usually more than once. And where if you get drunk and pass out on your lawn in January, you freeze to death.

In a year, only about a dozen or so things out there in the tropics ever turn into hurricanes. And most stay out at sea and just shake up the fish before they run out of gas somewhere off Canada. Even when they do hit land, the coastline is long. Maine to down here and up to Pensacola and over to Texas and back down. You have a better shot at getting elected president than having a hurricane come over your house.

But sometimes, the dice come up snake eyes. And you get a storm that just about wipes you off the map.

Some folks sweat bullets about it. Others just live their life. Much of South Florida is like that right now. The hammering and sawing hasn't stopped. Sometimes it's like they build a place in a day. Some homes are right on the water, and there's just a few roads inland from the coast, and what happens if the ocean comes up past your porch?

Seems to me the answer's somewhere in the middle. I look both ways before I cross the street. But I still cross the street.

Even though it was September, the worst month for hurricanes, we went about our business. On this particular night, our business was a strip of seedy storefronts up north of downtown, in Arch Creek. One storefront specifically.

A guy had come to see us. Said he'd left his kids' lunch money at a backroom craps game. Said he had a tingling feeling that some hands moved fast in the dim light, and the game wasn't on the up-and-up. When you're at a place that's already breaking the law, you don't have much of a beef with them if they rig the dice.

We got lucky and caught the operators off guard. Sometimes they get a tip that we're on our way, and they have time to hide the hooch in a locked cabinet and flip the craps table and cover it with sandwiches and lemonade. Not this time.

Customers swarmed for the door or tried to twist away from cops. Amid the shouting and shoving, a sergeant shouted, "Moran! Over here!"

In a corner, on a wooden chair, his hands cuffed in front of him, sat an old friend. He stared at the floor.

"Hiya Frank. Whaddya know?"

The sarge gave Frank Marte a poke, and he looked up.

"Oh. Hi, Moran. Sorry. I had a fight with my girlfriend. Don't feel much like talking."

I slid a candy cig into my mouth. "This your place, Frankie?"

He didn't answer.

I gave him that smile I give mopes that tells them that this time, all the good cards are in my hand.

"This looks bad for you, Frank. Not like you can deny it. There's the booze, and there's the craps table. This isn't thirty days in the city lockup. This'll get you five years looking through bars at the pine trees of North Florida. I hear it's pretty in the fall. But in the summer, even steamier than here. No ocean breezes."

Frank fidgeted. I knew the look. He's at the edge of the cliff, and the herd of buffalo is bearing down on him. When guys are in this spot, there's always the potential for added value. It didn't hurt to test the market.

"You know, Frankie, you give us something, maybe we could make it easier for you. Your call. Don't make us no never mind. We've got plenty to keep us busy."

I made a big show of shrugging. I twirled the candy cig along my tongue. I motioned to the sergeant to stay and the other cops to step away. I looked back at Frank and raised my eyebrows. Like I was saying, "What'll it be?"

Frank lowered his head. He mumbled.

"Pardon me?"

I heard, "Give you something."

I leaned in. Frank, still looking at the floor: "You cut me some slack, I give you something,"

I gave him that sumbitch smile again. "Well, Frankie. That's up to a judge. But we certainly can tell hizzoner the defendant was a valuable source of information on other crimes and might deserve some leniency."

I quit smiling.

"Course, that's as long as you're on the up-and-up. Long as you don't feed me a line. Send us chasing after wild geese."

Frankie fidgeted again. And fidgeted. Again, I shrugged. "Have it your way." I turned.

Another mumble. My eyes locked with the sergeant. "Din't catch that, Frankie."

He looked up. "Jimmy Chin."

He repeated the name. It meant nothing to me.

He shifted in his chair. He'd crossed the line. He couldn't go back. He looked at a spot in the back wall.

"Comes in here regular. Drops a lot at the table. He's a sucker for the yo."

I had to remind myself of all the games going on at once at a craps table. "Yo" was an eleven. Long odds. Big payoff.

"Jimmy was here tonight. He hit a couple yos and he was feeling good."

I smiled. "And you were about to switch to your special dice and end that run of luck. Can't afford those big payouts."

Frank's eyes narrowed. "Everyone's a comedian." Then back to the spot on the back wall.

I said, "Back to—what's his name?"

"Jimmy Chin. He's a regular. But no one knows a lot about him. Don't see too many Chinamen in Florida. I think he works in the railroad yard. Lot of his pay ends up here, either at the bar or the craps table. Tonight, he hit those two yos, and he was feeling that cabbage in his pocket and he…he…he was in the sauce but good. He starts getting a case of the talkies. About a palm tree plantation down in Redland. That place is so far, it might as well be the moon to me. I never been south of Coral Gables in my life. Farms ain't my thing."

I made a face that told him to get on with it.

"Jimmy was saying just how to get there. And was joking about how he goofed and left the shovel. We're all laughing too, ya know, like guys do. But then someone says, 'What. Did you bury something down there?' We're thinking hooch or moola. But…."

Frankie made like he was clearing his throat. He stared at the floor. I looked at the sergeant. Didn't like where this was going. Didn't like it at all.

"Umm, Jimmy's so drunk he doesn't skip a beat. He says, 'This girl. Picked her up coming out of the Catholic middle school. Skirt uniform and all."

I still heard background noise in the room. But it was muffled. Like, in our corner, all the sound had been shoved in a box, and the lid closed. My throat closed.

Frank Marte was sweating. Not from the heat. I was wet under my collar, too.

"Jimmy…uhh…he…he…uhh…he says, 'I made like to give her a ride home. She gave me a real hard time while I was doing her, so I was done with her.'"

I gripped the back of a chair. The sarge looked like he'd eaten a bowling ball.

Stay cool, Nate. Do your job. Forget for a minute you've got a little girl of your own.

It almost worked. Almost.

Frank still looked at the back wall. "I…uhh…like I said, Jimmy was blotto. He don't notice everyone at the table stopped laughing. No one's saying nothing. It's as quiet as a library. Then Jimmy laughs and hollers to throw the dice and see can he get another yo. Of course, I already had gave the signal—"

He caught himself and looked up at me.

"Frankie, we got you on booze and running a backroom craps table. Fixing the dice? That's your customer's problem. Keep going."

Frank sighed. "We…uhh…we set up Jimmy for the snake eyes. He just shrugged. Cashed in whatever he had left and wished us a good evening and stumbled out."

I said, "Did he say anything else about the girl?"

Frank shook his head: "No. And I didn't wanna know."

He wiped his face with the back of a shaking hand.

"Look, Moran. Maybe I water down the rotgut. And maybe I make sure the table ain't too generous. But I don't have button men or goons, and I don't ice people, or even have them beat up, even when they owe me money. Though God knows I know plenty of guys could use a few more holes. And—"

Then he looked right at me.

"I would never hurt a kid. Never. Anyone who does should get run over by a truck about twenty times. I ain't got none of my own. But I got a sister in Tampa. She's got a ten-year-old girl. That kid's like the sun coming out after a storm. I…I…I…"

Frank was sobbing. I looked up. The sergeant's face was as white as mine probably was.

I said quietly, "Okay, Frankie. We'll go back to the station, and I'll start writing, and you'll tell me what Jimmy told you. And where we might find him. And my chief will see what we can do with the judge."

Frank wiped his nose on his sleeve. The sergeant stared. Somewhere all the way down in Redland. A kid in the dirt under a tree.

At home that night, while the Missus snored, I tiptoed down the hall. I creaked open the door to the kids' room. Moonlight sent a white line across Anna's face. She breathed steadily. My right hand gripped the doorknob so hard my knuckles ached. I slipped back to my bed. For a good chunk of the night, while the Missus snored, I lay in the dark and saw my little girl's face on the ceiling.

Kids trust you with their lives. They think you're superhuman. The idea that you'd allow something bad to happen to them never goes into their noggin. But for you, it's there every second. Every.

As I slipped off, I was wondering if I'd meet Jimmy Chin. When Chief Burke woke me, I had a feeling I would.

* * *

"The McKenzies," Burkie was saying over the phone. "Yesterday, Julia didn't come home from the Catholic School. She's eleven."

I gripped the top rail of my kitchen chair.

"Chief."

"What is it, Nate?"

"Chief, this could be bad."

A pause. "Go on."

I told him about my night raid and Frankie and his story about Jimmy Chin. The chief didn't say anything for a few seconds. More than a few.

Then, "Nate, this could be a coincidence. Maybe your bar owner made up the whole thing to buy some slack. But maybe it is the girl. So not a word of it to the McKenzies. You got that?"

I said I did.

"They actually live not too far from you. Go by there first."

He gave me the home address. Said they were waiting for me.

"I told the McKenzies you're one of the best snoops we've got." A pause. "Which you are, of course."

He couldn't see me smile. "Thanks, Chief."

"I'll put out the word on this Jimmy Chin guy, Nate. We'll put the elbow on every pimp and pusher on the street. Tell them we'll make their life hell, they don't spit him up."

He sighed. "The girl's probably dead."

"Chief, we find a girl under the tree down in Redland, the only thing worse than it being Julia is if it's not Julia."

"I can't even think about that." Then, "Nate, you got that little angel yourself. Can you handle this?"

"Chief, someone gotta find that girl. Seems to me the best one to do it might be someone got a little girl of her own. Dontcha think?"

We rang off. I remembered Chief Burke had a granddaughter. She was around eleven.

My kids were up and already were loaded with pancakes and syrup, and ran around the house. I didn't feel particularly hungry. The Missus handed me a cup of joe, and I made a quick scan of the morning paper. A story about a storm in the Caribbean. And some procedural stuff on Mark Gregg's trial. It was dragging through the bureaucracy. The headline said "Gregg." Should say, "Monk."

Time to go. I couldn't put it off any longer.

The McKenzies lived in a modest home about four blocks from me. "Why, we're practically neighbors," Harriet said with a weak smile in the doorway. She looked about forty. Red hair. Dressed plainly but very pretty, in a simple, honest way. Phil was about the same age. Slim build. Modest but immaculate suit. Black hair. His face looked strong but haggard.

Phil was an accountant. Harriett stayed home. They were very religious. Had a photo of the pope in the living room. Julia was their only kid.

"She was a miracle child." Harriet handed me my second coffee of the day. "Doctors told us we couldn't have children. So, when I got pregnant, we were thrilled."

Phil McKenzie stared into his cup. Both these people were wound tighter than ship's cable.

Harriet reached into her apron pocket and held out a photograph.

"Fifth-grade picture. She wants to be a nurse."

Harriet let out a giant sob. Just one syllable. She pushed her face into the dish towel in her hand. And stayed there.

I stood. "I'd like to keep the photo if I can, ma'am."

Harriett still had her face in the towel. Phil gently pulled it away. "Harriet. The photo."

Her face wet and red, she looked at me like in a daze. Gears caught, and she looked down at the photo. She handed it to her husband, who passed it to me. Neither said a word.

Staring at the gray image, I wondered if she had the same red hair as her mom. The girl wore a striped dress with the school seal on the chest. She had a giant smile.

Phil led his wife to the couch. "Dear, I'm going to walk the officer out."

I laid my coffee cup on the kitchen table. "Ma'am, we'll do all we can to find your girl. I gotta little one of my own. She's an angel."

My jaw went tight. Maybe I said too much.

At the door, the dad tapped the photo in my hand with a forefinger.

"Just so you'll know. The uniform stripes are blue. Hair's red. Like—like her mom."

I pocketed the photo. McKenzie's face was steely. He spoke low.

"Detective, I just push numbers for a living. But I pride myself on being a good judge of character. I think you know something you're not saying. You're trying to protect us. Not load us up with bad thoughts when it might not be. I respect that."

I tried not to show any emotion. McKenzie looked somewhere in the middle of the room.

"Let me just say this. If some monster has taken my child from me, I—I—I don't know if I can handle it. I don't know if I'll be able to hear what might have been done to her."

His eyes came back to me.

"You can see I am a very religious man, detective. My faith teaches me to forgive. But -" His voice caught. "But if someone took my little girl, you need to make sure I never get near him."

I put a hand on his shoulder. He was shaking.

I started home. After about a block, I saw a bench. I sat and waited for my own shakes to stop.

In our front room, the Missus grasped my hand. "Nate, you gotta do your job. No matter how painful. A family is counting on you."

The more I hang out with that lady, the more I fall in love with her.

I called the chief and filled him in. I pressed for a road patrol guy and a car so I could get down to Redland pronto with the directions we'd gotten from Frank, the speakeasy boss. Burkie said he had a murder-suicide down in Coconut Grove that was more pressing; two bodies getting cold. Plus, he wanted to have Jimmy Chin in custody before we did anything in Redland. Chief wanted me to be able to take Jimmy with me. The sight of that little girl might get a confession out of him.

It's a ten-minute walk from home to police headquarters. I saw in the distance that the water in Biscayne Bay was flat. Of course, the bay's so shallow the waves almost always are flat. Skies were blue, and the breeze off the water was light on the back of my neck.

There's a federal weather office at the U.S. Post Office downtown. Every once in a while, the boys there send up the pole a red flag with a black square in the middle. That means a tropical storm, which is bad enough. Sometimes they put up two of those flags. That means hurricane.

I saw two flags.

A man out front used tacks to nail a printed notice to a wooden signboard. He had a short beard, and his suit looked like he'd slept in it. I tipped my fedora.

"That storm out in the islands?"

He turned to me. "It's coming."

"Whaddya mean, it's coming?"

"I should know. Name's Don Green. I'm the weather bureau chief."

I flashed my badge. "Nate Moran. Miami Police. Detective Division. Umm, the *Herald* said the storm was down in the Caribbean, and it was going somewhere else."

"You'll see my name in the story, detective. That's the word I was getting from Washington. But the *Herald* puts the next day's edition on the presses about midnight. I've been up all night, getting telegrams from the islands. Sometimes these storms make a turn we didn't expect."

I looked out at the bay. "How bad?"

"Nothing between the islands and us to weaken it. Or slow it down."

"How close?"

"Winds should be picking up tonight. Worst of it around sunrise."

"Can't you spread the word?"

He held up his palms. "Been doing that without a stop. Already let the port know. Too late for the ships to sail off somewhere safe; the storm's in the way. So, captains are tying up everything. The last edition of the *Daily News* is about four p.m., and it'll have what I just told you. And a lot more people now have radios. Carl Fisher's radio station's been putting out warnings all day."

"What can the PD do?"

He smiled. "Just got off the phone with your chief. Expect he'll have you doing something. Look. Sorry, but I gotta lot to do."

At headquarters, I saw a lot of officers and police cars outside. More guys inside. The place was humming. Chief Burke got to me before I could take off my jacket. He said, "Turn around. Go home."

"Huh?"

I'd talked to him on the phone forty-five minutes ago. What changed? Those two red flags.

"Do whatever you need to do for your family and your house. Then come back as soon as you can. In uniform. You'll be sleeping here."

I couldn't remember the last time I was in my old street uniform.

A little later, I had the Missus and the kids on a northbound to her cousin in Macon. The train station wasn't that busy. People either didn't know or weren't worried. Lots of new folks don't have a clue about these storms.

"Why do you have to stay?" Her hands were shaking.

"Hon, you know the answer." I ran my fingers through her blond tresses. She was as white as a jug of bleach.

"Daddy? You gonna blow away?"

I kneeled to Anna. Her little face showed that irrational fear of children who have no machinery for handling the unknown.

"Don't worry, sweetheart. We'll be in that great big police station."

Every day, when a cop steps outside his digs, his head tells him the odds are with him. But his heart goes right to the worst possible outcome. It's a hazard of the job. It's contagious. Spreads to cops' wives. I could assure the Missus until I ran out of alphabet. It wouldn't matter. I just gave each of the kids a hug and then gave Mrs. Moran one, a little longer and tighter. I waved until the last car of the northbound Royal Palm disappeared around a corner.

Back at HQ, Harvey Comeau met me at the front desk. He'd been around longer than me. Probably had more street smarts. I'll never say anything to anyone about Harvey's work ethic. It's just that, well, he does just enough to get by.

He'd switched to his old patrol uniform, too. But it'd been a while since he walked the pavement, and he visits the bakeries regular, and the outfit was tight.

Harvey motioned to the back, toward our desks. "Look who we found."

A man sat, head down. Hands cuffed. A chain led from his ankle to a bolt in the floor.

"Jimmy Chin."

I struggled not to show emotion.

"Patrol guys picked him up a couple hours ago. Tip from a pimp. Jimmy was passed out on a bus bench up by the seawall."

Jimmy looked up. Career drunks have a very specific morning-after look. Puffy eyes. Two-day beard. Scraggly hair. A look in the eye like they got run over by a trolley.

Jimmy wore a grin you wanted to rub off with steel wool. He said, "Nice duds." He eyed my uniform and looked over to Comeau. "You guys get demoted?"

Comeau saw me staring at a gap in Jimmy's mouth. "Nate, last year, over in Wynwood Park, a dad caught Jimmy peeking into his eight-year-old daughter's bedroom window. Cold-cocked him with one punch."

Hard to argue.

Comeau reached for papers on his desk. "I spent some tax dollars early this morning burning up the phone lines. Long-distance. To California. Got some folks out of bed out there. Turns out Jimmy left in a hurry a few years back. Still has some folks looking for him."

Jimmy said, "That's baloney. I just didn't like the earthquakes." He shrugged. "You just picking on me 'cause I'm a Chinaman."

Comeau read his scribbles. "Jimmy's family came over from China to work on the railroad. But that was a long time ago. Just after the Civil War. Jimmy can't speak a word of Chinese."

I gave Chin a look you give someone who pees in your bushes. "Jimmy, we're not picking on you because you're Chinese. We're picking on you because you like little girls."

Comeau handed me a page. "Been looking at some cold cases from around here."

I took a minute to read the thing and held it out to Jimmy. "Comeau here has a solid case that you're the guy molested a ten-year-old girl near Southside Elementary three weeks ago."

I held out a palm to Comeau. "Keys."

I unlocked Jimmy's cuffs. The ring around his ankle stayed.

"Jimmy, you might a' noticed we've got some other work to do right now. A storm is coming. So you just sit. Now, you're still stuck to the floor, but the chair ain't. So don't stand up or do anything else stupid."

I reached toward my desk and picked up my pack of candy cigs.

"Is that candy?" Jimmy said, contempt in his voice.

"The Missus don't like the smell of tobacco."

He rolled his eyes.

"Jimmy, I've had a long couple days."

He grinned again. "Sorry to hear. Romantic problems?"

This punk was trying to push my buttons. He was doing a good job. I stared at his grinning face. I counted to ten. Then I relaxed. Have at it, pal. I leaned in.

"Here's the score, Jimmy. Last night, we raided a juice joint in Arch Creek. They run a craps table in a back room. Know the place?"

Jimmy's eyes narrowed.

"A little bird told us about a rummy named Jimmy Chin. Said when he gets hot at the table, or gets some rotgut in him, or both, he flaps his gums."

The blood ran out of Jimmy's puss.

I twirled my candy cig in my mouth. "You were drunk, and you were laughing around the table about how you goofed and left the shovel."

I stood. My face was hard.

"Would that be Julia McKenzie you were talking about? Her folks are frantic."

He licked his lips. He swallowed a bunch of times. He looked away and said hoarsely, "Don't know the dame."

"She's not a dame. She was eleven. And when we drive you down to Redland later this morning, I suspect we'll pull her out of that hole you dug. You'll be taking the first step toward frying in that newfangled electric chair. The state bulls tell me it puts out quite the fireworks. Smells like hamburgers on the grill."

Jimmy bent his head. I wanted to throw up.

Across the room. Chief Burke was at his open door. I said, "Jimmy, you stay put. We'll chat more in a bit."

Burkie said, "Nothing we can do. Redland will have to wait. This storm is the only thing right now."

I looked back at Jimmy, chained to the floor. "He ain't going anywhere."

"Good." The chief eyed the room. "This place is solid. We've got jugs of water in case the faucets quit, and we'll get out our flashlights if the power goes. Once the winds get going, you and Comeau are with me at the front desk. Got it?"

A little later, a boy brought in the *Miami Daily News*. The headline used really big letters. It said what Green, the weather bureau guy, had told me. That "destructive winds" were expected that night.

I phoned the weather office. "Green; It's Nate Moran. The cop who stopped by this morning."

"I'm busy now, pal."

"We're just trying to figure out over here what we'll be dealing with in the city in the next few hours."

"The barometer's dropping like a rock. Winds already picking up. Tell the chief to get all your guys in off the street in the next hour or so. After that, you won't be able to walk outside, much less drive. Anyone calls you for help, don't go. They're on their own. Gotta run. Good luck."

The line clicked.

When I told Chief Burke what the weather guy said, he started barking orders.

Forty minutes later, all the phone lines would cut out. Then the electricity.

We wolfed down cold sandwiches for dinner. I walked to the front doors. They had an ever-so-slight rattle. I opened one.

Balled-up newspaper pages floated. A tin can noisily rolled down the sidewalk. A waste bin tipped and rotated in a crazy circle.

I took a step, and I was in the wind. It was going good now. I felt little stings on my cheeks and realized it was dirt. Maybe sand from all the way on the other side of Miami Beach.

I stepped back in and shut the doors. I was able to rattle both of them.

The chief was behind me.

"I don't know about these doors, Chief."

"I asked the mayor about them the last time we had a hurricane meeting. Said he'd put it on his wish list."

I rolled my eyes. I said, "What about Jimmy Chin?"

"It's too late now to take him around back to the holding cells, Nate. He'll have to stay in his chair."

For hours, everyone watched out windows as winds grew stronger and rain pelted glass. At times, we'd see something fly past. It seemed the longer the storm went on, the bigger the object. First, just palm fronds. Big chunks of broken roof tile. Then a crate. Then an outdoor table from the diner across the street. Then whole pieces of roofs.

A crash to my left. The front doors had blown in. The room exploded in a blizzard of white paper. Ledgers, table lamps, and desk chairs came at us. We all dove behind desks.

The chief shouted directions. We barely heard him above the roar. He motioned me toward my desk. Jimmy Chin and his chair both lay on their sides. Jimmy was grimacing. I'd forgotten about him.

I ran in a half-squat. Comeau squeezed his bulk out from under his desk and wrestled to his feet. We uprighted Jimmy and the chair. Jimmy had a cut on his cheek from where he'd hit the floor.

The noise was dropping. I listened. Yes. It was. Things still moved around inside the room, but not as much. A minute later, the room was as quiet as death.

In the sudden silence, Jimmy's voice seemed like nearly a shout.

"I gotta go to the can."

The chief nodded. I unlocked Jimmy's ankle and started to walk him to the john. He elbowed me and broke into a run.

"Jimmy! No!"

Before I knew it, he'd shot out through the tattered front doors and raced down the sidewalk.

I ran out. "The storm's not over! This is just the eye! Come back!"

I saw his form shrink toward Bayfront Park.

The chief walked over. "My fault."

"This won't end well for Jimmy, Chief."

I felt a prick of sand on my cheek. The wind was coming back. It seemed stronger. With the doors torn open, we were helpless. Another hour of it coming in that opening would have killed us all. But now it came from the opposite direction, from behind the building.

We watched a boat slide down the street. A boat! It slid about a block and then shot into the air and plowed into the tin garage door of Johnson Auto Repair and splintered. I wondered about my house. At least the Missus and the kids were hundreds of miles away.

From our vantage point, we watched the storm pick apart building after building. A glint of light made me look up. A corner of HQ's roof had torn away. The opening grew. Soon, rain poured in. People moved wastebaskets to catch some of it. My shoes were soggy, and I slogged through chunks of wet paper. It went on like that for an hour and a half.

Wait. Yes. The wind was lessening again. Then it stopped.

I stepped out where the front doors had been. One part of the sky was dotted with points. The stars had come out. The universe still was here.

"Everyone jake?"

It was Chief Burke.

A murmur indicated everyone was. One patrol officer had a gash above an eye from when a flying desk phone clipped him. Another had broken an arm when the front doors came in. But that was it.

A cop came out from the back, his arms heavy with white towels. "Found these in the supply closet." He handed them out until they were gone, which didn't take long. I got lucky. I wiped my face. My uniform was soaked.

The chief said, "Be daylight soon, men. I know we haven't slept all night, but you'd better not count on it right now. Moran. Comeau. Get out on the street. Take patrol guys with you. Take notes and send 'em back with one man at a time to let us know what you are seeing and where."

Outside, we walked over broken glass, chunks of concrete, and busted-up two-by-fours. Just a block from the station, we saw a dead dog. Another block later, we found our first dead person.

At the waterfront, to my right, a four-story apartment building had lost its wall. We saw right into kitchens and bedrooms. All I could think of was Anna's dollhouse. Sofas, stoves, and ice boxes had been flung out and down to the street. Also, people.

Around us, women walked around like they didn't know where to go or what to do. Some had had the dresses torn off them, and they stood, dazed, in their underwear. Some people had wrapped dish towels around bloody heads. I motioned for patrol guys to go help. Water in the street was up to our calves.

On the eastern horizon, the sky was lightening. We saw carnage up and down Biscayne Boulevard. Soon, we were up to two dozen bodies. Some were twisted into knots. Some were in trees. Some were so torn up you had to look away. I pulled out a pad and flipped to some mostly dry pages. I scribbled some notes. I tore out the sheets and motioned to a patrol guy to run them back.

I saw coming at me Green, the weather service guy. He had thigh-deep waders. That would have been a good idea. His eyes were filled with tears.

"I kept shouting that this was just the eye. The calm before the second half of the storm. People had driven over from Miami Beach to ogle. And to celebrate that they had survived. I said to go back. Go back. Go back!"

He shook his head.

"It was a tight storm eye. Not even twenty minutes. The second half doesn't build. It starts strong. They got caught. Some of them drove right off the causeway into the bay. Some were thrown when their cars rolled. Some were cut to pieces by flying whatever."

It occurred to me that I was really, really tired.

A little girl stood in the street. Couldn't have been more than twelve. She was barefoot. I leaned down.

"Sweetheart. I'm a policeman, and I need for you get home, or at least find some shoes. There's all sorts of broken stuff hiding under this water. You'll cut your feet up something awful. And get a nasty infection."

She wasn't listening. Her eyes were fixed on something. A fish flapped in the roadway in about six inches of water. Maybe a gray snapper. She wrestled it up to her chest. Its snout worked as it gulped for air. Probably hadn't expected it would end its day on Biscayne Boulevard. The girl ran off.

She made me think of Jimmy Chin. With him on the loose again, and police otherwise occupied, I worried about every girl in town.

My worry was for nothing. Two patrol guys would find Jimmy face down in two feet of water, just off the seawall in Bayfront Park. He was all twisted in mangroves. Chief Burke said later the guy probably drowned first, but it was hard to tell because of the beating his body took.

I can't say I felt sorry for him, and it did save the state the cost of a trial, not to mention the extra electricity to send the guy to hell. But Jimmy could have solved some mysteries. At least close things up, as horrible as it was, for some families.

Back at HQ, I told Comeau, "We'll still go down to Redland, when we can."

It would be a week. And that week was a blur. Snatches of sleep. Hours in the blistering sun. Rain and more rain. And standing water. I stank from my own sweat, and garbage, and rotted seaweed, and the saltwater that had come in from the bay. My feet barked from all the walking. A cut on my ankle got infected. I limped through it.

My house had lost a window. I got a board over it. The power didn't come on for two days, so the fans were useless, and even with the windows all open, the humidity was brutal. I tried to clean up the best I could, but I had to be at work. The house smelled damp and moldy.

The day after the electricity came back on, the Missus and the kids came back from Georgia. I met them at the station. There was crying. And so on.

She said, "I was in such a hurry to get out, I didn't check on Sandra and Nancy Monk. All alone."

"I checked, Hon. It's all jake. She got on a train to Baltimore the same day as you. She's back tomorrow. Maybe you'll look in on her."

When we got to the house, I was afraid the Missus would faint. But Charlotte Harper handles crises by taking charge. In twenty minutes, she had unpacked herself and the kiddies and had pulled out buckets and mops and sponges and was barking orders. I told her she had me for the rest of the afternoon, but I had to go back to work in the morning. I didn't tell her how little sleep I'd gotten since the day of the storm. Actually, since the night before, lying awake thinking about that little girl. But the Missus could tell how washed out I was. She told me to hit the sack. Said she and the kids had had it easy in Georgia, and it was their turn to do something. I was asleep as soon as I landed on the mattress.

The next morning, I was at the weather office. Plywood covered its smashed windows. Inside, the water had been swept out. But everything smelled sour. A floor fan tried to ease the stink.

Green, the weather guy, was out front with a gaggle of reporters. The heat and humidity felt like a blanket. The sun was relentless. Everything was steamy.

Green looked like I felt. But he was slogging on.

He was like a baseball manager giving statistics after the game. Stats is why I was there, too.

In mainland Miami, Green said, every building in a one-mile radius of where we stood had been damaged. Many were flattened.

"I never seen a storm's winds stay about a hundred miles an hour for a whole hour," he told the newshawks. "That's sustained, not gusting. We know they gusted to at least to one twenty-three before the gauge blew off the roof. I'm guessing they got to one fifty."

I thought about driving down the street at thirty miles an hour and sticking out my head into the wind. Then I thought about one fifty. I thought about the boat I saw fly into Johnson Auto Repair.

"Eight inches of rain in twenty-four hours. Storm surge up at Baker's

Haulover was fifteen feet."

Fifteen feet!

Green said water had been calf-deep three blocks in from the bay. It didn't drain back for days. Everything in every structure was soaked. Walls, floorboards, furniture, inventory. A surge had come up the Miami River, and warehouses on either side had up to five feet of brackish water inside. Everything was ruined. The losses would add up to a number I couldn't begin to figure out.

Most of Miami Beach's hotels and night spots got clobbered. All of them were waterlogged. I was thinking that the season would start in about ten weeks. How could they be ready?

Green said a hundred fifty boats sank. One had rolled and blocked the channel. It was loaded with construction bricks. No one would be sailing in or out for a while.

"This is the most profound hurricane that has ever struck southern Florida on record. And my office in Washington has declared it the worst hurricane, in both power and deaths and damage, that has struck the American mainland since the great 1900 Texas hurricane. And that's just from what we know now."

A reporter asked Green about total damage, in dollars. He shrugged.

Then he motioned to me to the front. I cleared my throat. This is the number they'd been waiting on. The body count.

I said my name and spelled it. I said, "Police Chief Burke and coroner Phil Purdy have asked me to announce." I paused. "Two hundred and seventy-three. That's as of an hour ago."

I scanned the reporters' faces for reaction. They didn't show surprise. They'd been out on the streets.

"Off the record, boys, the coroner said to count on that going over three hundred by this time tomorrow. Not people newly dying. People they're finding."

One reporter said, "What about injuries?"

"We'll never get a good number on that. Don't even bother."

A large man pushed through the reporters. They used the pause to run their hankies over their pates. I stepped aside. The man turned and faced the news guys. In his vest and tie, he looked ridiculous in the sweltering heat.

"Go ahead, mayor," a reporter said.

Hizzoner puffed up like a bicycle tire. He got that look that all politicians get when they know everyone around them is waiting to hear what they say, and they can take all the time they want.

"I predict," his voice boomed. "I predict that Miami will make a world-class comeback. It is the same people who have created the fastest-growing city in America who are now turning their energies and enthusiasm to the work of reconstruction."

He smiled at the reporters. Then he was off. I watched his receding bulk. Between him and the storm, I couldn't decide which had been more of a blowhard.

"Okay, boys," Green said. "That's it for now. We all got a lotta work to do."

As reporters scattered, they smirked at the mayor's optimism. I didn't blame 'em. The good times probably were over.

Southern Railway had announced free rides for anyone who wanted to go north, and when I'd picked up the Missus and the kids at the station when they came back from Georgia, I saw people packed in northbound cars like sardines. They wouldn't be coming back.

Mixed in with them, I suspect, were a lot of the guys who'd come down to buy and sell property like a board game. The folks up north, who'd been watching their money flow south for years, had been looking for a reason to badmouth Florida. Now they had it. A place that got flattened like this every few years was a lousy investment, they argued. It was more like every few decades. But it didn't matter. The fix was in.

The next day, Chief Burke gave the nod for Harvey Comeau and me to coordinate with the county sheriff and go get Julia McKenzie.

The storm had been tightly wound. Miami was smashed, but down south, it had stayed dry and sunny the whole time. Go figure. Just as well. I didn't want to think about pulling Julia out of mud.

She was about two feet down, right where Jimmy had said he planted her when he'd bragged at the craps table. She stared with dull eyes. She still wore her white socks and school shoes. And a plaid dress with the school crest. The plaid was blue. Her hair was, in fact, red. Jimmy had done things to her. Unspeakable things. And then strangled her.

I motioned for Comeau and the two county deputies to stop clearing the dirt from around Julia. We just stood, leaning on our shovels. Silently. For a long time. I really wanted to sit down.

An hour up the road, a storm had killed hundreds of people. But that was the whim of nature. This was something else.

Chapter Four: The Cemetery

The morning after we dug up little Julia McKenzie, and I had to tell her parents, I didn't want to go to work. The Missus would have none of it.

"Nate, I know you're hurtin' for that little girl and her parents. And, well, you're seeing her in your mind. But if it wasn't for you, they'd never found her. They'd gone to their graves wondering what happened." She topped off my coffee. "I know you didn't get the satisfaction of watching that—that—that animal get justice. But you can't do nuthin' about it. Best way to honor that little girl is to keep doin' your job."

I looked up. "Well, Charlotte Harper. If I didn't know better, I'd swear you were on the debate team in high school." Which she had been.

Police HQ was mostly back to livable after the storm. Like most of Miami, including my house, the stale smell of damp and mold hung on. It would take a while.

Somehow, my work papers mostly survived. Some had gotten wet, and they'd dried wrinkled, and they were making a mess of my file folders.

Chief Burke stuck his head out of his door. "Nate. Need you in on this." I stepped in.

"Got a call from Gary Johns, detective over at the county sheriff."

I'd worked with Gary on some cases that had parts in the city and parts out in the county.

"Wants you to meet him pronto up at Baker's Haulover."

"Why? What's up?"

"All he said is they found a boat up there, mostly buried in a dune."

I checked out a roadster from the motor pool and drove up Biscayne Boulevard. The road had been cleared, but junk still was scattered on either side of it for miles. I cut over to the north end of Miami Beach. I parked near the south side of the inlet. Guys stood at the water's edge, in an area all roped off. I got closer. They were county deputies. And Phil Purdy. The coroner.

Uh-oh.

"Hello, Moran." Johns stuck out his hand. Next to him was a tall guy with a short haircut. Looked military. I guessed Fed.

"Meet Bruce Keyes. Prohibition agent."

Bingo.

Keyes shook. His face was serious. "I appreciate all you did for Bailey Monk."

I said, "It was a privilege."

Johns said, "Now that the gang's all here, here's what we know."

He pointed at the boat. Deputies with shovels had cleared away much of the sand around it. It looked busted up. And weather-beaten.

"Couple of treasure hunters came by looking to see, maybe someone dropped something, and the storm surge brought it up on shore. Started digging with a little pail and shovel and hit something big and hard."

"The boat was covered? All of it?"

"Sure was, Nate. We dug around it and measured it. About thirty feet long."

I said, "Nice size boat."

"We're thinking maybe someone was crossing from the Bahamas the night of the hurricane and hadn't been listening to the radio," Johns said.

I said, "Didn't they notice everyone in Freeport taking their boats out of the water? Running for the interior?"

"Maybe they were cocky. Thought they could go around it. Or outrun it. Wouldn't be the first people to die from stupid."

I said, "And maybe they figured the best time to get back home to Florida was when the U.S. Coast Guard was too busy to look for 'em."

The Coast Guard had been beefing up patrols between the coast and the islands. Most runners come in at Palm Beach. It's where the peninsula bulges east, and that makes it the closest point to the Bahamas. It's a straight shot west from Freeport. Lots of empty stretches of beach. Some of the runners get close and then angle down to Baker's Haulover. Lots more potential customers in Miami.

The idea that this boat belonged to rumrunners had been the obvious choice from the get-go. But it's good for cops to talk it out.

I said, "Why's Purdy here?" Dumb question.

Purdy's skinny and pale and looks more like a chess player than a guy who cuts up stiffs. But he knows his stuff. He motioned us to the far corner of the stern. I saw something I still see in my sleep.

A face. Just the face. Bleached pale white. Surrounded by sand. Eyes open. Spotted with grit and dirt. No need to brush it away. Nothing bothered this guy now.

"I got two of my morgue guys on their way," Purdy said. "We gotta treat this like a crime scene. Get this guy out without disturbing the rest of the boat."

It took another half hour of us standing in the heat before the meat wagon showed. Two guys in white, using small shovels, carefully dug around the body until most of it was out of the sand.

There's a smell when a body's been in water a couple days. Don't ask me to describe it. And hope you never sniff it. We all backed up. I guess Purdy and the boys in white are used to it. They didn't flinch.

"Look here, Nate."

I placed my hanky over my nose—it didn't do a lot of good—and drew closer. The stiff had a rope tied around his waist. We pulled on it. It led to a giant burlap bale. Through the fibers, glass reflected the sun.

Well, well, well.

Johns said, "Wanted to save his load of hooch if it's the last thing he did. Which it was."

Keyes said, "I guess that settles what these guys were." He clucked his tongue. "Hope it was worth it. I guess he'd say no."

The men in white gingerly slid a stretcher under the body. I worried it was gonna come apart on 'em. Yikes. I watched them walk to their wagon.

Purdy said, "OK, gents. The boat's all yours."

I told Gary Johns, "Your turf. You lead."

We spent a solid hour. Nothing on the boat would give us a hint to the identity of the dead rumrunner. Or who he might have been working for, if he was working for someone. Maybe Purdy would give us a better idea.

This wasn't my last stiff of the week.

Ever hear the old saw that when it rains it pours? In this case, it had stormed, and we still were finding stiffs. And not in the usual places.

Around the turn of the century, around when I was born, a handful of pioneer families had laid out a small cemetery on the bayfront just north of downtown. It held maybe fifty plots. Because of that, it didn't get a lot of visitors. Some folks let their dogs run through it. Sometimes we'd have to run out a bum who'd built a tent in the back corner and didn't mind sleeping with the dead.

Since the hurricane, anyone who had someone planted there had been too preoccupied for a visit. But the morning after we found the boat washed up at Baker's Haulover, someone woke up around sunrise, before the mosquitoes, and came to the little graveyard.

"She wanted to visit Grandpa at the cemetery and tell him all about the big blow," Senior Detective Dirk Monroe said, hands around his morning cup.

"I give up being surprised at the stuff that happens in this town. She got close to the plot and just about fainted dead away. Guess why."

I couldn't afford to be a smart aleck to Dirk. I said, "Go ahead."

"A hand was sticking out."

Two days in a row. Not counting the little girl in the grave. The hurricane's dirt and smell and heat and water damage and all that death had given me a two-week headache. Smelling that waterlogged stiff at Baker's Haulover hadn't helped. Now I had to see another corpse, and I hadn't even hung up my coat at my desk yet.

Dirk said, "The granddaughter screamed. That woke up the folks in a nearby house, who called HQ, who sent the patrol guys, who reported to Chief Burke, who laid it on me. We told the patrol guys not to touch anything until you got there."

Dirk would give a lot of advice over the years. One of the best pieces: When he would send me out before I'd had my first cup of bad police coffee, or drag me out of bed in the middle of the night, he would shrug and say, "Crime never sleeps."

I set my fedora. "On my way."

One of the patrol guys had driven the poor lady home. She'd given him the name of the fellow who manages the plot. That guy, and the patrol guy, and me, all got to the place around the same time. The manager had brought some shovels. We wouldn't need them.

We were thinking maybe the storm surge from the bay had washed away the topsoil and pushed open the rotted wood of a twenty-year-old coffin lid. But that couldn't be right. After twenty years, Grandpa wouldn't have much of a hand. And soon after I got there, we knew it wasn't Grandpa.

I told the two patrol guys to push away mud from the hand. It was connected to an arm, inside the sleeve of a suit jacket. One of the coppers felt around and pulled, and there was a second hand and arm. I shouted, "Stop." I eyeballed the two arms, then picked a spot in the middle and cleared away mud. There was a face.

First, that poor girl. Then the soggy stiff at Baker's Haulover. Now another washed-out face of someone who's been under dirt for a while.

I reached around it and pushed away some more mud. Under the stiff was the original coffin.

"Well, I'll be," I said to no one in particular. I turned to the manager. "Any guess how long he's been here?"

The manager leaned over. "I'd say not too long. Suit's in good shape. As for the body, if it was embalmed, it can take months to look like this. I suspect this guy wasn't embalmed, still in his suit and all. Plus, he got really wet. You know what that does. I'd say it's probably a question for the coroner."

And there was Purdy, the coroner. Standing right behind me. For the second day in a row.

"Nice meeting you like this, Purdy," I said. "Usually by the time someone ends up at a cemetery, you're already done with him."

Purdy said, "This is a new one, even for me."

He dropped to a knee and reached into a bag and pulled out a pair of black rubber gloves. He slid them on and worked his fingers over the stiff's face. I swear it's like it was falling apart. It was hard to watch.

"Three weeks at most." He turned to the manager. "You're right. No embalming. Up in places like Minnesota, in the north woods, a corpse, if a critter don't get you, take several weeks to look like this. Down here, the summer heat and rain, I'd say no more than three weeks. Know for sure when I get him to the morgue."

"That's slick," Dirk Monroe said, cig in hand, leaning on the wall in Chief Burke's office back at HQ.

"Yep," I said. "Take someone out and bury them on top of someone else in a cemetery. Never get caught."

Dirk leaned back. "Unless you get a storm of the century."

I'd washed my hands in hot water three times, but they still smelled from that mud at the grave, and whatever god-awful gunk was in it. I wanted to go home and take a hot bath.

A tap on the jamb. My partner Harvey Comeau stuck in his head. "It's Purdy. Walked over from next door."

Burke said, "Send him in." He wanted to hear this.

Purdy dropped into a chair. He said, "Nate, you're the luckiest detective in Florida."

"How's that?"

"Well, I was thinking like a cop. Like maybe someone offed this poor mope and put him in the dead farm. Anyone go through that trouble is cocky no one will ever find the guy. But they're old hands. Still going to make sure to take any ring or watch and empty the stiff's pockets. Anything that could identify him."

"Purdy, you could teach at the academy. But if that's what happened here, how am I lucky?"

Purdy grinned. He was having fun with this.

"Well. We had to cut his suit off him. Turned out he had a little tear in the inside coat pocket. Probably from a pen or a pencil. A piece of paper had gotten through the hole and inside the lining and slid to the bottom. It was wet and muddy, but we were able to dry it enough to read it."

Purdy opened an envelope that had been in his shirt pocket and carefully handed the thing to me.

Ticket number 32059. King the Tailor. Twenty-one Northeast Second Street.

A block away.

* * *

"Hmm." Roderick King was thinking, palms on his counter. He dropped into a chair, spun it, and reached to a back desk for a ledger.

"That series of numbers goes back about, let me see…" His finger moved down the page.

His shop was thick with suits and dresses and jackets and slacks, all hanging on pipes that spanned each wall. I felt like I was in a water plant. I said, "Mr. King: Just curious. I know the storm surge came up through this neighborhood. How'd you save all your togs from getting soaked?"

He smiled. "Elevation, me boy. Elevation! That British know-how. That and metal sheets bolted to the windows to keep out the wind. And we were between two large buildings."

I was impressed.

"Also…" But King's mouth stopped. So did his finger.

"Yes. Here. Goes back to April."

I waited.

"Luke Crawford."

Next stop: HQ. Leo at the front desk, sifting through his own ledgers.

"Crawford, Crawford, Crawford."

From behind me: "I can tell you, partner." It was Harvey Comeau. "I know the guy. He's muscle for Mark Gregg."

Well, well, well.

Comeau motioned with his head toward Dirk Monroe's desk. "Let's go back."

Harvey filled in Dirk, who said, "Think maybe the Mosleys took him out? Some turf war thing?"

We knew all about the Mosleys. Gregg's biggest competitor. Claude's the leader. Oldest of a bunch of brothers and cousins set in the woods northwest of Palm Beach. Maybe got a place west of Miami, too. They make life hard for cops from Cape Canaveral down to Key Largo. Rumrunning, stills, robbery. Real nice guys.

Dirk shook his head. "Nah. Plenty of commerce to go around. These guys mark off their turf and mostly leave each other alone."

He looked at the ceiling. "Well. Mostly."

Now none of us was sure.

Chief Burke had walked over. We filled him in.

I said, "So who put Luke in the cemetery? Literally?"

Burkie leaned in. "Well, Nate, you're the one gonna find out."

Frank Marte still was in our jail, waiting for a judge to send him up to the state prison. The guard unlocked the cell and left. I sat.

"Thanks for letting me know about the little girl, Moran." Marte looked away. "Not that it mattered."

"Frankie, you did the right thing. You don't say something, maybe the parents never know. And maybe Jimmy Chin's doing it to some other poor girl."

He shrugged. "I didn't do it just to get a break. I did it because...."

"I know, Frankie. I know."

I slid a real cigarette out of my jacket pocket and held it out. I pulled out a matchbook and Frank leaned in while I lit the thing. He inhaled and I got that first whiff of toasted tobacco before the harsh smoke kicked in. I do miss it.

"Thanks, Nate."

Then he looked at me. "You want something."

I smiled. "I guess I need to work on my technique. Yeah, Frankie."

He let out a big cloud of smoke. "Will it get me more points?"

We both were smiling. I said, "See what I can do."

A long puff. "Go ahead."

I leaned in. Luke Crawford."

A smile. Smoke out. "A goon for Mark Gregg."

"Right. We knew that. Do you do business with Gregg?"

He shook his head. "Sorry, Nate. Won't tell you. Don't want to end up face down in the prison shower, a shiv in my back."

"Well, Luke's dead."

Frankie's eyes widened. "I'll be."

"Any ideas?"

Frankie took another long puff and savored it. I remembered what that was like.

"Well," he said. He looked at the cig. "I did hear a little on the lowdown just before you popped me. Like maybe Gregg caught Luke working both sides of the street."

Interesting.

"The Mosleys?"

He shook his head. "Dunno with who. Just that he was stepping out. Should've known better."

I'll say.

Chapter Five: Tamiami Trail

I've had some bad experiences with the courts. They can take months to bring a guy to trial. All the time, the mope is out on the street. But Mark Gregg felt good about his chances in court for killing my friend Monk, and he wanted to be done with this, one way or another. He had a business to run. So his lawyers pushed and pushed to move things up. But then we had the storm. So it still was a while. And the bad guys didn't slow down. Even Gregg's competitors. Especially them.

In the morning, I have time to help get the kids ready and pack their lunches before they head out for the three-block walk to school. Then a quick scan of the paper and a cup of decent joe, and I'm off to fight bad guys.

This Monday didn't work out. My phone rang at seven. It was Chief Burke.

"Tamiami Trail?"

I was in high school when I read about an idea to cut a road from Tampa down and then east through the Everglades to Miami. Why the name. Politicians talked about it and talked about it, but it took years for folks to finally start hacking through the jungle and swamp. The road opened a few years back. I've driven it a few times. Always pack a jug of water and a sandwich. A hundred miles of nothing. I pack my gun, too.

Because of where they built the Trail, nature's hard on it. Crews are always fixing or shoring up something. This time, the hurricane had taken out some bridges. Crews had been out there a few weeks. One crew showed up just before sunrise Monday, and the guys found a corpse. Thus, my early departure from hearth and home.

You get a good headache bouncing down a rocky road. Plus, an ache at the other end.

I saw tractors in the middle of the road and pulled off. Nothing but mud and standing water.

To my right, workmen sat in the grass between the roadway and a canal. They knocked back jugs. It looked from their stained overalls like the water they drank skipped a few steps and turned into sweat as soon as it hit their gullets.

Two patrol guys had been there for a while. They'd pulled the body out of the water and covered it with a blanket. The coroner was running late. Guess he'd slept in.

One of the coppers pointed to a flat wooden boat in the canal.

"Caught the eye of one of the construction guys. Floating upside down and all. He was eyeballin' it when he saw a hand slide out."

More hands sticking out.

The construction worker next to the cop said, "I wandered over to take a leak. I-I-I seen a lot of fellas get hurt on the job. I never seen no dead guy. Ever. Especially one looked like him."

The patrolman said, "Looked like he'd been in the water a couple days. Under the boat. Steaming. He looked like a poached fish. Never wanna see that again."

I suspected neither the cops nor this worker had had breakfast. Or if they had, they regretted it.

"ID?"

The cop shook his head. "Not exactly. No papers on him. But he was wearing Seminole clothes. And that's one of their flatboats."

I walked to the larger group. "One of you the foreman?"

A stocky fellow in overalls and a mustache stood. "Me. Ken Hearst."

I showed my badge. "Need to talk to the Seminoles. Can you help?"

"One usually comes around this time. Sells us frybread."

About twenty minutes later, a flat canoe emerged from the long morning shadows. A short, dark-skinned man with a bowl haircut, wearing regular work pants but a colorful shirt with horizontal stripes, worked a long pole that steered as much as it propelled. The canoe stopped. The man stared at the upside-down flatboat. Pretty much like his. He didn't say anything.

You don't like to judge a whole group. But it sure seems there's something in the Seminole culture that they keep their feelings close to their chests. Suspect the way we treated them the last hundred years or so is part of that.

Mosquitoes buzzed my ear. I saw their tiny black shapes around this guy's head. He didn't move.

No badge would do me any good right now. I pointed to the guy's basket. I recalled the word the construction foreman had used.

"Frybread?"

I dug into my pants pocket for coins and held them out. He counted out what he needed and dropped the coins into a pocket in the front of his shirt that I hadn't made out earlier. He bent and came up with a loaf of bread. I bit in. It was as dense as a rock. And delicious.

I made a big deal of showing how much I was enjoying the stuff, which wasn't a stretch. After what I figured was the right amount of time for decorum, I pointed to the body.

The man said, "Billy Tiger."

Now I pulled out my badge. He looked me up and down and wiped his hands on his pants. He was thinking about it.

"Umm, Billy was my cousin."

I looked at the boat and back at him. His expression never changed. Just a blank face.

He said, "Not an accident."

Okay.

I said, "How do you know?"

"We grow up on the water. Do this every day. Water is calm here. Not like the ocean. And the boat is flat. Nothing makes you flip. Nothing."

I took another bite and talked while I chewed. "You're saying someone killed your cousin?"

Another nod. This guy was some live wire. A real chatterbox.

He stood for a second. Nearby, something splashed. The black water swallowed the sunlight.

"You like the bread? Okay-okay?"

I said I did. More seconds passed. Something buzzed my ear. The man looked at something in the distance. I took another bite. Waited him out.

"Billy helped bring hooch out of the swamp." A pause. "For the Mosleys."

The Mosleys. Whaddya know.

"Moonshine?"

A nod.

"Why are you telling me this?"

A shrug. "Too late for you to do anything to Billy. Police never lied to us. Told us if they catch us with hooch, they put us in jail. But mostly they left us alone. Okay okay. But big Mosley lied."

"Big Mosley? You mean Claude?"

Another nod.

"Big Mosley said he'd give Billy big money to move hooch. Then he..." He looked away. "Then he killed Billy."

I said, "Did you see it?"

More mosquitoes buzzed my ear. The man pulled out a hanky and wiped his face. Then he reached for his pole. "No. Didn't see. Can't help you."

Terrific.

Then he surprised me. "Maybe someone saw something."

He turned the boat and poled into the hanging branches. In a second, they'd swallowed him.

Slap! A big one had stabbed the side of my neck.

I waited until the morgue guys came and took Billy away. Then I made the long drive back to police HQ and filled in Dirk Monroe. The senior detective took a big drag of his smoke. "Sure wish we could leave all this Prohibition stuff to the Feds. A federal problem that local cops gotta clean up. This ain't the first time."

"But Claude Mosley killing that Seminole. That's our problem."

"Another half mile west and it would have been the county's," Dirk said. Another drag. "Moonshine. Rumrunning. Banks. Payrolls. Murder. The Mosleys sure do diversify."

"A fancy word. Now you're showing off."

He smiled. Then he didn't. "They're slick. But maybe we can nail him on this."

"Hardly. If we can't collar him for a dead guy in a cemetery two blocks from here, how do we get him for drowning a Seminole out in the Everglades?"

"Have a little faith, Nate. Crazier things have happened. This is South Florida."

How many times have I heard that?

Dirk took another drag. "You might have a higher profile in not too long. Chief's creating a new position for me. Chief of detectives."

I'd heard rumors. "Maybe you're next in line for chief?"

Dirk doesn't mince his words. Got him in trouble sometimes, but mostly people respect his bluntness. I'm the same. Maybe that's we like each other so much.

"Probably," Dirk said. "Maybe even a lock. But not for a while. I'd say about five years. Chief Burke still loves what we do. But you know he's already got a granddaughter. Sure likes her company."

Dirk or the current chief, didn't matter. Both standup guys. I was proud to work alongside them.

The next morning, I hadn't even finished my first cup at my desk when my phone rang.

"Nate Moran. Detectives."

"Detective: It's Dennis Martin. I'm road manager for the company doing the work out on the Trail where they found that dead Seminole."

"Hi Dennis. I don't envy your guys. Between the heat and the mosquitoes."

"Right, Moran. They're good men. I'm calling because early this morning, one of our supply drivers told me he'd just dropped off some hardware out there. Said he bought frybread off a Seminole for the long drive back, and the guy told him to get a message to you. To be out there around noon today. That's all he said."

Another hour of bouncing. I pulled off at the bridge. A guy I recognized as Hearst, the foreman, stepped over.

"What's up, Detective? Thought you guys cleared out yesterday."

"Don't know, Hearst. Let you know when I find out."

I'd taken off my jacket and left it on the front seat of my police-issue roadster. The day still was toasty. I stood and sweated for twenty minutes.

Just like last time, without warning, a flatboat materialized out of the shadows of the branches hanging over the canal. It was the same Seminole. He didn't speak.

I looked him up and down. Then I reached into my pocket. "Lemme have one of those. And five for the other guys."

He took the money and handed me the bread. I walked it to the crew. I walked back, and the Seminole was moving some things on his boat. Sure didn't look like they needed arranging. I took another bite of my loaf. I was filling up in a hurry. Won't need lunch.

I waited.

The man still looked down. But he talked to me.

"Got another cousin. Mitch Cypress. He guided a hatkee—white—on Saturday. Night fishing. Bigmouth bass. I asked around this morning. He didn't wanna tell, but then he did. He seen everything. It was dark, but he knows Mosley. Worked for him a few times. Mitch says he pulled the boat into the trees and told the hatkee not to talk, or it would be very bad. The two of 'em kept quiet. Saw Mosley grab Billy with some other guys. They, umm…"

The man stopped. He looked at the floor of his boat, like he hoped to find something else to rearrange.

"Umm, they held Billy's head in the water."

A long pause.

"When they finished, they made it look like the boat flipped. Like you saw."

I swallowed a chunk of the bread.

"Why'd they do it? Did your cousin Billy double-cross the Mosleys?"

The man shook his head again. "No. Billy was mad big Mosley lied about the pay. Billy told Mitch the day before that he was gonna tell Mosley to pay what he promised, or he would go to the police."

Well. That was a mistake.

This is getting to be a pattern. Foot soldiers end up in jail, like Frankie from the speakeasy. Or dead, like Billy Tiger. And maybe Luke Crawford. But the kingpins skate.

"Will Mitch talk to us? Could help us send your cousin's killer to the chair."

The man shook his head. "Mitch don't want to go to jail himself. Or dead. He got new work. Far away from the Mosleys. He's scared of 'em."

I'd be scared.

"Mister"—I didn't know this guy's name. "If Mitch won't talk, can he at least tell us the name of the white guy he guided?"

The man's face showed no emotion. A pause. Then he looked over. My eyes followed his. In the direction of the road construction crew. I turned back. He already was turning his flatboat. In a minute, he was gone.

First thing in the morning, I called the guy who'd called me the day before: Dennis Martin, the road manager.

"Detective. What's doing?"

No time for small talk. "Mr. Martin, I have strong reasons to believe one of your crew out there at the Tamiami Trail bridge is a material witness in a murder investigation. I can shut you down. I suspect just one day of that would be very expensive to you guys. I've set aside this morning to do desk work. I'll wait for a call from you."

Martin sputtered. I cut him off. "I'll wait for a call from you."

A few hours later, Harvey Comeau said for me to come with him to drop off some papers at the courthouse, and then we'd stop at Rosedale Deli for corned beef. I asked him to bring me back a sandwich.

"Umm, can you spot me a five?"

"Didn't get to the bank, Harv?"

His face darkened. "Something like that."

Harvey left. I stayed. I had a hunch, and I didn't wanna to leave my desk. It was a good move. Five minutes after Harvey left, the phone rang.

"Nate Moran. Detectives."

"Dennis Martin."

He couldn't see me smile.

"Yes, sir."

"Will you be in your office in a little while?" Say, noon?

"I will."

"See you then." Click.

When Martin came in, he wasn't alone. Something had told me not to be surprised if it was Hearst, the foreman. So I wasn't. I found us an interview room.

Dennis Martin was sheepish. "Detective, I believe the best way to handle this is the way I do business. Straight and head-on."

"Suits me."

"OK." He put his rough hands palm down on the table and looked at the backs of them.

"For reasons of safety, and legal stuff, our contract calls for all workers to be off the site at sundown, which we check the time against the newspaper weather page. Naturally, we do not work weekends. No one is to be on the site ever, except our employees, and then only during working hours."

Hearst had his hat off. His forehead was red from the sun. He stared at the floor. He was like a schoolboy caught lifting jujubes at a five-and-dime.

"Our foreman here is allowed to take the company truck home on weekends. On Monday morning, he swung by the yard to pick up some materials before he headed out to the bridge. Right away, I saw the truck had a big dent in the back. Hearst said he'd parked it on the street outside his house, and someone must have clipped it and took off."

Hearst still looked at the floor.

"This morning, detective, after you called, I drove out to the site. I pulled aside every worker, one at a time. I saved Hearst for last. When I mentioned you, he cracked."

Hearst looked like he'd swallowed a spark plug.

"Told me that on Friday, he was talking to the injun who sells the boys bread. Made arrangements to come back out Saturday and go fishing with a Seminole guide. That night, on his way off the site, he backed into a dredge. That was the dent."

I said, "Mr. Hearst, I suspect you hit that dredge because your mind was racing with something you just seen and you wanted to scram."

Hearst was buttoned up.

I told Martin, "Sir, I wouldn't tell you how to run your business. But you have a golden opportunity to help us get a murderer to where he can't bother anyone. All you gotta do is make a deal with your foreman here."

Martin leaned in and folded his fingers on the table.

"Like maybe, we don't punish him for breaking company policy and damaging a company vehicle, and he agrees to testify to what he saw. In court."

I gave a big smile. "Either of you like a cup of coffee? I can fire up another pot."

For the first time, Hearst looked up. "Detective, I got a wife and a little boy. Those injuns tole me those gangsters drowned that redskin 'cuz he crossed 'em. If I help you, my name goes public, and maybe they come after me. My family."

"Hearst, I can't make you do this. And you're right. These criminals are bad dudes. I'm guessing they'd like to ice me sometime. Or my chief. One rumrunner popped a federal Prohibition agent. My friend. The thing is, we let them keep doing this, they never stop. I'm like you. I got a bride and three tykes. So maybe you help us 'cuz it's the right thing to do?"

Dennis Martin said, "Hearst, we'll back you all the way."

Hearst sat for a long minute. He exhaled. "Okay."

I told him he did the right thing. I didn't tell him nothing could happen to him. Wish I could.

Claude Mosley was so cocky he came into town two days later to buy provisions. We'd been watching his favorite haunts, and we were waiting. The chief called me, and I raced out to find him in the back of a prowl car. I leaned in. "Mr. Mosley. Nice to finally meet you."

He had this grin that made me want to punch him out.

"You'll never hold me."

∗ ∗ ∗

The phone. "Nate Moran. Detectives."

"Bruce Keyes."

"What's up, agent?"

"Last night, one of our guys ran in a snitch. The same one tipped Monk about Mark Gregg. One of many times he gave us a heads up on big landings of hooch. But everything's stopped for a while since the storm. So the snitch had to give my guy something. Throw him a bone."

I knew how that worked.

Keyes said, "You know Claude Mosley had two brothers."

I thought for a second. "Francis and Simpson."

"Right. We know they make the run to the dock at Freeport regular. This snitch says Francis went over right before the storm. Never came back."

I rang off with Keyes. I thought a minute. Then I called the morgue.

"Purdy? Nate Moran. Could you pull out that corpse from the boat that was in the sand at Baker's Haulover? Gonna bring someone down to you."

"Sure, Nate. Gimme twenty minutes."

I called down to the jail. Old Man Scheerer answered. Karl Scheerer's been our resident civilian jailkeeper for a dozen years.

"I'm coming down to check out Claude Mosley."

On my way out, I stopped at the front desk. "Leo: I need a patrol guy to walk with me to the jail. Pull out a prisoner. Walk him to the morgue."

"Hey Price." Leo motioned to a tall, stock kit at the end of the counter. The two of us walked around the back of City Hall.

"You play football?"

"Second-string defensive tackle. Miami High."

"My alma mater."

We met Scheerer at the front door, and he walked us down the hall. We shut the cellblock door behind us. I motioned to Scheerer, and he opened Mosley's cage.

The guy sat calmly, pulling on a smoke.

Price and I walked into the cage together. Scheerer closed the door behind us. Taking no chances.

"Get up, Mosley. Gonna take a walk."

"Where to?"

"Tell you when you get there."

"Go to blazes."

The towering patrol officer took one step forward. Mosley put up his hands. "Okay. Okay. I'm going."

I grabbed his wrists and cuffed them in front. Then I clicked a second pair, one on his right wrist and one on the wrist of the beefy patrol guy.

"Officer Price here is going to be attached to you until you're back here. Got it?"

Five minutes later, we met Purdy at his giant wall of corpses. The gangster still had that smug smile. But his eyes also showed confusion.

"Claude. You know anyone lost at sea lately?"

I didn't know a man's face could turn that white that fast. For a crook, he didn't have much of a poker face. He took in a deep breath. Almost a gasp. He sputtered, "Uhh. No. No. No one I know."

He looked like his finger was stuck in a light socket.

I nodded at Purdy. The coroner grabbed a handle and slid out a drawer. He flipped down the sheet.

Mosley stared down at the wrinkled, rotting, stinking corpse from Baker's Haulover.

Price's arm pulled taut. Mosley's knees had turned to rubber, and he hung from Price by the handcuff chain. I saw a look on Mosley's face.

"Need a bucket. Pronto!"

Purdy reached back to a shelf and grabbed a metal pail. He put it in Mosley's free hand. Mosley gripped it with white knuckles. His knees touched the floor now, and Price had to kneel alongside.

In seconds, Mosley was emptying his stomach. He heaved and coughed and gagged. His face leaned into the pail. Price had to lean as well, because he still was cuffed to the guy.

I motioned to Purdy. He slid the drawer shut. Then he gave me a funny look. Just sort of stared. Caught me off guard.

I nodded to Price, then at a bench. The patrol guy half lifted Mosley to it.

The gangster had stopped heaving. He still was the color of a bedsheet. Purdy grabbed a hand towel and wet it in a sink. He handed it to Mosley, who wiped his eyes and then his mouth.

I said, "I had to do that, Claude. I knew you'd never tell us it was Frank. And you didn't. Until your heart betrayed you."

Mosley had caught his breath. His look of terror had switched to something else.

"You're a bastard, Moran. You're evil. You got no soul."

I said nothing.

"I'll get you for this, detective. I swear. I'll get you."

We walked Mosley back to his cell. He didn't say a word all the way. But the stare…I'm used to dirty looks from thugs. This one spooked me. More than a little.

Back at my desk, I sat. Didn't say anything. Just looked at the ceiling. For a while.

Harvey Comeau had been reading reports. The body language of someone nearby not doing anything caught his attention.

"You okay, Nate?"

I kept my eyes on the ceiling. "Yeah, Harvey. Everything's jake."

Twenty minutes later, I heard Dirk Monroe's door open behind me. I turned that way. He motioned.

Inside, Dirk did something he'd never done with me before. Ever. He shut the door.

I stood while he walked around his desk and sat. He waited a minute. Then he put his palms on his desk.

"Nate, you're the best young detective we have. And I think of you almost like a son."

I had a feeling where this was going. My face flushed.

"I—I—I was wrong today."

I sat down hard in the chair across from him. I said, "Mosley." Then, "I—I…" My voice trailed.

Dirk lit a smoke and blew out.

"Nate, I just got off the phone with Purdy, the coroner. He's upset. You might want to call him later."

I kept my eyes to the floor.

"I'm sure you thought you had to do something desperate to get Mosley to confirm that the body was his brother. All good and well. But, well, I don't approve of your tactics."

He leaned in. "Son, scum like Mosley are, well, they're scum. Everyone knows that. But we cops are judged by how we separate ourselves from the scum we deal with every day. That we're better than them."

I sat with my hands on my knees. I didn't say anything for a while.

"I won't lie to you, Nate. This wasn't good."

I wanted to cry. I knew the feeling would pass, but right now I wanted to quit the force and go tar roofs. First, I wanted to go home and curl up in a ball in my bed.

"I...I..." It was nearly a whisper. "What about..."

"What about Mosley threatening you? Or your family? Or me?"

"Yeah. If he does something because of what I did, I'll never...I'll never forgive..."

"Look, Nate. I told you these guys are scum. What you did wasn't right. But don't think for a minute that if Mosley or one of his goons came after us, it just would be about this. He's someone who held a human being's head in filthy canal water until the man drowned.

"You don't have to worry about comparing yourself to him. And he already hates every lawman from here to Pensacola. And then some. You couldn't make it any worse."

I was ready for Dirk to pass sentence. His lip curled in a smile. "Don't worry. You're not getting fired. Or demoted. You're too important to this department. Burkie and I talked, and he feels the same way. And, well, I think maybe you're already punishing yourself."

The weight in my chest lifted. A little.

"I know you, Nate. You'll learn from this. Also, let me make it easy for you. Anytime you're not sure if something's hunky-dory, there's an easy way out. Run it past someone higher than you. Then—and here's the best part—if it goes wrong, it's their butt. Not yours."

Good advice.

"Take the rest of the day off, Nate. Tomorrow, we move on."

At home, I told the Missus everything. Everything. She sat for a while. She said, "Nate, I hope you know how lucky you are to have bosses like Chief Burke and Dirk Monroe. They handled this just right. And you'll be a better man for it."

I still spent a lot of the night staring at the ceiling.

Chapter Six: "I had a better year"

nna wanted to be a lion. She was resolute.

I said, "What's your plan?" The Missus said, "I got some yellow yarn. I can make whiskers and a tail. That'll be enough for her."

"She'll take it off five minutes after we get to the school, hon."

The Missus smiled and shrugged.

Matt and Zach were easy. Matt already had a cowboy hat. The Missus talked Zach into being a ghost because she had an old sheet. Our family is nothing if not resourceful. Of course, I would go dressed as a police detective.

My friends on the force who'd moved to Florida from cooler climes told me their memories of Halloween were of yards littered with leaves ripe for kicking. And, depending on where they grew up, it already was cold. In some cases, really cold. Not a problem in Florida. It was a month or so since the hurricane, and temperatures still were in the eighties. But the humidity had dropped just enough to make things livable.

I was wrong about Anna's whiskers. They lasted twice as long. A full ten minutes. Matt doffed his ten-gallon just long enough to bob for an apple, then slapped it back on. But Zach quickly shed the bedsheet for a large game of tag.

We surveyed the chaos two dozen youngsters could create in a small schoolyard. My gaze slid to each of my three kids. I turned to the Missus. Before I could say anything, she said, "Yes, Nate. Too fast. Way too fast."

All afternoon, the kids ran and ran and ran. And gorged on hot dogs and candy. They didn't touch dinner and were out cold by eight O'clock. Which allowed the Missus and me some private time on a Saturday night.

* * *

I have no beef with celebrities. Sooner or later, they all show up down here. Then they're followed by reporters and photographers. And hangers-on trying to make a buck off 'em. And fans. Sometimes crazy ones who fling themselves on 'em and say, "I want to have your baby!"

Sometimes, if the person's a big enough deal—actually, if the crowd is big enough—we have to assign a patrol guy. Or two. Or sometimes a detective. Thanks, Dirk.

My paperwork said, "Harold Crews." Like anyone called him that. Everyone knew him by a single name: Bull.

For the first six games of the pro football season, Bull and his New York team tore up the league. Every Sunday, he'd run over guys on his way to the end zone. And every Monday, he'd whine about the size of his pay packet.

Until this past Monday. When no one could find him.

After Sunday's game in Chicago, he dressed in the locker room, walked outside, stepped into a taxi, and vanished. All day Monday, he was the talk of the nation. Had he taken a westbound train to parts unknown? Had crooks kidnapped him? Would the team pay ransom? Are they dragging Lake Michigan for his body?

On Tuesday morning, he surfaced. Where? Not Chicago. Not Canada. Not France or Australia. You guessed it.

"He's at the Everglades Hotel," Dirk Monroe said. He handed me a scrap of paper.

"Jane MacDonald?"

"She's his, umm, PR person."

My eyebrows arched. Dirk said, "Bull's been separated from his wife for a while. This dame has a separate room at the Everglades, but I'll bet a sawbuck the maids don't have to make her bed."

"And what am I doing?"

"She's called reporters to the hotel at ten this morning to hear Bull publicly give his bosses the, uh, terms of surrender. Meet her in the lobby at 9:30. Then you stay with her, and Bull, until they get the heck out of town and my migraine goes away."

"If I can be honest, it's not the kind of work I'm used to."

"I'll let that one go, Nate. You know we all have to pitch in, even for grunt work."

I grabbed a Cuban coffee on my walk to the Everglades. The place was the bee's knees. When you stayed here, you made sure to brag it to everyone. I couldn't even afford to sleep in the cloak room. The place wasn't my style anyway.

You couldn't miss Jane MacDonald. She stood in the dead center of the lobby, in a very businesslike dress, with a businesslike hairdo, and a businesslike face that stared down the people in front of her, a gaggle of guys I knew to be newshounds.

I flashed my badge. She said, "I expected you ten minutes ago."

A nervy dame. She caught me off guard. I stammered, "Uhh, the chief told me 9:30." Was I really talking like a schoolboy who was late for home room? She said, "9:20!" She let out an exasperated sigh. "Never mind. Follow me while I escort these gentlemen"—her face made it clear she used the word advisedly—"to the ballroom."

Bull sat, like a king in his court, in a groaning folding chair on a raised platform. He was a walking floor safe. His paws were as big as a bear's. Looked like he could squeeze me so hard my head would pop off.

A side table held a pitcher of lemonade and a plate of cookies. Bull hadn't touched 'em. As the reporters took seats, I saw more than a few eye the plate.

I stepped up onto the platform. "Nate Moran, sir. Detectives. Miami police. Here to, uh, protect you while you're in town."

We both smiled at the absurdity of my statement. He was as big as three of me.

The man put out one of those paws. "Shouldn't be any trouble." He leaned in and dropped his voice. "Don't want the newsboys to hear this. You probably won't have to worry about me too long. I'm guessing the bosses in New York is peeing their pants right now. I expect to be on a northbound train tomorruh."

I'd read that he grew up in Pittsburgh. His voice was as solid as that town's steel.

In front of us, Jane faced the reporters.

"Mr. Crews will read something. Then he will answer a few questions."

"Not a lot," Bull piped up behind her. "I got a tee time at Miami Country Club." Then he flashed that big Bull smile. The reporters all laughed. This guy was a bull, but he could melt ice.

Jane leaned to hand me a piece of paper and motioned to give it to Bull. He surprised everyone in the room by reaching into his suit jacket for a pair of specs. He cleared his throat.

"During the offseason, Miss MacDonald and I spoke repeatedly with team owners, both written and in person." He said "POY-sun."

"But it was to no…to no…" He handed me the paper. I ran my finger. I leaned and whispered, "To no avail."

"To no avail." He gave that big smile again. Then he quit reading off the paper.

"Look, boys. I played the first six games as a show of good faith. But now I'm ready to stay away until my demands is met. If the team is ready to play ball, I am ready to, well, play ball." He smiled at his cleverness.

"I can be in New York in plenty of time and be ready for Sunday's game. Or not. I got a telegram yestiday fum the folk over in Sarasota. They said they'd hire me right now to be announcer for the circus."

The reporters did chuckles and mumbles.

"I's serious, boys. The team needs me more'n I need them. And you can put that in your stories."

A man in the second row stood. "Bull. You never said how much you want."

Jane started to say something. Bull blurted out, "Eighty thou."

The girl turned to glare at him. Guess he wasn't supposed to let that out of the bag. He gave her a shrug. The newsies were like ants had crawled up their trouser legs.

A guy stood and shouted, "Bull. That's more than the president makes."

Bull smiled like he'd been waiting for this.

"I had a better year."

The reporters exploded into guffaws. They'd just won the grand prize. They'd gotten the quote of the day. Maybe month. Maybe year.

"That's it, boys," a flustered Jane shouted. But the newsies already had their backs to her. They were racing for the bank of phone booths in the lobby, shoving each other aside. In twenty seconds, the big ballroom was empty except for Jane and Bull. And me.

"Well, mister, uh, Crews…"

"Bull, brother. No one calls me by my real name."

"OK. Bull. I'm supposed to stick with you. I guess I'll follow you to the golf course."

It was a glorious fall day. The summer heat had broken. Bright blue skies and bright sun. What we call "Chamber of Commerce weather." Still, I was steaming in my suit as Bull, togged up in plaid plus-fours and a brightly colored shirt, a tam on his noggin, mugged for the photographers. As per my assignment, I walked with the guy through all nine holes. After the first two, I slipped his caddie a buck to hold my jacket. My dress shirt was damp. So was my forehead around my fedora.

Bull had joined up with some local bankers. I gave the foursome their distance. At the end of the game, I took a load off on a bench at the Nineteenth Hole Club and waited while the golfers ate roast beef sandwiches and knocked back lemonades. They probably were lemonades. Maybe.

All this time, Jane was nowhere to be found.

Bull and I walked out the front, and he gave his ticket to the valet.

"Umm, sir, your lady friend done took that car 'bout an hour ago."

Bull got a confused look. I stood with him for about twenty minutes. His roadster came around the corner, Jane at the wheel. He leaned and said something, and she slid to the passenger side. Bull smiled back at me, opened the door, and climbed in. I didn't hear what the two said. I hopped in my car and followed them back to the Everglades.

Out front, Jane turned to me. "Bull and I will be resting the rest of the afternoon. We're fine."

I walked them in and made sure they were in their rooms, guessing Jane wouldn't be in hers for long. Then I excused myself and drove back to HQ. I stopped for a late barbecue and brought it to my desk. I checked my messages and did some paperwork until it was time to knock off.

"How'd you like bein' around royalty, Nate?" The Missus was eating it up. She knew I could take celebrities or leave 'em.

"Just doin' my job, ma'am."

* * *

I've been on more than one assignment that led to my being woken up by the phone out in the kitchen. This one hadn't looked to me like it would be one of those. I was wrong.

"Get down to the Everglades Hotel. Pronto." It was Dirk Monroe. I looked at the clock. Three in the AM. A cop gets a call at that hour; it can't be anything but bad.

"What's up, Chief?"

"Jane MacDonald. The Bull's lady friend. He woke up to find her hugging the commode. Then she fell over on the tiles and stopped breathing. For good."

"On my way."

I threw on my suit from earlier in the day and walked fast down to the waterfront. Even at this hour, Biscayne Boulevard had more than just a few cars. I turned into the lobby. A patrol guy named Hughes stood by the front desk. He waved me over. We raced up a fancy staircase to the Mezzanine and down a hall of rooms. One door near the end was open. I recalled it as Bull's. Another uniform guy stood in front of it.

Bull sat on the edge of his bed, sobbing. I leaned in and spoke quietly. "Mr. Crews. Bull. It's me. Nate Moran. The police detective."

Bull lifted his swollen and wet face. The giant who lived up to his nickname, who could drag three tacklers across the goal line, was gone. In his pajamas, Bull looked like a little boy. He pulled his bedsheet and used it to wipe his nose. He talked to the ceiling.

75

"We'd spent the afternoon readin' on the balcony. She said she didn't want dinner. Not hungry. I dint think nothin' of it. I skipped it too. At bedtime, she crawled in next to me. I already was just about asleep. I woke up, and she was coughin' and gaggin'. Said she couldn't see. She got up and staggered into the can. I heard her pukin'. Then I heard a thump. I ran in, and she was on her side. She—she—"

I laid my right hand on his big shoulder. A shadow slid into the doorway. I made out a man who looked official. I said, "You a manager?"

The man was about fifty and weighed about as much as one of Bull's legs. He looked like someone had just dumped a pot of sewage in the lobby.

"I'm, uh, the night manager."

I motioned, and we stepped into the hall.

"Think you can find another room for Mr. Crews? And get someone to move his stuff over?"

He nodded wordlessly. His face was as white as Bull's bedsheets.

I walked back to the bed. "Bull: These folks gonna take you to another room. If you want, I can get a doctor, give you something to help you sleep."

I helped him up. It wasn't easy. I felt every pound of him.

Two bellhops had materialized. One took each elbow. I saw a robe on the bedpost and handed it to Bull. He slid it on. Then he stood straight and waved off the bellhops. His form filled the door frame as he stepped out.

Two guys in white showed up. Danged if they weren't the same morgue guys I keep seeing. Or maybe they're the only ones Purdy's got. The three of us stepped to the bathroom doorway together.

Jane MacDonald lay on her side against the white toilet. She stared at nothing. All sorts of body fluids that I didn't wanna know pooled around her. What a way to go.

One of the coroner guys leaned over and brought his face close to the dame's mouth.

"Hooch."

Not surprised.

I said, "Umm, maybe bad hooch?"

"That's my guess, detective. Purdy'll know more when he gets here."

I told the two men what Bull had said about Jane's last minutes of life. They made notes. I watched them slide the poor lady on a stretcher. When everyone had left, I walked the room. Nothing of import. Closet full of Bull's wardrobe. Drawers of his undies. Soda bottle in the wastebasket. Some chocolates on the bedside.

The night manager still was in the hallway. I said, "Can you open Miss MacDonald's room?"

He walked me over. I was right. The bed looked like she'd never pulled back the spread. I eyed the room. Closet, drawers. The usual dame things. A lamp. A bedside table. And...

That's odd.

"Did you guys take the wastebasket out?"

The manager said, "No one's touched this room, Detective."

I looked in the bathroom. Nothing. Balcony. Nothing. Closet. Bingo.

There was the wastebasket. And in it, a clear glass bottle with no markings. Empty.

I pulled out a hanky and said, "I'll be taking this."

I dropped the bottle at PD and went home and got a few hours of shuteye. I got up and washed up and had some scrambled eggs and two cups of the Missus' strong java and felt almost like a new person. Almost.

Before I reached my desk, the phone I shared with Harvey Comeau was ringing.

"Nate Moran. Detectives."

"It's Purdy. C'mon over."

* * *

"Moonshine," he said. We stood next to Miss Jane, now on a slab. Looking at the ceiling but looking at nothing.

I said, "You solved that fast."

Purdy held up the empty bottle I'd pulled from the wastebasket.

"This wasn't any commercially made booze, Nate. I'll bet my medical license on it."

I said, "Moonshine's nasty, but it doesn't usually kill people."

"You know, sometimes it does, Nate. Moonshiners sometimes make their stuff with methanol. Wood alcohol. Cheaper. They figure it'll boil out, but sometimes it doesn't. Or they don't care. Enough of it, it'll take down anyone. Especially a dame. The thing about her puking and not being able to see. That just about sealed it."

There's lots of different kinds of murder. Some people look someone in the eye when they shank 'em or plug 'em. Some leave a bomb in a locker at a train station and never know, or care, who they kill. Some make moonshine with wood alcohol. Maybe not trying to kill anyone, but if someone dies, it's no sweat off their nose.

Purdy said, "Nate, I'd recommend figuring out where this lady was about twelve hours before she croaked."

That would be around the time she pulled up to the golf course valet after making a drive that was a mystery even to her boyfriend.

I walked back to HQ and filled in Dirk Monroe. He said, "Let's call Keyes."

The Prohibition agent picked up on the first ring. Dirk filled him in. I listened on another phone on the desk.

"Well, Dirk, I'm not a bettin' man. A hand of penny-ante poker with the boys sometimes. But I'd put my money on one person. This ain't the first time we found poison in his moonshine."

I had a good idea as well. Same guy. Keyes and I would turn out to be right.

I walked back over to the Everglades and showed my badge to the desk clerk. He had a bellhop walk me to Bull's new room. The door was ajar.

"Hello? Mr. Crews? Bull?"

The balcony door was open, and a breeze blew in a curtain. In the bright midday sun, Bull sat, his back to me.

I took the second chair. "How are you doing?"

Below us, cars made their way down Biscayne Boulevard. Lunch rush. Bull looked out, but not at anything. He let out a big sigh.

"I'll be okay, son."

I said, "Miss MacDonald. How long were you, were you…"

"About two years. We weren't gonna get married or nuthin. But I did—I did –"

His voice trailed off. He sounded like nothing mattered anymore. Nothing.

"Bull, I know the timing stinks. But—"

"No. That's fine. You got a job to do. A job I want ya to do."

"Did Miss MacDonald—"

"Yes. A lot." He shrugged and, for the first time that day, looked at me. "She had a…a…problem."

"Sorry. Gotta ask. What about you?"

He smiled and shook his head. "This body is my bread and butter. It's gotta last a long time. And stay good the whole time."

"But Miss MacDonald—"

"I told her she was puttin' away more than just for fun. She said the usual things. Dint have a problem. Could quit anytime. She knew she could get arrested anytime she went out and bought a bottle, but she said not to worry. She…"

His voice cracked and he stopped.

"Bull, we have reason to believe Miss MacDonald—"

"Please. Call her Jane. That's how I want to remember her." His eyes welled.

"We have reason to believe she bought illegal alcohol. Homemade."

"Moonshine?" His face was a mask of confusion and pain.

"Did she ever buy it before?"

He shook his head. "At least, not that I know. When we go on the road, it's usually a decent-sized city. Someone can find you a speakeasy. When I saw Jane had left during my golf game, I figured she'd found one here. I'm guessing there's a few in Miami, Detective."

"Keeps me busy." We both smiled.

I said, "Someone must have steered her to this stuff. Told her it was the best hooch she'd ever have."

Bull said, "Who would do that?"

"I have an idea. There's a local gang, sir. Mosley. Far as we know, they're the biggest moonshiners. We've had our eyes on them for a while. Their leader's in jail now. Murder."

Bull shook his head. "My biggest worry at work is a cheap shot to the knee. You guys deal with human rattlesnakes."

"Are you going to stay in town?"

He shook his head. "The team called. Offered me sixty-five. I started thinking that the best way to honor Jane is to get back to work. Keep my mind off—off –"

"OK, Bull. As long as you're a phone call away." I stood. "Sorry to say you're part of a long line of victims of these guys. They take up a big part of our day. But that's what we do."

A weak smile. "Ever in New York, detective, I get you a couple tickets."

I grasped his giant right paw and stepped back. I fitted my fedora. "Appreciate it. Let you know."

On my way out, I stopped at the desk again. "Your day manager in?"

The clerk picked up a phone, and a minute later, an older guy came out. Name tag said "Hopkins."

I leaned in. "Can we speak privately?"

He opened the gate and led me behind the front desk to his office. "Coffee?"

I said, "Sure." A place this ritzy, it had to be better than the stuff back at HQ. He picked up a phone, and two minutes later, a girl walked in with a tray. It was a lot better. I waited for the girl to step out.

"Any bellhops quit in the last day or so?"

Hopkins' face blanched. "How—how—"

I waited.

"Yes. One."

My eyes told him to go on.

"Hudson. Been here three months. Kept his nose clean. But not a very, uh, gregarious type."

"Ever see him acting suspiciously? Around guests?"

He shook his head. "But that don't mean anything. I don't really keep an eye on the bellhops unless someone complains."

"Did he give notice?"

Hopkins shook his head again. "He got off Tuesday night around midnight. Supposed to come in at three Wednesday afternoon for his shift. I come back from lunch Wednesday, and someone had dropped a note for me at the front desk and left. It was Hudson. Said he quit. Said not to worry about his last pay packet. Goodbye and good luck."

He put out his palms.

I said, "Got an address for him?"

"I looked in his file this morning. Looks like, uh, whoever hired him here didn't bother to check anything." He slid a paper from his desk and handed it to me.

For home address, it said 3100 East Flagler Street. The middle of Biscayne Bay.

A bellhop who used a fake address to get hired walks away. No forwarding address. Leaves a couple days' pay. In a court of law, my lawyer friends tell me, jurors can consider flight not a direct admission of guilt, but at least a circumstantial one. For me, the bar's even lower.

Now I had to find him.

Chapter Seven: The Roof Garden

The phone rang. At his desk, detective Harvey Comeau watched me pick up.

"Nate Moran. Detectives."

Harvey couldn't hear the other end, but he saw my eyes widen.

"A trash bin?"

I hadn't had my second cup yet, and already my day was ruined.

"Okay," I said. I jiggled the hook. "Leo: Nate. Dirk in with the chief? Can you send my call in to them, please?" A pause. "Hi, Chief. Workers found a stiff in the big trash bin behind the Columbus Hotel. I'm heading over."

I gulped my java and walked the few blocks to the Columbus. I'd been inside it many times. Never been around the back.

A patrol guy waved me through. Three more stood next to the big, square bin, its metal lid braced open. I walked right up to the lip, which came to about my chest, and leaned in.

The guy was down just past the ends of my fingers. Good looking. Dark. Age maybe thirty. He looked like a pencil. Like if he turned sideways, he'd disappear. Except his upper arms were nearly as big around as his waist. They pressed against his shirt sleeves. His clothes were ruffled but not torn. He had black slacks. They weren't typical pants. More, well, flexible. Stretchy. They had loops for a belt or a waist cord. But there wasn't one. The man wore no jacket. No tie. The front of his white shirt didn't have the kind of big red splotches you usually see when you're looking at a stiff. Knife. Gun. Nothing.

"Hiya, Nate."

Sergeant Mark Ginze. Forty-ish. Not as dumpy as Harvey Comeau. But, well, just as slobby. Mustache had those nasty flakes in it. He looked like he slept in his clothes. But he was good at his job.

I said, "How long?"

"Workers said they found him at seven when the garbage truck came for pickup. Before that, no one had any reason to look in, since they dumped the last of the hotel garbage about midnight."

I looked down. "But looks like he's lying on top of it."

Under the corpse were table scraps, steak bones, broken wine bottles, empty rice bags.

Ginze said, "Yeah. I also found that interesting. It would mean he was dumped after the last garbage. So we have a seven-hour window."

I scratched my scalp under my fedora rim. "Dumped on top."

"Beats me, Nate."

"Did you move him at all?"

Ginze said they hadn't. They'd been waiting on me.

I asked did anyone have some kind of stool. A hotel worker brought over a wood crate. It was a little rickety, but I got up. That let me reach the body. I gingerly rocked it. Lotsa black and blue. But no signs of bleeding. I scratched my scalp again.

Alongside the stiff was a giant burlap bag nearly as big as he was. A corner had torn open, and I saw potato peels, steaks chewed mostly to the bone, and pieces of half-eaten dinner rolls. I tried to lift the bag. I guessed forty or fifty pounds. I stepped down and away from the stench of the garbage and slid out my candy cigs.

It took some doing, but the morgue guys got the stiff out of the bin and onto a stretcher. That let me get a closer look at him.

They were the same two morgue guys I keep seeing. I said to one, "Marshall, right? You're an old hand at this?"

"Five years."

"Look at this guy. Something funny jump out at you?"

He smiled. "Probably the first thing you noticed, detective. Lots of bruising. But no holes. Bullet. Knife. Nothing."

"Right." I pointed to the stiff's throat. "And no marks there, so he wasn't strangled or garroted. And I don't think he died of the flu."

Marshall leaned and manipulated the head.

"Know for sure when Purdy cuts him open. But—" He jabbed. "I'd say broken neck."

My face scrunched. "Neck?"

He shrugged. He and his partner rolled the guy to the truck.

Most of the garbage stink was carried off by the late-December breeze off the bay. The cool air was refreshing, but I pulled my jacket closed. South Florida natives like me have a low tolerance.

"Moran!"

Ginze stood on the other side of the loading dock with a patrol guy who waved wildly and pointed up the side of the hotel, which loomed over us and blocked the morning sun. I stepped over.

Ginze said, "Today's our lucky day, Nate. We get to go see a lady up on the twelfth floor."

"What about?"

"She's dead, too."

In the Boom, businesses did a lot of one-upping. The guys who built the Columbus made sure it was seven stories taller than its next-door neighbor, the McAllister, which I think opened six years earlier. The McAllister had been right on Biscayne Bay when it opened, but then the city fathers dumped fill in the bay, and now it isn't. The McAllister folks weren't happy about it. The Columbus folks were all about beating their chests. They boasted forty-seven shops down in the arcade. And three hundred guest rooms. Including Room 1205. That's where I was headed.

I walked around front. The lobby was impressive. Two curving marble stairways, with wrought iron rails, leading from street level up to the main floor. Tall columns. Tile floors. Thick rugs. Long leather couches.

At the front desk, Ted Forman wore a concerned look but still managed a smile and a nod every time a guest walked by. I said, "Good to see you, Ted. Looks like the move from the Royal Palm was a good call."

"How's that drop-dead gorgeous wife of yours? One of my best bookkeepers ever."

Forman's a sweetheart to the Missus and me. He's old enough to be our dad. In fact, he was quite a father figure when he was her boss at the Royal Palm.

I said, "Tough business up on twelve."

"A fancy place like this, stiffs aren't good public relations, Nate."

"Especially two of 'em. The one in the garbage bin, people won't know about. The lady on twelve, a little tougher to hide."

He scrunched his face. "I'll take you up."

The twelfth-floor hallway was lousy with uniform guys. Ginze had gone up ahead of me. Inside the room, it was just Ginze and me. And Forman in the doorway. And on the bed, the girl.

I get the misfortune of seeing dames when they're not their best. No matter how thick a cop's skin gets, this never gets easy. They're someone's daughter.

The girl looked in her twenties. She was naked. She lay flat, hands halfway to her throat. As if she could have stopped it.

She'd been quite the looker. But now the cord around her neck dug into the skin. The area around it was mottled dark red and blue. Her eyes were open.

I slipped another candy cig in my mouth.

Ginze was at the window, running his hands up and down a curtain.

"All the cords are here. Killer must have brought his rope with him."

Premeditation.

"ID?"

Ginze shook his head.

"So, we're behind the eight-ball already. Clothes?"

Ginze pointed to a little black dress crumpled on the floor. Ladies' underthings lay about a foot away.

I pivoted to Forman, still in the doorway. He said, "Way ahead of you, Nate. Room is registered to Nils Freeman. Car parts distributor from Houston. Checked in two days ago."

"Where is he? Can we talk to him?"

"Holy crap!" It was Ginze. He'd opened the bathroom door and looked in. He rubbed the back of his neck. He motioned me over.

"Well, Nate, looks you can't talk to the guy."

Ginze stepped back to let me look. This was the gift that keeps giving.

An expensive business suit lay in a pile by the commode. A large, dumpy man wearing only boxers was on his knees at the tub. His right cheek lay against the rim. His eyes were open. A lot of dark smears and wet spots on both him and the porcelain.

Someone had smashed his head against the rim until he was dead.

When something is that brutal, it's about one thing: love.

I looked at the tub. No way he'd ever have gotten into it. He probably was twice the size of the girl. Wonder how that would have worked out, romance-wise. Not my business.

I called out behind me, "Anyone see anything? Maid? Front desk?"

I heard Forman: "My house dick found her. He'd been making rounds and found the door ajar. He's checking around with the staff."

"He didn't think to open the bathroom door?"

Ginze said, "To be fair, Nate, we were here for a while, and we didn't either."

Had me there.

I used a coat hanger to lift the girl's dress. Under it: A small handbag. The crime gods had cut me a break. Inside was a small red card.

"MEAL TICKET. Fiesta of the American Tropics. Cast."

The Fiesta was an attempt to put Miami on the map, the same way the Rose Bowl was a showcase for Southern California. Parades, pageants, and a college football game. The thing ran on New Year's Eve and the first two days of January. Mostly downtown. I remember reading in the *Miami Daily News* that the highlight on New Year's Day was a big show along the bay, ending at sunset with fireworks.

Back at my desk at HQ, I found a newspaper. A story listed some jugglers from Cuba and a dog show from Key West. And: "Acrobatic troupe from Ringling Brothers and Barnum and Bailey winter headquarters in Sarasota."

Those strange pants on the guy in the garbage bin. Yeah.

I found a telephone number at the bottom of the page. The organizer was a guy named Dutton.

"Yeah, detective. A few years back, after the last of the other Ringling brothers died and left just John, he moved the off-season winter HQ from Connecticut to Sarasota. Wouldn't you? They been sending a troupe over to Miami every year since we started up."

He told me the acrobats were camped out in tin can trailers up the Miami River. Gave me an address. And a contact: Andre. No last name. I didn't say anything about my visit to Columbus. Dutton had enough to worry about with New Year's Eve a day away.

I checked out a squad car and drove up Northwest North River Drive to where five trailers surrounded a clearing. In the center, the troupe had set up a contraption with ladders and hanging rings. It was about fifteen feet high. I got dizzy just looking up. People were doing trapeze things on it. A man hung, his knees wrapped around a swing, while a woman dangled, her wrists tightly clasped around his upper arms. Which were as big as my calves.

Where had I seen someone with arms like that?

A guy had his heel up on a stump and was stretching the back of his leg. I flashed my badge. "I'm looking for Andre." He smiled, but he didn't say anything. I repeated, "Andre." He pointed at himself and said, "Oui." Uh oh.

The man dropped his heel and held up a finger. He jogged off and returned with a little girl, maybe twelve.

"Andre, my papa. Speak no English."

She was as lithe as her dad. Her modest shift dress, covered in flower designs, billowed out. Her smile was as sunny as her light blond hair, tied in a ponytail. Same color as Andre. And, by the way, same color as our Anna.

"Where you from?" I'm talking to a twelve-year-old kid.

"Quebec."

Why the language thing.

"We live Chicoutimi. From Montreal, umm, in car, one day."

Her English was passable. My French was non-existent.

"Are all the people here from Chic-Chic—"

"Chicoutimi. Yes. We family. Two people non family."

"How many in all?"

Her ponytail bobbed as she ticked off the numbers in her head. "Ten and six."

"How many are children?"

"Huit. Umm, eight."

"You're doing great, sweetheart. What's your name?"

"Juliette."

A breeze from the river tickled my neck. Juliette didn't flinch. For her, this is a balmy day in Canada.

I looked to Andre to signal I wasn't a threat, then took a knee and looked Juliette in the eye. "Ask your papa is anyone missing."

Her eyes scrunched.

"Anyone not come back last night?"

She said something in French. Andre's smile vanished. He said something to Juliette. I reached out in desperation, but he'd sent her away.

"Papier?" He motioned scribbling. I pulled out my notepad and pencil. The handwriting was flowery, but I could make it out. The first name was easy. Gabrielle Tremblay. I wrestled with the second one. "Phillipe Gag-non."

He smiled. "Gan-yon."

"Trapeze?"

"Gabrielle, oui. Phillipe, oui." He pointed his index fingers up and touched them together. Gabrielle and Phillipe were trapeze partners.

Then, "Phillipe non family."

"Boyfriend?"

He didn't understand. I wrapped my arms around myself and made a kissing face. "Gabrielle, Phillipe?" He gave a grave nod.

So maybe that's Phillipe in the trash bin. I'm thinking more than maybe. And in the hotel room...

Then Andre said, "Ehh, où est Phillipe? Où est Gabrielle?"

Uh-oh.

When I was on street patrol, French-Canadian tourists would stop me, pointing to a building and then a map. I learned the French word for "Where is?" Like, "Où est Miami Beach?"

This is when guys like me should get double pay. I felt confident about answering his question. But not yet. It was midday now. I pointed to the ground, then my watch. I held up six fingers. Hope he got, "I'll be back here at six."

He held up six and pointed to what I knew was east. "La baie de Biscayne."

OK. They'd be practicing on the waterfront at six. By then, I should know something. I already had two names.

At headquarters, I filled in Ginze.

"We have a math problem."

"Right, Ginze. Gabrielle, figuring that's her, didn't strangle herself. Our auto parts rep didn't smash his own head on the tub. And if that's Phillipe in the garbage bin, even if he did the murders he didn't then climb in there and snap his own neck."

Ginze took a deep pull on his cig. I got that quick whiff of sweet tobacco, and then it was gone, replaced by harsh smoke.

I rang up Purdy in the morgue.

He said, "Marshall, the meat wagon guy, he's a smart cookie. He'll run this place when I retire."

"Purdy, you'll never retire until you're on one of your slabs."

"That's good, Moran."

"What's the call?"

"Like Marshall said. Broken neck." Then, "But, like Alice said in Wonderland, it gets curiouser and curiouser." So the guy liked the classics. Or maybe he just liked to read the book to his kid. Hope he washed his hands first.

"Curiouser? How so, Purdy?"

"He also had a broken back."

"Broken back?"

"Like someone took a two-by-four or a thick metal pole. Nearly separated the spine. That or the broken neck killed him. Maybe both. I don't know. Either would have."

Curiouser and curiouser.

I'd gotten lucky with that meal ticket in the girl's handbag, and the luck of the New Year still was hanging around. An hour after I rang off with the coroner, I was finishing the first half of a barbecue beef sandwich when the phone rang again. It was Forman at the Columbus.

"The Roof Garden."

"Your restaurant?"

"Bender, our night manager up there, came in early today to do some bookkeeping on the holiday rush. He saw all the cops still hanging around the garbage bin. Your boys were their usual discreet selves."

I laughed.

"Bender asked what's up, and I gave him a few details. He said he maybe saw the Houston auto parts guy just before closing. Big man. Hard to miss. Saw him with a girl."

"On my way."

I offered the other half of my sandwich to my buddy Comeau, who said it would be a shame to waste it. I walked the few blocks back to the Columbus. In the lobby, Forman told the elevator kid, "Roof Garden."

It seems all the hotel elevator guys are pimply teenagers. The kid worked the elevator crank. When we got to the top, he reached past us and pulled open the gate.

The Roof Garden sure is as advertised. Strings of colored lights overhead. Potted palm trees. Slim waiters in black slacks, white shirts, and bowties. Busboys in all white getups, smoothing out white tablecloths and placing silverware, plates, and glasses.

To my left, past the tops of the big office buildings, I could follow the river out to the Everglades. Straight ahead, I could follow Biscayne Boulevard. The sweet view was to my right. Across Biscayne Bay, all the way to Miami Beach. With the midafternoon sun sparkling off the water, you could see what a paradise this rooftop garden would be for someone who'd come down for New Year's Eve from Albany or some such icebox.

At the long bar along the side, a man in a full tux. A strange sight in mid-afternoon. He eyeballed papers on a clipboard.

"Bender, this is Moran, the police detective I told you about."

Bender led us to a table right near the edge of the roof and far enough from the noise of the dinner prep. Forman said, "Go ahead."

"The guy came in with the girl about nine. I don't want to sound harsh. But a guy built like a sedan has a girl on his arm who's so tiny you're afraid he'll snap her in half? It catches your eye."

I said, "Was it the dead girl?"

"Your sergeant gave me a look at her when they rolled her out. It was her." Bender shook his head. "I know looks shouldn't matter. Just as evil to murder a homely girl. But a pretty young thing like that. To do that to her…" He shrugged.

I nodded for him to get back to the story.

"So last night, she and the big guy looked like they'd stopped first at a speakeasy. He already was soused. Probably the girl, too. The guy slipped my maître d' a fiver on the way in, so probably he'd be dropping some dough. The waiters and I have signals, and the maître d' motioned with his head for me to make sure the big man gets extra attention. I sent out our best waiter, and I stopped by the table myself. The big man said he was on an expense account, and he'd sold a giant contract to a car dealership opening next month in Coral Gables, and he was feeling good."

"You sure he did all his drinking before he got here?"

Bender looked at Forman. The manager said, "Can you mix me an iced tea and lemonade? And one for Nate."

Forman waited until Bender was across the garden and behind the bar. He spoke low.

"Nate, you've been like a son to me. And I'm madly in love with your bride. And those cute kids."

"I feel the same way, Ted. But I swore an oath."

Forman leaned back. "Up to a few months ago, we had secret stashes locked away in a safe. Not anymore. I swear."

I smiled. "Glad to hear. I can't bust you for what I don't see."

Ted lit a cig. I allowed myself that sweet smell. It dissipated in the breeze. He exhaled.

"Why'd you stop, Ted? Any of my colleagues wise to you?"

"No. Mark Gregg."

Yowsa, yowsa, yowsa.

"I played stupid, Nate. Never asked our old restaurant manager, Kopp, who our supplier was. Turns out it was Gregg. When Gregg shot those two agents, Kopp must have decided the guy was too hot. Kopp wanted to close the account. Gregg musta told him that would be very hazardous to his health, because Kopp quit us the next day. Poof. Confessed about Gregg on his way out."

I said, "Your old manager forgot the rule. You lie down with dogs, you wake up with fleas."

Forman looked over to Bender, who still was at the bar. He was taking his time making the drinks. Giving his boss time.

Forman said. "Now I had to get a new guy. Bender was a catch. I stole him from Palm Beach. Had a girl down here. In the week and a half before he finishes up in Palm Beach and gets down here, I'm working the restaurant on top of my regular manager stuff. A guy comes by. Never said who he works for. He's offering us hooch. I play dumb about the deal with Gregg, and I tell him thank you, we'll pass."

"Why are you telling me this?"

He put out his hands in surrender. "Right now, hooch is the least of my problems. I've got a stiff in my dumpster and two more on the twelfth floor. Bad for business. It's good to get this cleared up pronto. Plus, I trust you."

I said again, "But I swore an oath. You gotta stay clean."

Forman said, "Promise on my mother's chicken soup. This Prohi won't last forever. In the meantime, we'll take a chance on losing customers to hotels who break the rules. Cops is bad enough. Guys like Gregg, they're just too scary."

Bender had come back with the ice-tea-and-lemonade concoctions. I took a sip. Man, that was good. Forman nodded for Bender to start up again with his story.

"Like I said, I checked on the big Texan myself. He wanted our fried chicken. Most popular thing on the menu. The girl ordered Florida lobster, but no butter. Said she was in a show and had to watch her waist. I said,

'Knock yourself out.' Me, I can't eat it without melted butter. I—"

I said, "Me neither." When I had it. Which was rarely. It's a luxury. I said, "So she spoke English."

"Decent, but with a thick Quebec accent."

"How'd you know it was Quebec and not France? Or the islands?"

Bender said, "Alexandre, my maître d', is from Montreal. He's tried to teach me a little French, for when the high-roller Québécois come by, but I'm hopeless. Spanish is hard enough."

I said, "You and me both."

"So we bring the Texan and the dame their chow, and they're tucking into it, and everything's hunky-dory. After about an hour, he's made a pile of chicken bones, and she ate about half the lobster. They're laughing a lot. I'm sure by then the booze has set in solid, and they're loopy. I'm thinking this will end up in a bed, but not before the car parts king has run up a big tab with us. But then a strange thing happens."

"Go on."

"The waiter's standin' over them, and I'm watching from the bar. I look over to the front. Alexandre—"

"That's the maître d'."

"Right, detective. He catches my eye. Real subtle like. That's how you do things at a fancy place like this. I learned that from the best."

Bender nodded toward Forman, who smiled.

"Just in front of the entrance, where the elevator opens, is this young guy. Skinny, like the girl, but strong arms. Thick upper arms. Like he lifts weights or something."

Well, well, well.

"He's pacing. Back and forth. Wants to come in. Wants to see is his girl there. Thinks she came in with another guy. Alexandre's telling me all this because the guy's jabbering in French."

"Quebec French?"

Bender nodded.

"I tell Alexandre to give the guy the bum's rush, but nicely. Alexandre's the best at that. He has to run people off all the time. But he makes you feel like he's your best friend when he does it. Real magic.

"The two of them go on some more, in French, of course, and the next thing I know, the guy's gone back to the elevator. Crisis over. Alexandre asks should we let the girl and the big guy know someone was looking for them? He—"

"How'd Alexandre know that's who the guy was looking for?"

Bender said, "He described her to a T."

"Did the guy say his girl's name?"

"He didn't."

"What about his own name"

Bender said, "Yep. For Alexandre to get a message to her that he came by."

"Did you?"

Bender shook his head. "We didn't owe this guy anything. Not our place to get in the middle of a triangle. Bad for business."

"What was the jilted boyfriend's name?"

"Phillipe."

Back at my desk, I found Comeau working a jelly-filled.

"Leo brought some in," he said, his mouth full.

This was after his regular lunch and the half-barbecue sandwich I'd given him. If he wasn't careful, he'd end up as big as our dead Texan. He was getting there.

I rang up Ginze, and he walked over. I filled him in. He said, "Sure sounds like Phillipe is our killer. Crime of passion. You saw the Texan's busted head against the bathtub and how tight the cord was around the girl's throat."

"But we come back to our math problem."

"Yep." Ginze lit another smoke.

I leaned back and stared at the ceiling. The two of us sat in silence.

I sat forward. "Sergeant, my first week in the detective bureau, Dirk told me something. When you hit a dead end, sometimes the best idea is to go back to the beginning."

I rang up Forman at the Columbus. I stopped for a café con leche, then met him out back of the hotel, at the garbage bin. With him was a guy shaped like an icebox. His arms were like a ship's anchor cable. He blocked out the dang sun. Forman said, "Gus is in charge of everything out back. Everything."

Someone had brought over a crate, and I stood on it, my hands on the rim of the trash bin.

"Gus: Has this thing moved since we found the body in it?"

Gus was all Brooklyn. "On garbage day, the city guys roll it up a ramp and tip it. Before we got this thing, it took twenty minutes just to get all the garbage out of the building."

"But you always roll it back to the same spot."

Gus said, "We gotta."

He pointed up. I followed his finger.

About five feet above the garbage enclosure, the hotel's second floor did an overhang. It had a big hole in the middle, maybe four feet by four feet, surrounded by metal cowling.

Holy mackerel.

"It's a garbage chute."

"Yep."

"Does it go all the way to the top, Gus?"

"Right up to the Roof Garden."

Gears turned.

"Ted: Can we go to twelve?"

We stepped off the elevator. In my head, I tried to line up where the bottom of the chute might be twelve floors below me. Gus knew what I was thinking. He pointed. A few feet down on the right, I saw a door. No sign or any words on it. A plain metal knob in the usual place.

"Can you open that, please?"

Forman pulled a keyring off his hip. I peered in. A lip of maybe two feet. Then blackness. My belly twisted.

"Ted: If a person didn't know better, could he open this door, thinking it's the elevator or the stairs, only it's the garbage chute?"

Forman's back arched. "Nate, as soon as you open the door, anyone with brains could see there's just a drop."

I said, "What if you're in a hurry. You're panicking. Because you just murdered someone."

Gus shrugged. "I guess."

"Who uses this door?"

Gus said, "Just the maid supervisors. They got a key."

"Do they sometimes forget to lock the door?"

Gus made a face. "All the time. Once a week, I sends out a note to remind them."

I looked at the inside of the open door. "Where's the latch?"

"Only on the outside."

I looked at Forman. He said, "Yes. Bad design. Someone could get stuck in here. It happened a couple times. Maids. They press against the door and hang their toes on the lip for dear life and bang until someone opens up."

"Ted, I won't say anything to city code enforcement. Not today. But that has to get fixed."

Then, "I'm thinking out loud. In the circus, Gabrielle's role is to hang from Phillipe's forearms fifty feet up. She trusts him with her life. But this night, she doesn't mind making him the fool. Especially when her head gets turned by the bright lights of the Magic City. And a high roller with a fat wallet who maybe came by when she was practicing at the Bayfront and offered to show her the town.

"Phillipe tails 'em to the Roof Garden. He spots his girlfriend yucking it up with this salesman. He'd love to confront the two of 'em at their table, but Alexandre won't let him. The guy tells Phillipe he'll pass a message, but Phillipe's sure he won't. His blood's boiling.

Gus said, "Where do I come in?"

I pointed to the garbage chute door. "Phillipe makes like he's leaving, but when Alexandre gets distracted, the kid slips out back into the shadows. Sees the hot-blooded couple get in the elevator. Hears the Texan say twelfth floor. Races down the stairs to twelve and hides in the stairwell until Gabrielle and the Texan come off the elevator. He can see they're lit. He's right behind them and gets his foot in the doorway of 1205, and they don't notice. He waits ten minutes and then pushes in. The girl's on the bed naked. He blows his top. Pulls the cord from around the waist of his trapeze pants and jumps her, and she's dead before she can scream.

"He pushes into the bathroom. The Texan's in his boxers and freshening up in anticipation of a night of love. Now Phillipe's really loco. Then the big man's dead.

"Now it sinks in what he did. He bolts into the hall and sees this door here. Thinks it's the elevator. Or the stairs. Jumps in and the door shuts behind him. He sees he's in the garbage chute. His toes are on the lip of a big hole. Twelve floors down. No latch. He's in a full panic. He can't bang for help. He just iced two people. One's his girlfriend. With the cord from his pants. Which I'm guessing we'd have found somewhere in the garbage bin.

"Phillipe is thinking the cops'll finger him in five minutes. He says, 'Wait. I'm a gymnast. The chute isn't that wide. Maybe I can just spider my way down against the walls.' He starts heading down. It's scary. But he has no choice. Then—"

Gus said. "Oh, no. The Roof Garden. The night's garbage."

I said, "The last sack of the night. I tugged a corner of it downstairs. What's it weigh?"

Gus said, "I weighed one for fun. It was somethin' like forty pounds."

I said, "And it drops all those floors from the top. In the dark. Phillipe doesn't know it's coming and can't brace for it. Not that it would have mattered. Forty pounds of steak bones and stale rye bread slam down on his noggin. If that didn't kill him, he's dropping now, and he buys it when he comes out the bottom of the chute and his back slams into the rims of the garbage bin. Him and the bag of garbage."

Forman grimaced. "What a way to go."

The next day was New Year's Eve. After dinner, we let the kids pretend eight O'clock was midnight. We got out pots and pans and lids and they went at it, all around the house. My ears rang. That wore the kids out but good. They were asleep in minutes. The Missus and I weren't far behind. So much for puttin' on the Ritz.

On New Year's Day, I took the Missus and the kids to the waterfront for the big event of the Fiesta of the American Tropics. The troupe from Ringling performed brilliantly. Lots of oohs and aahs. Those guys were dealing with a brutal double dose of death. And the loss of a big chunk of their act. But they were pros.

Near dusk, we made our way to the water's edge to get a good look at the fireworks. I spotted the acrobats. They'd changed back to street clothes. I found Andre and Juliette. The Missus had had some high school French, and she did okay. I used her to explain to Andre what we'd found out. He said the troupe had heard. They were sad. But the show goes on.

Chapter Eight: Hypocrite's Row

A while back, soon after I had made detective, Dirk Monroe stopped by as I was about to head home.

"Start your shift tomorrow after lunch. We've got an evening activity."

"Oh yeah? What's that?"

"You get to meet El Gordo."

He saw the name meant nothing to me. "See you tomorrow." Then, "Crime never sleeps."

The Missus and I packed an early lunch and drove down to Coconut Grove, to Dinner Key. You know, that's how it got its name. Picnickers. It was a cool day, and we weren't the only ones with blankets and baskets. We had a lovely time. I drove her home, left the car, and walked to work, enjoying the breeze. Dirk told me we'd grab a sandwich late.

The sun lay low behind us as our unmarked sedan crossed County Causeway to Miami Beach. The blue water of the bay sparkled. People up north hand over every nickel from their cookie jar for just a few days here. We live here. Shame on me, I ever forget that.

Dirk steered with his right hand. His left elbow leaned on the car's windowsill. He looked straight ahead, but he talked to me.

"You speak Spanish."

I held my thumb and forefinger to indicate a little. I actually know more than a little. After all, I am the grandson of a Cuban beauty.

Dirk said, "El Gordo."

"The fat one."

"Antonio Paseo."

Name meant nothing.

Dirk said, "When Spain gave us Puerto Rico after the Spanish-American War, our government nationalized the island's sugar businesses. Didn't ask first. It wiped out the Paseo clan. Young Antonio decided if the Yanks could give his family the skunk, he could return the favor. He came to South Florida and became a gangster. It's all about semantics, I guess. Who's robbing who?"

Dirk kept his right hand on the wheel and moved his left from the windowsill to the right inside pocket of his coat. He slid a cig out of an unseen pack and slipped in his mouth. He reached in again and pulled out a small cylinder. I'd seen these. It looked like a bullet. It was a bullet. Doughboys in the Great War had made them into lighters.

Dirk never talked about the war, and the cough he got out on the North Sea that never quite went away. And he never talked about the flu that killed his first kid, a little boy. Everyone in the department knew you didn't bring up either topic.

Dirk looked down just long enough to get the lighter to the end of his cig. A flick, a breath in, a breath out. The first sweet smell of tobacco, before it's replaced by the harsh odor of smoke.

Dirk's lighter's flame lit the dark. The ball of the sun had dropped, and the sky was bleeding from blue to navy.

"El Gordo stays away from running the booze. He just likes to have it available. Pays the big suppliers a premium to keep a steady flow going. Flow. Get it?"

I did.

"The guy's business model is elsewhere, Nate. He's got his hands in Bolita." That's the Cuban lottery. "Also, bordellos. And protection. And murder."

Another puff.

"His hobby is poker. In Miami. Or with the cigar barons in Ybor City over in Tampa. Or the society snakes in Palm Beach. I don't have to tell you, five grand a year is a decent salary. El Gordo would play that in a night. Sometimes he'd win a grand. Sometimes he'd lose it.

"The guy makes his own rules. Sometimes he'd take three of his paid girls upstairs for some kinky, then send them home and play cards until dawn. If some guy made a bad joke at his expense, the next thing you know, the mope is taking a one-way ride to the Everglades, where no one will find him."

I said, "How does the guy keep skating?"

"It's funny how many doors money can open. It also buys people. He's the butter-and-egg man in so many operations, and he's not afraid to spread around some mazuma, or lay on an elbow, to make sure witnesses shut up. Or evidence vanishes. Or crooked cops conveniently forget things. I wish it wasn't the case."

We'd crossed the bay to the south end of Miami Beach and worked our way down the side streets. In the fading light, it was hard to make out street signs or the wording on storefronts.

Dirk pulled into a spot. Across the street was a sprawling restaurant with a big sign: Jack's Crab. Even from across the street, we heard the tinkle of glasses, the hum of talk, and now and then a burst of laughter.

A while back, people figured out the sweet meat of stone crabs. And how you didn't even have to kill them. Darndest thing. Just catch them in a crate, tear off their big claw, and throw them back. They grow back the claw, and you get another crack at them. It didn't take long for the cuisine to go from roadside stand to black tie.

Dirk leaned and reached across me, pointing with his cigarette hand out the passenger window. It brought the tobacco smell right up to my beezer.

"That's him."

My eyes followed the cigarette hand out the window to the courtyard. I counted eight people at a large round table. And three waiters hovering. Even in the dim light, I made out El Gordo. You couldn't miss him. He took up about twice the space of anyone else. He leaned back, and I made out the red glow at the tip of his fat cigar.

"I wanted you to see what he looked like, Nate. Now you're a detective, you need to learn the regular cast of characters. You'll be dealing with them at some point or another."

Dirk sat up at the wheel. He pointed. His cigarette, still in his hand, was down to nearly nothing. We watched El Gordo and his entourage get up. He crossed the street, a gorilla on either side, and guys and girls trailing. He walked, oblivious, just a foot in front of our car's grill.

After they were out of earshot, Dirk said quietly, "He's just like Rudolph Valentino. Got his own fan club."

"But Valentino's doing the sleep now."

"Valentino had a ruptured ulcer, Nate. I suspect the big man will go in a more violent fashion."

Dirk: You win.

* * *

Probably once a week, somewhere in South Florida, cops raid a speakeasy. Sometimes it's a low-rent blind tiger. Sometimes it's a black tie.

One night, long after I'd met El Gordo, I found myself out on the street in a rare cold night. Rare for South Florida. At least at home, I'd be under a blanket and could hear the Missus' soft breathing. Instead, I shivered in the shadows of a storefront, in a row of businesses along the Miami River, along with a half-dozen patrol guys.

Mostly, the raids are a waste of time. Anyone prominent, or heavily invested, gets hustled out the back as the cops are busting in. Any customer drunk or sloppy or stupid enough to get caught with a drink in his hand gets off with a fine. Operators hide most of their inventory off property and never set out more than they can afford to lose. Whatever doesn't magically disappear just before we arrive, we pour down a street drain. Operators are looking at a fine or a short stint in the pokey. Cost of doing business.

As I watched from across the street, a ratty-looking punk in a suit that didn't fit him stepped out of one of the storefronts. A small beam of dull light shot out, and just as quickly vanished when the door shut behind him.

I said he was ratty. In fact, we called him Ratso. He worked the Bolita. He made a nice buck. He spent it all on rotgut. We'd tailed him a couple of days. Now we knew where he bent his elbow. But he wasn't our prize. He was bait.

102

A cab pulled up, and Ratso got in. We waited another three minutes. Then we walked across the street and huddled to the side of the front door Ratso just left. It was one of those doors with a little window and an outside that was all cushiony padding. I guess in case a bouncer had to knock you around, they didn't wanna have to explain a cracked skull.

I nodded to the sergeant. He turned on his flashlight and flung open the door.

"Nobody move!" I shouted. "Miami police!"

I stopped cold, my mouth open. The place was empty. Except for a kid back in the corner with a mop.

"What's your name?"

"Norman. I-I-I-I'm just the cleanup guy."

He looked about seventeen. Trying to grow a mustache but doing a lousy job. Looked like he weighed less than the mop.

I reached into the bucket. The water was hot. Just poured.

The sergeant came up. "Nothing behind the bar but bottles of Coca-Cola and birch beer."

We'd been played.

Ratso must have gotten wise to us and tipped the operators. Everyone had scrammed out the back. The night's hooch probably was in some vault that, even if we had the key, we couldn't open without a warrant.

I looked at Norman, the mop boy. "Tell your bosses they're smart. But their luck won't hold out."

He gave a scared look. After I turned, I discreetly looked toward a mirror behind the bar. The kid didn't see me looking at him. I could make out a smirk.

Like Monk, I don't drink. Like him, I don't like Prohibition. But it's the law. And it was one thing for a hard-working guy to keep a flask under his kitchen sink. It was another for guys to make big bucks and, on occasion, kill a lawman. For them, it wasn't about the hooch. It was about feeling like there's two sets of rules.

There's a place called Hypocrite's Row. Where patrons who used a secret hallway could get their snorts. For a year, Palm Beach cops knew about it, but not which hotel. They couldn't catch anyone red-handed. These are places where no one talks and things stay private, and everyone benefits. Until someone gets croaked. That's how Hypocrite's Row finally did get found out.

It's a funny thing. When you mix money and gambling and gangsters, you sometimes get somebody dead. In this case, it was El Gordo. Cops found him bleeding out on the floor, still in his shiny tux. Then it became my business.

Knocks on the door after midnight never are good. Two days after Ratso and the failed raid, I got one.

I threw some clothes in a bag. Somehow, the Missus stayed asleep. The patrol guy who'd knocked on my door drove me to headquarters, where I checked out a department jalopy and made the long, lonely late-night drive to Palm Beach. Miles of silence. I crossed the bridge from West Palm to the island and pulled up to the Palmetto Hotel. An elevator boy ran me to the tenth floor. A Palm Beach policeman guided me through the secret hallway that suddenly wasn't secret anymore.

No one had moved anything. It was cool outside the hotel, but in here, the stifling heat added to the feeling that everything was suspended in time. That went for El Gordo as well.

He sprawled on splinters of a chair he'd crushed when he had gone over. His nice black tux mostly was unwrinkled. But just below his nice black bowtie, three red dots painted the front of his nice white shirt. A fourth shot had ripped his nice polka-dot cummerbund.

I dropped my fedora on a side table. A tall man in plain clothes stuck out a hand. "Deputy Chief Clarke. Thanks for coming up so fast, Moran."

"Not stepping on your business, Chief. Just here to help. El Gordo is sort of on our dance card."

"Right. That's how they explained it to me."

Across the room, another guy in a tux sat, a big bandage around his lower leg.

"Bullet went through," Clarke said. "Not serious. But it kept him from scramming with everyone else when the lead started flying."

The man's tux jacket was off, and his shirt was slick with sweat.

"No name. Had a hundred in his pocket."

I whistled. I've never had a Ben Franklin in my wallet in my life.

The guy's eyes met mine, and he quickly looked away. Not quick enough. I gave one of the special smiles I reserve for my favorite punks.

"Small world, Skee."

I turned to Clarke. "Horace Kowalski. Grifting. Booze. Mostly gambling. I've busted him, lemme see, three times for running a Bolita operation in Coconut Grove."

Back to Skee. "Surprised to see you up this way. I saw your friend Ratso the other night. You guys were altar boys together, right? He was at a blind pig on the Miami River. Lots of his friends got away. I wonder if you were one of them."

Then my eyebrows raised. "Wait a minute. Shouldn't you be in your luxury suite at Raiford?"

Skee gave me an oily grin, and I saw his missing front incisors. I had to remember I knocked them out after he came at me with a blackjack during the raid that sent him up to Florida State Prison.

He mumbled, "They shaved off two months." I could smell the booze on his breath. "I was the top license plate producer."

"Congratulations, Skee. Did you give the trophy to your momma?"

His smile vanished, and he lunged for me, but his bum leg stopped him.

God, I needed coffee. And, once, I'd have gone for a smoke. I reached into my coat pocket for my candy cigs. Skee knew about them from our last dance. He didn't blink an eye. Clarke did a double-take.

I said, "Skee. Where'd you get that C-note? I know you won't own up to playing cards, here at this card table, with these cards, and those poker chips, that I can see with my own eyes. I'm sure that hundred in your pocket goes straight to your sharks as soon as you get back to Miami."

Skee actually snarled. "You putting the screws on me?"

I felt some of the spittle, but I didn't give him the satisfaction of wiping my face. I leaned in.

"You're in a tight spot, Skee. You're a repeat offender. And here we have you in a room with illegal hooch and illegal gambling. And one stiff. Your pal, the fat man, is missing a lot of motor oil. Last time I checked, putting four holes in somebody was illegal, too. And here you are, with a hole in your leg, not five feet away from the dearly departed. What a coincidence."

I twirled the candy cig, narrowing it to a sharp point that poked my tongue.

"Did you owe him? Was he pressing you for the vig?"

Maybe it was the pain in his leg. Maybe not. Skee was squirming, but good.

"Never met the guy."

I laughed. "C'mon, Skee. You run his numbers franchise for him."

"Go ahead and prove it, Moran. I say I don't know the guy."

Skee fingered his gums where I'd knocked out his choppers.

Clarke pulled me a few feet away. He spoke low and into his hand.

"I got a math problem."

Oh, no. Not another one.

"How do you mean?"

"I got two guys with holes in them. That means two guns. We've scoured this room. Can't even find one." He motioned toward Skee. "No gun on this bum. No hooch on him. No cash on the table. Can't hold him."

Damn.

Clarke turned. "You can go, Skee. The house doc said you can walk if you go easy."

I said, "You're a long way from your clip joint in the Grove. How you gonna get home?"

"I got a room here."

I wondered how Skee could afford even a broom closet in this place.

"I'll take the train down tomorrow." Skee stopped. "Hell. It is tomorrow."

I picked up my fedora. "I'll tell my guys back in Miami to keep an eye out for a gimp."

Skee glared. Two patrol guys got him under his arms and helped him to his feet. He limped out.

Clarke said, "Got you a room across in West Palm, Nate. Downtown on Clematis Street. At least you can get a few hours."

"You got someone can tail Skee back to Miami? Someone who's good. Skee's been tailed before."

Clarke said, "Way ahead of you. A Palm Beach County deputy. He won a bet with me once. Said he could tail me for two hours and I'd never know it."

The candy cig was down to a nub.

"Chief, I don't have to tell you Skee knows more than he's letting on. The dark side is no place for loyalty. They're your blood brother one day and stab you in the back the next."

Clarke started to say something. A thin, sallow-faced man, in a suit he looked like he couldn't afford, appeared at the doorway. Clarke smiled. "Well. Mr. Ingraham. We found Hypocrite's Row."

Ingraham had a hanky out and was wiping the back of his neck.

Clarke motioned to El Gordo. "This dead guy is a bit of a problem for you. This room isn't supposed to exist. We can't keep this murder out of the papers. We can tell reporters these guys were playing bridge and drinking lemonade. Probably won't believe us, but maybe. But this little drinky-drinky room is out of operation. Starting right now."

Ingraham wrung his hands.

"And we will want to talk to everybody on staff." Another stare at the squirming manager. "Everybody."

Ingraham backed up and vanished from the doorway.

Clarke said, "Go get some shuteye, Nate."

Three hours of sleep just ain't enough. That had been my life when the kids were really little. I don't miss it. I had scrambled eggs at the diner next to my hotel. My head pounded. At least I'd washed up and changed clothes. I waved for more coffee.

This was West Palm Beach, not Palm Beach. A roomful of businessmen on a Tuesday morning. Nifty guys, with trimmed mustaches angling down their chins and watch fobs dangling from their vests. Making big deals. Deals that would mean more of the tall buildings I already had seen along the street from my hotel window.

I spotted Clarke at the front door and waved him over. I waved to the waitress and pointed to the empty cup across from me. She was there with the pot even as Clarke sat down.

"Ma'am, you are an angel." He smiled at her. "Just a couple of pieces of toast, please." Then back to me. "How'd you sleep?"

"Great, but not enough."

"Don't plan on a nap today."

The toast was out promptly. Clarke slathered on butter and jam. He said, "Skee might spill if we make a deal. Or he might worry about someone finding out he ratted and giving him the shiv. Sure would like to know who hightailed out of that room before we got there."

I put down my cup. "Yep. The problem here is too many suspects. Subjects unknown."

Clarke drove me back over the bridge to Palm Beach. In daylight, I could get a better look at the town.

It shouted one word: money. Not the kind I like. I like people who get rich on smarts and hard work. Good for them. This was old-family money. Lots of the people here were rich when they fell out of their mothers. They had lucky bloodlines. They never worked a day in their lives, and their only worry was keeping their chums waiting on the tennis court. Or how much to pony up when their daughters were ready to be debutantes. These people were night owls because they didn't have to be anywhere in the morning. I'd rather have my life, without the riches, than theirs. Maybe you don't believe me. Not my problem.

Clarke pulled into the circular drive of the Palmetto Hotel. Up came a valet with a phony smile that faded when he saw who it was. He motioned to a corner of the drive. Clarke parked there. The kid dragged a small pylon over and set it behind Clarke's bumper.

I figured the kid was irritated that he wouldn't get his quarter tip. But I've been in this show a while. Something else caught me up. The kid seemed jumpy. He avoided eye contact with Clarke. I got a hunch.

Clarke had his back to me, heading to the front door. I pulled a single from my wallet and slid it to the valet as I passed. The kid showed surprise. I said under my breath, "What's your name?"

"Danny."

"When's your next break?"

"Twenty minutes."

"Some place we can talk privately?"

"You a cop?"

I said I was, but not local, and all I wanted to do was find out who chilled the big man. Anything else that happened on Palm Beach was Clarke's problem.

Danny thought for a minute. "There's a shack for the golf caddies right over there, about fifty feet behind the valet stand."

Clarke had stepped back out. I said, "Kid's giving me recommendations for lunch on the West Palm side."

When Clarke and I got to the front desk, he asked for Ingraham. The manager's attitude had switched overnight from nervous to belligerent. Yeah, the hotel admits to Hypocrite's Row. Yes, it's shut down for good. Yessss, he knew who El Gordo was. A regular who stayed in the penthouse and dropped a lot of dough. No, he didn't know the guy was a gangster. Okay, maybe. But the management asked no questions so long as a patron was running a tab.

Clarke asked could we talk to the hotel staff who worked the room. Ingraham said he would have to get an okay from the owner, who was up in Ormond Beach, looking at some hotels he might buy, and he wouldn't be back until the next morning.

Clarke was losing his cool. "By then, pal, I'll have a search warrant."

Ingraham shrugged, "And I'll still have a job. Do what you gotta do."

Clarke asked could he at least look around the lobby and the grounds for a half hour. Ingraham said, "Knock yourself out."

I told Clarke, "I gotta go to the john. Might be a while. That coffee."

Clarke headed toward the French doors leading to the big lawn. Ingraham pointed me to the john, then busied himself with paperwork. Just before the washroom, I made a hard left and was out the front door. Ingraham was oblivious.

I followed the path behind the valet stand. In a minute, I was at the lip of a putting green. To the right stood a small shack and a bench. Five minutes later, here came Danny.

He looked all around him. "They catch me talkin' to you, it's my job."

My second and middle finger, resting on the back of the bench, held a tightly rolled bill. Danny slid the five from between my fingers. His eyes widened.

"Who was here last night, might have gone up to Hypocrite's Row?"

Danny shrugged. "Well, El Gordo already was checked in here. You already knew that. His Duesenberg's parked in the back lot. Don't know what'll happen to it."

"Who else?" I knew I had him just until the end of his break.

He looked out over the golf course. "That guy Skee. Pulled up in a taxi." His nose scrunched like he smelled a sewer. "A real weasel."

The kid was a good judge of character.

"You know a guy named Mark Gregg?" Danny didn't. It was worth a shot.

"Anyone walk in with El Gordo?"

Now Danny fidgeted. "I gotta get back."

I looked him over. "Who, Danny?"

More fidgeting.

"Danny. What's her name?"

"Umm, I gotta get back."

"Danny."

He stood. "I gotta go."

I laid a hand on his forearm. "Son, if this dame was mixed up in this, she's already in trouble. Better to be mixed up with the cops than mixed up with whoever cooled El Gordo."

He said, "Maybe. But also..."

Oh no.

"You're dizzy on her, Danny. You fell hard."

He didn't answer.

I stood. "Tell her to meet me today for lunch on the mainland. I'll buy. The diner two doors down from the Pennsylvania Hotel. If she thinks she's not in danger from this mess, I'll never see her. Except maybe in the morgue."

Not a big reaction. Just a tic in the right eye. It was something. His mouth stayed buttoned.

"Sorry to be so blunt. But you know this world she's playing in."

Silence.

"I need a name, Danny."

Nothing.

"OK. Just the first name."

Another pause. "Lara."

I slipped back into the lobby just as Clarke came in from the lawn. He said, "I have to deal with something at the north end that just came up. You can hang out here, or taxi back over the bridge. Your call."

No need for me to tell him about Lara just yet.

A cab ran me back over the bridge. I got in a couple more hours of shuteye after all. Then I walked to the diner. It was five minutes before noon. I ordered a coffee and opened a *Palm Beach Post* I'd picked up that morning. I read it front to back and even got through the funnies. I looked at my watch. The waitress already had refilled me twice.

"You the cop?"

The voice came from the booth behind me. I didn't turn. "Lara?"

She came around and sat down. Maybe in her mid-twenties. Maybe early twenties. She was a blond, but not really. I saw the black roots. A little makeup but a lot of true beauty there. And a body and gams that didn't quit. Apologies again to the Missus. I'm a cop. Just stating facts.

She slid a smoke out of a silver case. "Do you mind?"

As she brought the cig to her lips, she tried to hide the tremor. But when she came up with the lit match, she used two hands. Our eyes met.

"How bad?"

"Don't know what you're talkin' about."

The waitress had materialized. I pointed to Lara's coffee mug and said, "And two roast beef sandwiches, hon."

I leaned in and talked low. "Lara, there's a valet over at the Palmetto Hotel, thinks you're the cat's meow. And that includes worrying about you."

She pulled hard on her cig. "He's a sweet kid. But he's a kid."

"You guys are about the same age."

Her sad smile came from someplace far away.

"The valet kid is cute. And he fell hard for me. But I didn't want to start anything there. He's a bunny. He's an innocent. Come down from Jersey to get out of the ice. Parks cars and lies on the beach."

"And he doesn't like the world you live in."

She shrugged. "It's exciting. And I get a lot of, uh, benefits."

My eyebrows went up.

"No. Not that. I'm hands off. That was the deal. When El Gordo did want hanky-panky, he just rang up one of his call girls. Me he just wants hanging on his elbow."

She pulled hard on the cig.

"These guys, when they're putting on the Ritz, they want to be seen with a fine dish, all dolled up in the best glad rags. Someone to sit next to them at dinner, or walk the lobby with them to show how they have a spiffy tux and a hot babe. Or to put an arm on their shoulder at the card table and make a big gasp when they win a big hand."

I said, "And in exchange, the big man slips you twenties and buys you necklaces and lets you run a tab at the dress shop."

"Something like that. But I ain't no gold-digger. I take just enough. For now, I just hung out with all these disgusting crooks and took the big man's money."

"How long were you gonna ride that gravy train?"

She shrugged.

The waitress was back with our plates, refilled our mugs, and was off. I reached over and made an "O" around Lara's thin wrist. My fingertips met. And then some.

"Was it El Gordo who started you on the junk?"

She yanked her hand away. Took another hit of the cig. She was trying hard to control her shakes. She reached for the sandwich. Took a couple bites. Washed it down with some coffee. I waited her out.

An exasperated sigh. "Skee."

Well. Whaddya know.

I leaned back. "How well did you know him?'

"The guy's a ghost. I know he lives in Miami, but that's about it. Takes the train up here every weekend. He can't afford El Gordo's table. But some of the guys sometimes run a second table in the room. With lower stakes. I, umm, I think Skee cheats."

Skee? Never.

"And the heroin?"

She looked out across the room.

"C'mon, Lara."

Another puff.

Finally. Here it came.

"Skee was slick. He could tell I was getting bored. And I liked the dough, but the whole thing was starting to creep me out. He knew I liked to have a drink. He said, 'Forgot the hooch, baby. I got stuff, it will take you somewhere.' I was stupid. El Gordo had won big, and he'd gave me a big wad. I figured, what the heck."

What the heck. How many times I've heard this.

I said, "Next thing you know, you were an involuntary customer of Skee."

No expression.

A bite of my roast beef. "But one day you decided you didn't like being a junkie."

She had more of her sandwich, then more coffee, then more cigarette. I could tell this was painful.

"I, uh…well, I got where I was waking up in the morning and thinking of it first thing. Being hopped up. That's when I knew I was in big trouble."

How many times did I hear this, too? People like Lara were the lucky ones.

I said, "Danny, the valet, wanted to help. You told him you were fine. He knew different, even though he wasn't in your sphere, you being a high society dame and him being just a car runner from New Jersey."

Got her. She gave a little smile.

A light went on in my head.

"But El Gordo figured out what Skee was doing."

She didn't say anything.

"And him being your sugar daddy, he didn't like Skee damaging his asset."

She stared at the tablecloth.

"Tell me how this sounds. El Gordo confronts Skee at the card game. Blows his top. Maybe the big man says that while he might do a lot of shady stuff, even he doesn't make money off junkies. And he says people like Skee are worms. How am I doing?"

She picked up the sandwich, then laid it back down without taking a bite.

I said, "And Skee snapped. And he pumped a bunch of lead into the fat man's pretty white tux shirt. El Gordo got off one shot into Skee on the way down. And then everyone else ran out like cockroaches. Until it was just Skee with his leg. And you. Standing over the corpse of your benefactor, sobbing like a schoolgirl."

She nodded ever so slightly.

Another light went on. "Holy cow. Skee made you dump the guns."

She looked at me like I'd found out her underwear size.

I said, "Dang. He told you to take the two guns and head down the secret hallway and out the back. Dump them in the lake. Even made you take the spent shells. Didn't even give you time to grieve. With his knee, he couldn't run away. He said your meal ticket had gone to the great beyond, and you'd better do what he said if you wanted your next fix. And you'd better not squeal to the cops if you wanted to see another sunrise. Sound about right?"

She looked up at me. "What are you, a wizard?"

I shook my head. "It's not complicated." Then, "How long have you gone?"

She smashed out the cig. "Two days. I'm really shaky."

"Look, Lara. I'm no goody two-shoes. Well, I am. Part of my job description. But I've watched the morgue guys collect bodies out of the gutter who still had the needles in their arms. You don't gotta take my word for it. You stick with this stuff, you die."

I leaned in. "You're feeling balled up right now. But I can get you help. Get you to a place where they can get you off the stuff. Won't be easy. But I know a sweet kid who's carrying a torch for you. He'd give his last two bits of tip money from the parking lot to stand with you the whole way."

She stared at her roast beef, like it she was looking past it. I let her stew. Took another sip. Then she slid her cigs into her bag and stood.

"Thanks for the sandwich."

She stood at the booth. Body seemed to be swaying ever so much.

"Let you know."

After the girl left, and I paid, the waitress directed me to a phone booth in the back, and I called over to the Palmetto Hotel. Ingraham's tone was not obliging. He said Skee checked out. I asked did the mope give a forwarding address. Ingraham allowed as how he did not.

I hung up and called Clarke.

"I got a lead. I think it's Skee after all."

"Who tipped you?"

"A chick. Hope I can leave her out of it."

"You find Skee, I don't care about a broad."

Uh oh.

"Whaddya mean, find Skee?"

Clarke sighed. "My guy lost him on the train to Miami. He saw him go into the john, but it turned out to be a baggage room that had a door at the other end. Skee must have moved to the next car and jumped off at one of the other stations. Maybe around Lauderdale. First bird my guy ever lost."

Terrific.

I said, "Just maybe he's dumb enough, or cocky enough, to go back to one of his old haunts. Maybe even back to that blind tiger I raided the other night. Maybe he'll figure I'm still up here, sitting by the pool."

Clarke thought for a second. Then, "Okay. I'm with you, Nate. Miami. These guys might have their fun up here with the society swells, but we both know they do most of their day-to-day business at your end. And that is his base. Ingraham, the hotel manager, wants to protect his bosses. He knows we have an ace, if you will pardon the pun. He's already lost the secret of Hypocrite's Row. That'll be on the front pages tomorrow. But the manager might be telling the truth when he said El Gordo just rented rooms and everyone looked the other way. It's a slog here. You find Skee down at your end, make my job a lot easier."

I checked out of the Pennsylvania and started the long drive back to Miami in the blazing sun, with nothing around me but scrub and dirt and a small burg every few miles. The sleep I hadn't been getting was like a gallon of milk hanging from my neck. I got home in time to wash up, take a quick nap, and have dinner with the Missus and the tykes. I do enjoy their company.

At least three times a day, I muse on the double life I lead. A peaceful home with a wife and kids. And walking the streets, poking around amid the dregs of society.

The Missus walked me to the door. She said what she always does.

"Make sure you come home to me."

I told her I would. And then there was some other stuff.

It had rained, and the air was cold and clammy. The streets were slick. I stopped about a block from the blind pig. Threw on my coat and tightened my tie. Put on my fedora. The Missus makes fun, but my momma always told me to look right in public. Even in front of a juice joint.

I walked to the corner across from the place and hid in an alcove outside a print shop. Right about now, I'd be lighting up. Instead, I slid in another candy cig. Forty minutes later, I'd gone through three of them and was getting sugar jitters.

A cab pulled up. A man stepped out. He wore his fedora low. I saw a limp. Bingo.

The goon at the door followed him in. Now no one was out front. I raced across the street to an alcove at the shop right next door to the speakeasy. Deep enough to swallow me.

Skee had come by cab. So he probably would leave that way. But cabs wouldn't be trolling for fares on a weeknight. Not in this neighborhood. He'd have to call for one. And wait for it.

I ran my hand over my revolver, snug in my shoulder holster. Have to wait longer. And I was out of candy cigs.

It was another forty minutes before Skee limped out. He checked his watch. I slid behind him and poked him with my gun.

"Hello, Skee."

His hands went up. He turned. He grinned. "Hi, Nate."

"It's up, Skee. We have the sheba. She's ready to get off the smack. You lost your hold on her."

"Sorry. Don't know nothing about no junkie dame."

"Okay. You're coming in anyhow."

A noise behind me. A cab pulled up. It distracted me just long enough for Skee to bolt.

I didn't want to shoot him down in the street. That headache I didn't need. But I did take a step toward him. His face showed the terror of a man who didn't want to go back to the big house, because this time it might be for good. Looking back at me was his fatal mistake. His bum leg froze up, and he slipped on the wet street and dropped right in front of the cab. The front right wheel popped him in the noggin. Skee was dead where he fell.

* * *

Clarke took the train down at midday. I bought him a late lunch at a diner on Flagler Street. Dirk Monroe came along.

Clarke leaned back from his coffee and lit up a smoke. It smelled delicious.

Dirk said, "One would think this wraps things up nice and neat. But we know it doesn't. With El Gordo off the table, we can count on a battle for his turf across the state. Also, I'm wondering if Mark Gregg, the rumrunner we're watching, just lost a big account. We'll all be busy."

"You're right," Clarke said. "But when Skee's melon hit that tire, it did tie up some things at our end, in Palm Beach. You'll see it in the papers. Ingraham, the hotel manager, panicked, and everything came out. The hotel wasn't oblivious. Looks like the town wasn't either. Last night, my guys booked a town councilman. And the mayor. Which is kind of awkward because the guy signs my paycheck."

I said, "Well. At least that will be the last elected official in Florida to succumb to the lure of corrupt money."

We all three smiled. Clarke said. "Oh yeah, Nate. The last one."

Clarke spent the night in Miami. The next day, he went with me to a local service for Prohibition agent Fred Paxton, who had died with Bailey Monk. Paxton had been buried up in Georgia around the time of the storm, so we hadn't had a chance to send someone.

I was thinking that neither Clarke nor I had known Paxton at all. Of course, that didn't matter.

Chapter Nine: The Gulf Stream Pirate

The silence. That's what gave me the heebie-jeebies.

At the dock at the U.S. Coast Guard station in Fort Lauderdale, the man at the helm of the patrol boat cut the engine, and it coasted up. Lashed to it: An empty thirty-footer that only could be a rumrunner.

I heard the thunk of the boats' sides touching the wood of the dock. The slap of the tossed rope slamming onto the deck. And the lapping of water. Nothing else. No one spoke.

As the Coast Guard patrol boat slid into my view, like a float in the Rose Bowl parade, I saw the men, laid out on the deck like landed tarpon. Saltwater mixed with blood sloshed up and down the seventy-five feet of deck boards and channeled in rivulets around the bodies.

In the pilot house lay the skipper. Blood and gore soaked the wooden walls. A Secret Service agent sat against a gunwale like he was napping. Enjoying a nice day on the Atlantic. His nice white shirt was pocked with giant red splotches, each dotted with black stuff that I didn't wanna know.

The sun, low in the sky behind me, threw harsh light across the gunwales. They were striped with streaks of red-brown old blood. Two Coast Guardsmen leaned on them, moaning. One guy, Holland, had his right eye and much of his face blown away. The other one, Landry, had what I'd find out later was a bullet in his back, stopped near his spine.

Four other lawmen stood in the boat, unhurt but stunned.

Around the mount that held the boat's one-pound gun, two guys were trussed like rodeo calves, with handcuffs and rope lines.

I'd learn names later. Dustin Wiegel was alert. But Henry Ward was half-conscious. He'd been stabbed a half dozen times with an ice pick, stomped in the ribs, and smashed in the head with fists, a pistol butt, an oar, and a barnacle scraper.

Ten Fort Lauderdale cops stood at their cars. Near them, a man shouted to Coast Guardsmen who had leaped onto the patrol boat as soon as it had come to a stop.

"Careful. This is a crime scene!"

The Coast Guardsmen tried to work around the mess. But they had to get the dead and almost dead onto the dock, where wagons waited to take them to Miami. As they picked up Landry, one man slipped in blood and seawater and nearly dropped the guy. It wouldn't matter. In four days, Landry would be dead, good guy number three.

The man who'd shouted at the Coast Guardsmen turned. "Tim Garrison. Bureau of Investigation."

"Nate Moran, Miami PD."

We shook.

"This is ours, Nate. All federal. But glad to have ya. Appreciate your chief loaning you out. You know the territory. And the players. I don't. Been here all of two weeks. From upstate New York. The ocean? I'm clueless."

America is a sieve. The borders with Canada, and in the desert down by Mexico, are bad enough. Miles of unpatrolled stretches. Here it's open water. In a fast boat, you can be in Bimini or Freeport and back in just a few hours. With no one the wiser.

Garrison said, "I'm sure you already know this. The rumrunners break no British law by buying the hooch in the Bahamas. The Limeys know it's going right back across to Florida. They could not care less. In fact, it's one of the best things that ever happened to them. Prohibition's not their problem. They think it's stupid. But it's letting them sell to smugglers at a premium."

I knew the story all too well.

The stretchers made their way up from the dock to the lined-up ambulance trucks. There was my old pal Purdy, the coroner.

"Out of your turf," I said.

"A favor to my colleague up here. He doesn't have enough facilities for all this….” Purdy's voice trailed. Then, "We're taking everyone, living and otherwise, down to Miami. The ones who are still alive won't die tonight."

Garrison said, "So we have some time. We'll talk tonight up here to the ones who aren't badly hurt. Then we'll head back to Miami in the morning for the rest of 'em."

Purdy gave a sort of salute and got back to the loading. Garrison said to me, "We'll stay at the New River Hotel here in town. Mr. J. Edgar Hoover will pick up the tab."

We drove our two cars to the hotel. I called to let the Missus know her dinner would go on without me. Figured she'd be steamed. Instead, she said, "I'm not having nearly a bad as day as the families of those guys." Meaning the lawmen who'd bled out on the patrol boat. Why I married her. At least one of the many reasons.

Garrison and I knew this would be a long night, so we had an early chow at the hotel. The stew wasn't bad, but it wasn't the roast chicken the Missus had been working on. And the business we discussed didn't make for a pleasant dining experience.

Garrison drove us back to the Coast Guard base. A supervisor left us in a small room and returned with a man who looked like he'd been run through a cotton gin. His face was as white as cotton as well. He'd washed and changed into fresh Coast Guard service duds.

Garrison introduced himself and me. The man's name was Robbins.

"Funny thing," he said. "We weren't going over about smuggling. We were going over for funny money."

I said, "Counterfeit?"

"Right. On Friday, a Secret Service agent came by the base. Name of Webster. He—"

Garrison turned to me. "Dead." A sigh. "Good man."

Robbins said quietly. "Yep." He took a deep breath.

"Webster said the rum merchants at the docks in Bimini and Freeport accept U.S. cash from the rumrunners. Love it. He said that last week, they complained to the American embassy in Nassau that they were getting dirty bills."

How's that for irony? When Americans who are breaking American laws pay with counterfeit American currency, the Brits want us to do something about it.

Robbins said, "We left around ten in the morning. About two-thirds of the way to Bimini, we hear a motor coming from the east. The boat clears the horizon, and we hail it. No response. The skipper gets out his Springfield rifle and fires three shots across their bow. That's when they stop. Skip asks where they're headed. The main guy—Ward—says Miami. Skip asks is there anything particular in the boat? Ward says no. Skip can tell this is hooey. He jumps over to the other boat. He lifts the hatch cover and sees the hams. About twenty of them."

Garrison said, "Hams?"

I said, "Burlap sacks. Each holds a half dozen quart bottles wrapped in straw."

Garrison said, "The smugglers in Quebec used something like that."

Robbins reached for a pitcher on the table. He poured water into a glass, knocked it back, and wiped his mouth with his sleeve.

"So, um, Ward says to Skip, 'What's your authority to come on my boat?' Skip says, 'On the high seas, the Coast Guard boards any boat if we suspect a crime.' Then the other bad guy—"

Garrison said, "Wiegel."

"Wiegel pipes up. Says this is his first trip, and he's got a wife and two kids starving back in Miami. Can't Skip just take the hooch for himself and let the two of 'em go? Skip says sorry, can't do that. He orders the two off their boat and calls to the rest of us to start unloading the hams. Then—"

Robbins stopped. He just stared into space like he was frozen solid. Garrison and I looked at each other. A few seconds ticked off. Tears started to fill the Coast Guardsman's eyes. Garrison leaned and put a hand on his wrist. "Go ahead, son."

Robbins opened his mouth to say something. Instead, he lowered his forehead to the table and sobbed into his crossed arms, his body shaking. Garrison held out two palms to me. Wait.

Robbins lifted his face and wiped it on his sleeve. Garrison handed him a hanky, and he blew. Garrison waved to say Robbins could keep the hanky. He poured more water for Robbins, who gulped it down, took several breaths, and hiccupped.

"I'm sorry," he said. "Been in the service less than a year. Worst thing I saw before this was a floater we pulled out of the water near Baker's Haulover after the hurricane. Nothing made me ready for this."

He breathed in. Long. Then out. Long. He gave a nod to indicate he was ready to go on.

"So, umm. Skip's watching me lug one of the hams and has his back to Ward. The sumbitch got a gun from somewhere. Before I can open my mouth to warn the Skip, Ward puts a bullet in his back."

Robbins squeezed his eyes shut.

"We….uhh…Landry's right next to me. He reaches for his service revolver. But Ward's got the jump and shoots him. Landry falls back through the engine hatch.

"I saw a wrench. I grabbed it and threw it at Ward. He dodged it and pointed his gun at me. Without thinking, I dove over the side. Came up for air and thought I saw shark fins. I swam around the side of the patrol boat, and Ward motioned for someone to pull me out. He had his piece aimed at all of us and he tells us to put the hams back on his boat. Then he herds us all to the stern. Then I hear him tell Wiegel to cut the gas lines, that they're going to burn up our patrol boat and all of us in it. But—"

He stopped again. He looked hard at Garrison. "Sir, I don't know if you and your colleague"—he nodded at me—"are religious. But I believe God decided it wasn't my day to burn to death on my own boat."

We waited.

"We're standing there, waiting for Ward to shove off, set our boat on fire, and us in it. Would you believe the engine on Ward's boat wouldn't start? Go explain that."

The jury's still out for me on this divine intervention thing. But who am I to contradict a man who's sitting in front of me while his pals are in the morgue?

"Ward aims his gun at everyone while Wiegel messes with the motor.

Nothing. Can't get the thing to turn over. That's when Webster, the Secret Service guy, takes his chance. He rushes Ward. But—"

Robbins squeezed his eyes again.

"But Ward sees him and shoots him right in the chest. The Fed goes down. Ward turns and shoots Holland. Holland goes in the drink. But Ward was distracted just enough that the rest of us were able to jump on top of him and the other guy. We—"

Garrison said, "You what?"

Robbins said nothing.

The FBI man leaned in. "Son, we can see how beat up those bad guys were. If you crossed a line, your bosses will deal with it. I suspect they won't be gung-ho to make a case, seeing as how seconds earlier these guys had gunned down your pals, who happened to be officers of the law. You might as well tell me. It'll come out anyway."

Garrison got Robbins another glass of water. He gulped it. Expect he'll be spending time in the john.

"We beat them up but good. Then we dragged them back to our boat and tied them to the gun mount and radioed for help. You know the rest."

* * *

Back at Miami PD, Garrison shook hands with Dirk Monroe.

I said, "Garrison's been here two weeks. From upstate New York. Still doesn't know a lot about South Florida."

Garrison said, "Tell me about Ward."

Dirk's chair squeaked. He looked at the ceiling and blew out some smoke from his cig.

"Well, my dad came down here from New England in the late 1800s. Try to help a wife sick with the TB. My mom. Dad knew this would be his home, and he tried to be part of it. But a lot of people come down here for what they can get. From the land. From crime. Whatever.

"I know bits and pieces about Ward. Most of his work was up toward Palm Beach or in the Everglades. Way outside our territory. But naturally, he came into our world now and again. And I talked about him a lot with my colleagues around the state."

Garrison said, "Tell me what you can. It will get me started."

"Henry Jefferson Davis Ward. His mom was a diehard daughter of the Confederacy from Tennessee. Came down to Lee County, near Fort Myers.

I said, "What better place in Florida for her to live than a county named for Robert E. Lee?"

Dirk gave me a glance.

Sometimes, when the Missus and I are with friends, I go off on a tangent. Then I feel a toe silently rub against my shin. That's the Missus giving me a signal. Sometimes I think she's too quick on the draw, but most of the time, she's spot on. I got a feeling she was rubbing my shin right now.

Dirk said, "The family had a place down south near the Everglades. In no-man's land. Heck, there's even a thing called Lostman's River down there. They call the area the Ten Thousand Islands. That's no exaggeration. Down there, it's almost impossible to know where the land ends and the ocean begins. That was the way with Ward and his life of crime. Even he can't tell you the day he crossed over to the bad side.

"When he was a teenager, he helped the family with its little farm on whatever high ground they could work. They fished, of course. Crabbed. Sometimes a rich Yankee would hire Ward as a guide. Maybe for tarpon. Maybe hunting a black bear or a panther in the woods.

"Ward has a wife and three kids. He enlisted during the Great War. But he never left Florida. He worked a desk job up in Fort Myers. After that, Prohibition changed his life. It was his ticket."

I said, "It doesn't take long for rumrunners to figure out Florida's the land of milk and honey. And this side of the state is even better than the Gulf side. Right next to the Bahamas, and a lot more potential customers. So Ward set up in Coconut Grove."

Dirk said, "Not far from my family spread."

Garrison leaned in. "In our business, there are no dumb questions. If he was right under your noses, couldn't you nab him?"

Dirk smiled. "In another life, Ward might have been a college professor.

One of the smartest guys I ever saw. Reads three newspapers. He worked the speakeasies and learned everything he could about smuggling. He already knew boats. The rest was easy. Staying one step ahead of an undermanned police force was a piece of cake."

I said, "And Ward had a lot of help."

Dirk said, "Exactly. We grabbed him a couple of times trying to slip in at the south end of Biscayne Bay, where there's not a lot of people. He paid some fines. Went to jail a few times. A month. A week. One time six months. Didn't matter. He was just right back at it the next day."

Garrison leaned in. "You told me about this other guy. Mark Gregg? The one who killed the two Prohibition agents."

Dirk shook his head. "Best as we can tell, the two never worked together. Same thing with the Mosleys."

I said, "Considering that stiff we found in the cemetery, looks more like everyone was competitors."

* * *

Dustin Wiegel had taken a dozen stitches in the back of his noggin where one of the Coast Guardsmen took a club to him. Lucky he didn't end up fish food. The ambulance had taken him to Miami with the others who were in bad shape. But doctors told us we probably could take him to jail in a day.

We squeezed into Wiegel's hospital room. He sat at the foot of the bed, a big white bandage covering his head like a Jew's skullcap.

A doc, older guy, told us, right in front of Wiegel, "The Coast Guardsmen opened up his head pretty good. But his faculties are all there. He could drive a car right now if he wanted. Talk to him all you want."

The doc looked Wiegel in the face, even as he talked to us. "I took an oath to save lives and relieve pain. But I don't have to like the people I treat." Then he was out.

I waved Garrison to the only chair and leaned against a wall. Wiegel said something in a small voice. I leaned in. He repeated, "Can one of you butt me?"

Garrison slid out a deck of Lucky Strikes and pulled out two. He handed one to Wiegel. The mope's paws shook. Garrison flashed his lighter to both smokes. He looked over to me. I pulled out a candy cig. "Missus don't like me smoking."

Garrison said, "Wiegel, Nate here is Miami police, and he's just helping out. I'm federal. It's our case."

The Fed leaned back.

"I'll be square with you. You're in a fix. We've got you in a vise, dontcha think? I mean, there's not a lot of gray area here. We have you on all the hooch. That's serious enough. But…."

Garrison stopped to take a puff. He was letting the guy sweat. Wiegel looked like he was about to pee himself.

"What do you do for a living? I mean, when you're not violating the Volstead Act?"

Wiegel had started in with the shakes. We waited for him to calm down.

"Umm, boatyard mechanic."

Garrison smiled. "Well, now, that's convenient, isn't it? Mr. Ward needs a helper, but maybe he'll pay extra for someone who's also handy if the engine quits in the middle of the ocean. The Bahamas run is like taking candy from a baby. Three or four hours on the high seas on a beautiful day. Unless your boat stops. You could drink the hooch, but not really. You'd die of thirst before anyone found you. I expect Ward paid you well for your expertise."

Wiegel actually turned a weak smile.

I tagged in. "But sometimes things go hinky. And when Ward wanted to burn and sink the patrol boat, with everyone in it, he couldn't get your own engine to start. Even with your expertise."

Wiegel looked out the window.

"Ward shoulda let me turn over the engine. He was impatient. He flooded it. That sumbitch."

I glanced over to Garrison. I said, "Yes, Wiegel. Mr. Ward is a sumbitch. But you're in the soup with him." I was talking through teeth clenched around the candy cig. I took it out and held it. "Look. Don't be a sap."

Wiegel's voice rose. "Listen. I'll cop to the hooch. But I never planned on hurting anyone. When Ward got the jump on the Feds, he told me if I didn't help him ice 'em, I'd join them at the bottom. I didn't plug nobody. Never even lifted a boat hook. On my mother's life."

I said, "That might all be true. Here's the problem. You work with boats, not the law, so you probably don't know about a thing called felony murder. Tell you how it works. You and I commit a felony. Say, rob a bank. Or shoot up a speakeasy. Or, I don't know, run a boatload of rum from the Bahamas. In the eyes of the law, any murder that happens while we're committing that felony, both of us can get charged for it. Even if you didn't do anything. How am I doing, Garrison?"

The agent said, "You nailed it, Nate." He turned to Wiegel. "It gets worse, pal. This isn't just plain old local felony murder. No offense to my Miami friend here, but this is federal. Felony murder of both a Coast Guard captain and an agent for the U.S. Secret Service. And we're not hearing good things about Landry's chances. You can forget about prison. You and Ward will be able to hold hands when you swing."

It was so quiet I heard nurses talk in the hall and a cart wheel squeakily past our door.

Garrison said, "Ward's done for. But you can dodge the rope."

He took a big drag of his cig, exhaled, and crossed his arms.

Wiegel looked back and forth at us. We both were stone-faced. Sweating him out. I've done this so many times. I fought the urge to smile. I twirled my candy cig in my mouth.

Wiegel lasted about a minute.

He let out a big sigh. "What's the play?"

Garrison said, "Attaboy." Then, "It's simple. Like I said, you can clam up. And you and Ward do the dance together. Or you sing. Testify against Ward. Go to Leavenworth for thirty years. But you're alive. And maybe you get out early. Your choice."

* * *

Cops learn early in their careers that crime happens in seconds, but justice takes longer. Which is frustrating when you're waiting on justice for fellow cops. And Feds, at that.

It would be weeks before Henry Ward would go to trial in federal court in Miami for killing those Feds at sea. But after a long time, Mark Gregg's trial for killing my pal Monk was about to start. That sumbitch.

As I climbed the white steps of the Dade County Courthouse, I saw Franks, the Miami Springs police chief.

"Ya think he really might get off?"

Franks shrugged. "It won't be the first time a wet turned into a folk hero. And I long ago gave up trying to figure out juries."

At the top of the steps, I straightened my tie. I instinctively reached for my rod, then remembered we couldn't take them in. God, I felt naked. But I did have the candy cigs. All that sugar, I get a headache if I eat too many. But they mostly keep me from thinking about the smokes.

I said hi to the bailiffs by name. One, Jimmy Hudgins, was a patrol cop before he blew out a knee chasing a mugger who'd knocked down an old lady and cracked her head. I showed Jimmy the candy cigs. He laughed. I slipped one into my mouth and took my seat one row behind the prosecution table.

Sandra Monk and her daughter? They'd stayed home. Sandra said they couldn't bring themselves to hear those horrible details again.

A few rows behind me, I saw the neighbor, Mrs. Grimsby. She looked tough as nails. I nodded, and she smiled. Her eyes shifted, and her expression changed. I followed her look. Mark Gregg had emerged through a doorway. The white undershirt he'd been wearing when he gave up his shotgun to the Miami Springs police chief had been replaced by a white button shirt with decent trousers. He also wore a cocky smile.

It sticks in my craw how a dog like Gregg could gun someone down, then get good lawyers who will use every trick to help a guy walk who they know is a murderer. But that's the way the justice system works, and I guess it'd be bad the other way around.

"All rise."

Things went bad right off the bat.

Stan Horton, a neighbor. Said he'd been drinking lemonade across the street from Gregg's. Said two agents come up to the house, and he saw Monk get a full shotgun blast in the face. I saw a juror wince. Behind me, I heard Mrs. Grimsby muffle a sob.

"I just had heard the officer call out, 'All right, Gregg. Open up. We've got a search warrant.' Something like that."

The state attorney said, "Mr. Horton, are you sure he used the words 'search warrant?'"

"Yes, sir. Absolutely."

"Your honor!" It was Lenny Rubini, Gregg's shyster. I eyeballed his nice suit. When I saw Rubini in court, I knew two things from the get-go about his client. Rich. And guilty.

Rubini held up a piece of paper inside a plastic sleeve. The red splotch in the lower right corner was my friend's blood. I bit through my candy cig.

"Your honor, we move to strike the search warrant from the record."

The crowd buzzed.

"Your honor, this warrant was for daytime only." Rubini lifted from the table a folded newspaper. "I have here the *Daily News* from the day of this unfortunate incident. May I approach?" Rubini handed the newspaper to the clerk.

"According to this fine publication, the official sunset, as obtained from the National Weather Bureau office in downtown Miami, occurred sixteen minutes before these federal agents knocked on my client's door. I have verified this with the weather service and can bring someone in to testify if needed."

Rubini stood near the jury box. "I argue that this warrant thus was invalid, and the agents' presence was an illegal incursion. My client had a right to defend his home from an invasion by strangers."

The state attorney was on his feet.

"Your honor: This is outrageous! For defense counsel to suggest his client didn't know who these men on his porch were is ridiculous. We can show Gregg had numerous dealings with all of these federal law enforcement officers. And we have witnesses who will testify to attempts by Gregg to bribe Agent Monk with a new car."

"Hearsay!" Rubini shouted. Even I know he was right. The only person whose version of the bribe would be allowed couldn't talk. He was on a slab in Arlington, Virginia, where he'd be buried with full military honors in a few days.

The judge rubbed his chin. He pulled out a handkerchief. He looked straight at the state attorney.

Then he turned to the twelve men in the box.

"Gentlemen, any information about a search warrant will not be part of this proceeding, and jurors are to disregard it during your deliberations."

A dagger.

Defendants don't have to testify. The burden's on the state to prove guilt. Every kid learned that in high school civics. Why take chances? But Lenny Rubini was cocky now. He called Mark Gregg.

"I was sittin' in my livin' room, just readin' the paper with the wife and the kid. All sudden-like, I hear a bangin' on the front door. Liked to jump out of my chair. I looked in the back of th' house, toward the kitchen. I seen a man with a gun. I jump up and grab my shotgun and run toward the front of the house, away from the man with the gun. When I got to the front door, someone was putting his shoulder to it and was fixin' to stave it in. I had to protect my family. I fired through the door. Then I wheeled and saw the other man's head stickin' aroun' the corner. I shot him."

Rubini waited a second for Gregg to catch his breath.

"Did you know they were lawmen?"

"No suh."

Gregg dropped his head in his hands like his heart was broken. I'd like to reach in and break it with my bare hands. I hoped and hoped the jury would see through this baloney. I wasn't sure.

They didn't.

I called Burkie from the courthouse lobby. "Jury took only twenty-four minutes, Chief."

There was silence on the other end. Then, "OK. Come on back."

"Hey, Chief? The judge told the courtroom not to react. But a couple people cheered anyway. Cheered a murderer. A cop killer."

My knuckles were white on the phone piece.

More silence. I heard Burkie clear his throat. Then, "Nate, we can only do so much. Come on back." Then: "You're getting on a train tomorrow."

A train?

* * *

Sure wish I'd gotten a sleeper berth. But this was cutting into Chief Burke's petty cash as it was. And the seat was comfortable. And it leaned back.

It was thirty brutal hours to DC. On top of that, I'd never been out of the state of Florida. At least it was November, and I wouldn't have to deal with snow, about which I also am clueless. At least, I hoped I wouldn't.

I did watch trees fly by. First, they were just palm trees. Then mixed with pines. Then all pines.

In the Carolinas, a jolt woke me. Out the window, the passing trees were an explosion of orange and red. It was other-worldly. I'd never seen anything like it.

Another nap. Another jolt. We rounded a turn, and I saw, in the distance, buildings I recognized from high school civics textbooks. The Washington Monument. The Capitol. And the memorial to Abe Lincoln that opened just a few years ago.

The train slowed and stopped. I stood and stretched. Everything ached. I reached to the upper rack for the overcoat I'd borrowed from my partner Harvey Comeau. I'm proud to say I didn't have a need for one before now. But Comeau sometimes went to New England to see family for Christmas. New England in December? That's love.

Comeau said he probably had to get a new overcoat anyway. This one was a little tight. Wonder why, Harvey.

I walked into the cavernous Union Station and got a face full of big city. A hum bounced through the atrium. Folks walked fast, not looking. One clipped me in the shoulder, mumbled a "sorry," and kept going.

I braced myself and stepped outside. The cold hit me and I pulled Comeau's overcoat tight.

Friends from the north often told me the thing about winter that made them want to eat a shotgun wasn't when it was January and ten below and gray. It was when it was nearly April and still cold. And, for some, when it was November and already really cold. I'm happy to say I don't deal with any of that.

I'd seen traffic on Flagler Street. It had nothing on Washington. I saw a line of roadsters bumper to bumper. I knew how to hail a taxi in Miami. I figured it worked here as well. To my left, I saw a line of cabs. I raised my hand, and one lurched toward me.

"Where to?"

Where to? I had an afternoon to play tourist. I'd figured I'd need to go right to sleep. But I'd managed to get in some good shuteye on the train. Somehow, I can snooze anywhere. Don't ask me where I learned it, but it comes in handy.

I thought for a second. "Lincoln Memorial."

I'd seen the place in magazines. But it was something else looking at it up front.

My great-grandfather had run a stockyard up in Chicago. He was a great admirer of this son of Illinois, and when Lincoln was killed, the big guy took it hard.

"Sorry, Abe," I said, looking at his eyes, cut in white marble. "We got rid of the slavery thing, but the colored thing's still a mess. Don't know that we'll fix that any time soon."

Dang. I was tired after all. I saw another line of cabs. I waved, and one pulled up. "Willard Hotel."

In the hotel lobby, I read a display about how people had met here just before the war broke out. Politicians, preachers, the works. For three weeks, they tried to stop what was coming. And failed.

That war was bad for my family. Some of them did things they'd regret, and some of them got killed. But, I thought, otherwise I might be a cop in Chicago. Freezing Chicago. I'm selfish. What can I say? I got my room key and went upstairs. I was out in minutes.

I was up early. Had some breakfast and read until it was time to go. Got a cab and crossed the river into Virginia.

You can't miss the cemetery. It's up on a hill. The saying is that everyone in Washington, including the president, has to look up at these heroes.

Headstones covered the hills. There were just too damn many.

Bailey Monk didn't die in combat. He died for a stupid law. But it was the law. And the criminals didn't break it out of principle. They were out to make a buck. And to hell with whoever got in the way. Someone needed to stand up to those punks. I guess Monk did die for his country.

People walked past me. No one talked. I made my way to the amphitheater. I saw Sandra and Nancy. Sandra gasped. She hadn't known I was coming. We all hugged a long time.

"You don't know how much this means."

"All the local police chiefs got together and decided to send one guy." I paused. "It is a privilege."

I teared up. She did too. Ditto Nancy. We all hugged again.

A breeze moved across the large field. It was damn cold. I pulled Comeau's overcoat tight. We walked a long pathway between rows. Far off, I saw a casket above the ground, surrounded by men in uniform.

Sandra and Nancy took chairs. I stood.

The director of the federal Prohibition agency stood at the head of the casket. He was preaching to the choir. But he knew some reporters were here. The shooting had been national news. Two Prohi men gunned down together. And the guy gets off. Well, Gregg had gotten off for Monk. He still had to stand for Paxton. And then he could get hit with all sorts of federal charges. But I watched him walk on Monk. It made my stomach turn.

The Prohi director didn't hold back.

"Perhaps the man who killed this hero and his colleague might not have acted, had he not been emboldened by the many inflammatory comments people have made about our personnel. Which leads weak-minded criminals to attack honest and efficient officers acting in performance of their sworn duty."

An officer in U.S. Navy dress kneeled in front of the sitting Sandra and Nancy. He held, horizontal, a U.S. flag folded into a triangle.

"Please accept this. With the thanks of a grateful nation."

Sandra and Nancy sobbed. But they sat straight. The wind chilled the tears running down my face. I didn't move.

Rest well, old friend. I'll get you justice. If I have to chase Mark Gregg to Pensacola and back.

Back at Union Station, I made a collect call to Chief Burke.

"How'd it go?"

"Sad."

"Thank you for representing the department."

"This ain't over for me, Chief."

"Me neither, Nate. Me neither."

Chapter Ten: The Mosley Gang

I got back to Miami Saturday afternoon and took it easy all day Sunday. The Missus and the kids were glad to have me back.

On Monday morning, I handed Comeau his overcoat.

"Had it dry cleaned in Washington. Charged it to the department. Chief okayed it."

Comeau smiled. "You got out all the doughnut jelly."

I rolled my eyes.

I said, "You know, Harvey, Mark Gregg walked, at least for now. But we know he hasn't retired."

Comeau nodded. "Indeed."

In the next weeks, I went back and forth to Miami Springs to pow-wow with Chief Franks. His boys still tailed Gregg, carefully. The guy was keeping on the straight, as far as Franks could tell. For now.

* * *

"Nate Moran. Detectives."

"It's Dennis Martin. The crew boss over on Tamiami Trail."

"Hiya, Martin. Hey. Thanks again for your help with the Billy Tiger murder."

"Well, we kinda got caught in the middle of that."

"What can I do for you?"

"Just wanted to give you a heads up, detective. One of my boys tells me the other day, right around quitting time, he heard something strange off in the sawgrass."

"Strange? How?"

He swore it sounded like an aeroplane engine."

"Aeroplane?"

"That's what he said."

"OK. Maybe I'll take a ride out there in the next day or two. Check it out."

"Detective, Ken Hearst still is ready to testify against that Mosley guy. He's a brave man."

I said, "Not to worry, Martin. We got Mosley all locked up."

I was at my kitchen table. Sunlight streamed in while I read the Sunday morning paper. Looking for anything. Some minor incident that might provide a clue about what Mark Gregg was up to. He was like a catfish in a murky canal who you couldn't see, but you could see the bubbles coming up, so you knew he was there.

Someone was ringing the doorbell. I shouted, "Come in." The mope kept turning that knob on the ringer. I yelled again. "Come in!" He kept at it. Brrring. Brrring. Brrring.

I stood and walked to the door and threw it open. No one there. I looked over to the ringer. The knob was turning by itself. Brrring. Brrring. Brrring.

That's when I realized I was dreaming. I woke in darkness. I stumbled to the kitchen and reached for the ringing telephone.

"Got a jailbreak."

Chief Burke.

Through the open bedroom door, I saw the Missus stir and roll over.

"Claude Mosley. His brother Simpson sprung him. Killed Old Man Scheerer."

My knuckles went white against the phone.

"Shotgunned right in front of his wife."

Scheerer.

"There's more," Chief Burke said. I waited.

"Lummus."

I fell back, and my butt just caught the chair.

"Jumped on the running board of the getaway. Simpson was driving and

Claude turned and got Lummus between the eyes."

Don't cry. Don't break. You're a cop. You're a cop.

Burkie paused. I guessed he was working his jaw. That's what I was doing.

"This department never lost a man before, Nate. You know that."

I did know.

A little later, I stepped into the front room where Scheerer and the wife lived. It was just outside the lockup. No one had moved poor Scheerer. At least someone'd put a handkerchief over his face. Mrs. Scheerer sat in her chair. The frau looked like she'd cried herself out.

Old Man Scheerer dealt with more boozehounds, pickpockets, and two-bit hoods than I can remember. Always kept his sense of humor.

He'd been razzed during the Great War, being German and all. It got ugly. But his family had come over in the 1840s and he was as American as the next guy. He never let the insults bother him.

And he never worried about a jailbreak. Who'd be that stupid? Unless you thought you were smarter than the law. Which Claude Mosley did.

I knelt in front of Mrs. Scheerer. She gave me a sad smile. She always had cookies for the patrol guys when they dropped guys off. Always a kind word for me. How's the Missus? How's the kids? The latest on her two grown daughters, both nurses at Jackson Memorial. Now she had the look of someone who didn't know what to do next. I had no answer.

I whispered to the chief, "Can we get the body out before the daughters show up? Bad enough for the old lady."

He said quietly, "The wagon'll be here directly."

Burkie motioned me back outside. The sky had lightened a little while I'd been in Scheerer's living room.

"Simpson came up and knocked on the door. Told Karl someone had been hit by a car. Scheerer opened up an inch, and Simpson pushed in and fired the double-barrel. Karl fell back on his bedroom door. Mrs. Scheerer was trying to push in from her bedroom, but her husband's body was in the way. Harvey yanked the key ring off the old man's waist and was out and into the cell block before Mrs. Scheerer finally got the door open."

Burkie motioned me to his sedan. We drove about two blocks to where a gaggle of patrol guys stood in the street. Rope had been run between lamp posts, to keep the curious out. The patrol guys parted. I looked down. Paul Lummus looked back up at me. Except he didn't. His face was something I still see. I'd never laid eyes on a dead copper before. And this was one I knew.

I croaked, "His mom."

The chief sighed. "Heading there as soon as we…finish here." Then, "I'll leave two patrol guys with her."

Lummus was just out of high school. Had his eye on a pretty young thing who worked at the dispatch desk. The Spanish Flu had cut down his dad. It was just him and his mom. And now it was just the mom.

Chief Burke had a look I didn't see very often.

"This is yours, Nate. You bring me Mosley. And his pals. All parts attached or not. Understand?"

His hands twisted the rim of his fedora.

"The man's big on bluster, Nate. You know that. That's how we get him."

Mosley once had left a bullet at the teller's window during a robbery, saying it was for Burkie.

"Do you think he'll lay low for a while, Chief?"

"I dunno, Nate. Maybe. You saw how his brother drowning shook him up."

I flushed.

"Nate, Dirk told me all about what happened. That's water under the bridge."

I wanted to say, "Thank you." But decided against it.

With Claude already in the can, Frank lying in the sand at Baker's Haulover left the family operation in a jam. A drowned breadwinner. An expensive boat out of service. And all that inventory lost. The Mosleys would need some moolah, and soon.

I said, "What about the getaway car?"

"Hot. Simpson lifted it from the dealership over on Brickell. Still had the dealer's paperwork in the glove box. A patrol guy found it two blocks from here. Checking it over now. They were sloppy. This was anything but a clean break. You got plenty to work with, Nate. Got any idea where to start?"

"Actually, I might, Chief. Tamiami Trail." I told him about my call with Dennis Martin, the crew boss. "It's a long shot, Chief. But somewhere to start."

The sun was up now. A black truck emerged from the low glare and eased to a stop. I saw the two morgue guys. Things were different this time. No one spoke. The guys strapped poor Lummus to a stretcher. The patrol guys stopped and stood at attention. So did I. So did Chief Burke. We stood that way until the truck drove off.

I remember hearing a reporter tell me once there was no bigger story than someone killing a cop. Someone would bump off a cop, no one was safe. Made me feel good, I guess, in a creepy way.

Chief Burke knew Claude Mosley. Knew his brothers. Had stood jaw to jaw with them. Looked in their eyes. I had my moment with Claude. And the drowned Frank. The rest of the gang was an abstraction. Faces on a wanted poster. Tales told around the coffee percolator. And now I had a weeping frau and a colleague lying in the middle of a dark street.

I would make it my business to make the acquaintance of everyone in the Mosley outfit.

I swung by the diner for a quick omelet and a cuppa and headed to the motor pool.

Another drive out to the Tamiami Trail bridge. Another hour banging my tailbone. Another meet-up with Martin. He put two fingers to his mouth and let out a loud whistle. It rang through the trees. Five minutes later, the mystery Seminole boatman materialized from the shadows. I held out some coins. He reached into a basket and handed me a loaf.

"Claude Mosley busted out."

He already knew. These guys are magicians.

More seconds passed. Something buzzed my ear.

I said, "You know where he's making the hooch."

Silence.

I ripped another corner of the bread. Something else buzzed my ear. I waved at it.

The boatman said, "Mosleys knew you and me talked about Big Mosley killing my cousin. So, well, no one's safe."

"You got that right, brother."

The man pulled out a hanky and wiped his face. I took another bite of the bread. Slapped my neck another time.

"Okay, okay. I'll take you to the still."

Wow.

"When?"

"Come back nine tonight. Bring your own boat. Two more police. Just two. No more. Bring guns. I'll take you almost there. Okay, okay?"

I said, "Okay. Okay."

* * *

"Whap!"

Dirk Monroe's hand came up on his neck. He wore a contraption of a hat with mesh hanging from it. He would have looked silly on a Miami street corner. Now he just looked like someone fighting a losing battle. The cop next to him, Raulerson, wore the same getup. He was working his elbow as well. Whap, Whap, Whap.

It was warm for this time of year. And, as always, the mosquitoes were in charge.

Why did they mostly leave me alone and go after others? Who knows? Maybe other guys' skin stinks from smokes or hooch, that attracts them. Maybe it's that Cuban blood that came down from my great-grandmother. Whatever it is, I ain't beefin'. I was wearing long sleeves. I used one to wipe a sweat droplet from the tip of my nose.

Raulerson stood in the boat, working the pole as we slid between trees. He'd grown up around Lake Okeechobee, and as a kid, he worked the shallows for bass. Why we brought him tonight.

It was nearly a full moon, and we could see a lot. The night was quiet, but not quiet. A million crickets chirped. Unseen birds cawed in the dark, and others responded. I heard the deep tuba of bullfrogs. And every once in a while, something splashed alongside us. Too close for my liking. And, of course, that buzzing around my ears. And Dirk slapping his neck.

Just as I was wondering how far in we were from civilization, a flatboat materialized out of the dark. Billy's cousin. I still didn't know his name, and I didn't plan to ask unless I needed to. He lifted his pole from the water and turned it horizontal. His boat slid to a bank and stopped. Raulerson pushed his boat pole, and we slid alongside.

I couldn't see the Seminole's face. He spoke in his monotone. "About a half mile ahead. I wait here." He turned to me. "You get Mosley. I hope dead."

No one spoke. We drifted past the Seminole. I looked back and saw him watching us until we rounded a bend.

It was like the tunnel of love at the carnival. Except even darker. And smelled from weeds and funky water. And was silent, except for Raulerson's pole. I barely saw the water in front of it. Sure glad to have Raulerson.

I wished I still did the smokes. I didn't have any of my candy cigs. I'd slopped my hands with grease to keep off the skeeters, so the candy wouldn't have been a good taste combination.

I heard it.

Low. Muffled. But close. Too loud to be a boat motor.

I put my hand on Raulerson's shoulder. He brought the pole horizontal. We slid near a big mangrove that was half in the canal. The thing was so big we saw it even in the dark. I wiped my hands dry on my pants and lifted my long gun from under the bench. Raulerson took the long step to the canal bank. I handed him his rifle, and he laid it down, then pulled me up. The chief did the same. We crouched in the palmettos. No one made a sound.

We'd cleared the tree line. We were out of the black tunnel.

Three large tents. Then, to one side, a large metal contraption that spewed steam in the moonlight. It had an aeroplane propeller on the back.

First time I had seen one of those airboats. Chief Burke had put in for one. They're not cheap. But out here, where the water averages about eighteen inches, a regular boat and its prop will just stick in the mud. Looked like the Mosleys had made a smart investment.

I saw only silhouettes. I counted. Two goons standing in the water loaded crates. A third person walked around the boat from the front. A fourth, face hidden, stood near the giant propeller, its blades inside a wire safety mesh.

Dirk motioned for Raulerson and me to flank him. We still were in shadow.

Dirk stepped out.

"Police! Give up, Mosley!"

The two goons stood, stupefied. But the man near the propeller came up with a long gun.

I saw a flash and heard a grunt. To my right, Raulerson dropped.

Dirk fired. The man near the propeller dropped to the deck. Even as he did, the prop noise got louder, and the boat began to move. The goons, their mouths open, watched it slide off without them.

Dirk started to run after the boat, but it had picked up speed, and he was slogging calf-deep in swamp. The boat had melted into the dark. Dirk whirled and trained his rifle on the goons. They flung up their hands.

A glaze on Raulerson's left shoulder shone in the moonlight. He grimaced. I said, "Gotta get you out of here."

The two goons walked toward us, Dirk behind them, gun at chest level. I said, "That guy was ten feet closer to us, we'd be putting Raulerson in a bag. As it is, he's shot up pretty good. Shoulder full of shot." As if on cue, Raulerson let out a grunt.

Dirk motioned to the two goons. "Carry him to our boat. Any funny business, and you get shot escaping. Understand?"

In the moonlight, I got my first good look. Neither looked like much of a goon. They looked like scared teenagers.

With Raulerson down, I had to work the pole. But it was one canal. No turnoffs, thank goodness. Between groans, Raulerson talked me through it. Push and steer. Push and steer.

We came around a bend and saw Billy's cousin. He stayed in the shadows.

"These boys see my face, I gotta kill 'em."

I said, "No more killing."

I turned to the two teens. "Faces down or this Indian puts his pole through you."

Billy's cousin led the way from there. Soon his flatboat slid to the bank. "You're okay from here. Okay okay?"

I said, "Okay okay."

I never would see the man again.

Raulerson had stopped moaning and appeared passed out, or nearly.

Dirk said, "Nate. I probably iced the man in the back of the airboat."

One of the kids, still face down, said in a muffled voice, "That was Mosley's dad."

I gulped. Dirk said nothing.

We'd left some patrol guys at the spot where we'd put in, and when they saw us, they scrambled to get Raulerson off and stretched him on the back seat of their car. Then they tore off toward town.

Dirk and I helped the two kids climb out and sat them in the back seat of our car.

I said, "By now, Mosley's stopped and seen Pops gave up the ghost. He'll be all hornets and bees. He'll really be all on us now."

Dirk shrugged. "Already was. And I'm all on him. He broke out of our jail. And killed Sheerer. And killed Lummus. And now he nearly got Raulerson. Or at least his dad did."

Dirk lit a cig and exhaled. "I popped his dad in the line of duty. Seems to me it ain't the same thing as what he did to Lummus. I know he won't agree. But it ain't."

* * *

Davie is a cowboy town on land that not so long ago was scrub. Like a lot of South Florida. It's surrounded by big beef and dairy ranches, and buildings on the main street are made up to look like it's a western town.

It's got one bank, and the town's so far out in the middle of nowhere that the armored car comes out just once a week.

On a Friday morning, not long after we raided the Mosleys' still, Homer Robbins, proprietor of the Davie Cattleman's Bank, got to work a little before eight in the a.m. His teller came in ten minutes later.

Robbins was in front of his open vault, morning mail in hand. He heard the front door open. Through the grate that separates customers from the teller, a woman approached. Robbins dropped his mail when she opened her mouth and said, "You being robbed." In a man's voice.

I was at Dirk Monroe's coffee percolator. He was giving me the latest on Raulerson. Off the street for about two months.

Chief Burke stuck in his head.

"Nate: Get down to the motor pool and check out a jalopy. Bank holdup."

"Where to?"

"Davie."

I moaned. "That's halfway to Tampa."

Burkie said no, it was west of Fort Lauderdale, and the road up to there isn't too bad, and it shouldn't take more than an hour or two, and quit griping and get a wiggle on.

"That's way off our turf. Mind telling me why I'm going?"

The chief puts up with a little sass. Not much. But he didn't want to take the time to lecture me. "It's the Mosleys."

Eyebrows up. Me and Dirk both.

Dirk said, "Chief, how we know?"

Burkie wasn't smiling. "They left a bullet at the teller's window."

Those guys get points for moxie.

It seemed all the dust in South Florida came in my car window during that long drive. The road barely was wide enough for one vehicle. Only once did I see another, a southbound truck loaded with peppers. I pulled onto the shoulder to let it pass. Then I put my car back in gear. But my back right wheel spun. I was stuck. I remembered the trick about rocking. I heard the gears grind as I went back and forth. I was in a panic. Help might not drive by for another hour. But the wheel caught, and I was back on the dirt road.

It was another half hour before I saw the sign for Davie. I counted about ten buildings on the one street. Reminded me of Miami Springs, except for the western thing. I saw a diner. My stomach growled, and I looked at my watch. Ten after noon. Have to wait.

At the very end of the street stood the Davie Cattleman's Bank.

A Broward County Sheriff's deputy stood at the front door. A hand-scrawled sign said, "Closed for audit." I'll say.

I showed my badge.

"Heard you was coming." Waved me in.

I counted twenty steps from the front door to the lone teller's window. Its vertical bars were just narrow enough to block a hand, even a sideways one. But maybe not a pistol barrel.

Behind the grill, Homer Robbins sat, his forehead sunk into the fingers of his right hand. Beside him sat his teller, a pretty, plump twenty-something, her eyes red and swollen. Next to them stood another Broward deputy and a stocky guy in plainclothes who must be a detective.

I showed my badge. The detective opened a gate, and I came around. He stuck out his hand. "Fran Lotesta. Welcome to the prairie. I'm the only Wop for ten miles."

We both smiled. You know the rule. You can make fun of your own ethnic group. Because you're really making fun of the people who make fun.

Lotesta leaned. "Mr. Robbins: I know you told us a couple times now. But we think the robber was part of a big gang that's making a ruckus across the state." He pointed to me. "This copper came up all the way from Miami. Do you mind…"

Homer groaned. "I'm ruined." Down went his head again.

I spoke quietly. "Mr. Robbins. Please. Could use your help. These guys murdered two people during a jail break. The jailkeeper. And a cop. Both of 'em were my friends."

Two beats. He sat up and straightened his coat. Like he was trying to gin up whatever dignity might still be left for a bank owner who just got cleaned out.

"Mr. Robbins, sir?" It was the teller. Her voice still was shaky. "You want I should leave you alone?"

"No, Daisy," Robbins said. "You might have something to add."

He looked up at me. "Five thousand dollars. This is the end of me."

Five grand. That's a year's pay for a lot of people.

"You can see this is a tiny bank. I use the vault for anything important. In this morning's mail were some documents for me to hold for an investor. He's building a small hotel at the south end of town. And not a flophouse, by any means. I had just opened the vault to put 'em in when the…when the…"

His voice trailed.

Lotesta said, looking at Robbins but talking to me: "What also was in the vault: A rancher here had sold several head of cattle to Cubans. They paid him in U.S. currency. They got it from the casino in Havana. Fifty one-hundred-dollar bills."

I whistled. "C-notes? That'll hurt the Mosleys. Won't be easy to pass."

"Right," Lotesta said. "It's not like you use one to buy a soda pop. We been spreading the word up here to all the PDs to keep an eye out, and also the folks up in Palm Beach. And your chief is doing the same in Miami."

I asked Robbins, "Any reason to believe the Mosleys got wind you were holding this guy's cash?

"I guess it's possible. But—"

Lotesta jumped in. "I vote for just dumb luck."

Robbins nodded in agreement.

I turned back to the teller. "Ma'am, can you describe the man?"

She sniffled. "I gotta be straight with you. Mostly all I saw was that giant gun pointing at me."

"Don't apologize. That's what most people say. Been in that spot myself."

She pulled a hanky from her sleeve and wiped her nose.

"And the dress."

Dress? I looked at Lotesta.

The girl said, "It was a floor-length black skirt. I recognized the pattern. My cousin has one just like it. It's her Sunday church outfit." She smiled. "Ruffled white shirt, all tied up at the throat. She—I mean he—had a bonnet and a veil."

"Can you describe the face at all?"

Her mouth turned into a frown. "No. The veil. And, like I said, I saw just the gun. Then I saw just the dress."

I said, "That's why they did it."

Lotesta said, "Yep. They knew she would remember just the dress. They are clever."

Robbins said, "He aimed the gun through the slats and told Daisy to come around or she was dead. I stepped forward from the vault, and he turned the thing on me. I—"

He still was shook. "I opened the gate."

"Did he say anything else?"

Robbins shook his head. "He just motioned toward the vault. He could see it was half open. I feel like a chump. All morning I've kicked myself for not slamming the thing shut as soon as I saw him at the teller window."

I said, "But then he just would have told you to open it, or he'd kill your girl. You were in a fix. How'd he leave?"

"He slipped the cash down the front of his dress," Daisy said. "He musta have had a lookout, because just as he threw open the door, a car pulled up."

"Can you describe it?"

"I probably saw it for three seconds. That's it. Just that it was black."

Black. Like just about every car in the world.

I nodded at Lotesta and tipped my fedora to Robbins and the teller. I turned to leave. I heard Robbins say, "Oh. Wait."

He held out his palm. The bullet.

"He said to let the police down in Miami know that this was for the chief. Burke. Compliments of Claude Mosley."

* * *

Dirk Monroe stopped at my desk. "You done with Davie for now? Can you talk to Mosley's, uh, assistants?" He handed me a file folder.

I walked around the block to the jail. Scheerer's furniture still was in what, at least for now, remained a living room. The widow had said to give away everything or sell it for charity. Workers crawled over the place. Three patrol guys stood by. Chief Burke was giving instructions.

"The setup with Scheerer went back to when Miami was a quiet village," Chief Burke said. "It ain't anymore."

He pointed to a new thick front door. "Solid oak. And no more resident

148

jailkeeper. You step inside, there's a patrol guy at a desk. Armed. Another door behind him. A patrol guy behind that." He looked at me. "It's a new world."

"What about Mrs. Scheerer?"

"The frau didn't wanna spend another minute in this room. All she could see when she closed her eyes was her beloved bleeding out. She's moving in with the older daughter down in Coconut Grove."

Down the hall, in their cell, the two teens sat on the floor. They looked as scared as when we'd dragged them in from the Glades.

I pointed at the first one. "Wanna talk to you."

"W-w-w-what about?"

"Routine. C'mon." I eyed the other kid. "Deal with you later."

The kid struggled to his feet. He looked pale. I can't say I'd look too good after days in the cooler, most of it in the dark.

The patrol guy who'd walked us in handed me a clipboard. I signed a paper and handed it back. I walked the kid to the end of the cell block to an interview room and sat him down.

"What's your whole name?"

Silence.

"You're gonna make me work? After all the trouble you're in? Okay. Suit yourself."

I opened the folder Dirk Monroe had given me.

Andrew Hudson.

Oh, no.

"You the Hudson used to work at the Everglades Hotel?"

He looked like he'd swallowed a razor blade.

I closed the folder and leaned back. Gave him that "You're in trouble now," cop smile.

"You got the football player's lady her moonshine. From the Mosleys. Who had cut it with wood alcohol. I guess you know it killed her. Sure you do. Why you terminated your employment."

The boy's mouth opened, but nothing came out. He gulped like his lungs had stopped working and he couldn't take in air. Then I heard a big rush as he inhaled. And a scream. Terror. Anguish. I don't know. I'm not a head doctor. But this guy was in a lot of pain. Not physical. He kept shrieking until I jumped up and put my hands on his shoulders. The patrol guy burst through the door. I waved him off. He quietly slid back out.

The shrieks stopped. The kid's head dropped to the desk, and he began to sob. I waited him out. After a few minutes, the racking stopped. He brought up his head. I handed him my hanky. He blew and snorted.

I spoke calmly. "Tell me about it, son."

His shoulders shook. I heard him sniffle.

"I—I—I." He coughed and blew his nose.

When he started talking, his face still was pasted to the desk. I had to lean to hear him.

"I grew up near the Mosleys. I knew what they was. Many times they asked my ma could they use me on jobs. She said she'd never let me get mixed up with crooks like them. But then my pa died and things got real rough and Claude Mosley come by with a wad of cash. When he left, my ma said, 'Son, sometimes we gotta do the wrong thing if we wanna eat.'"

Another good blow of his nose. Time to say goodbye to that hanky.

"I didn't wanna have nothin' to do with the Mosleys. Honest. Not 'cause they was bad. But 'cause I knew how I'd end up. Dead. Or like this. Cuffed in a jail cell."

Smart kid.

"I told Ma I'd rather quit school and get a real job. She said okay, we try that for a while and if'n it don' work, we go back to the Mosleys. I came downtown and got the bellhop job."

"Why'd you use the fake home address, Hudson? Middle of Biscayne Bay?"

He shrugged. "Just being a smart aleck, I guess. And in case I ever had to bolt."

I nodded for him to go on.

"Mosley come by the house one night and said he'd heard I got the job at the hotel. He said he'd pay me to find hotel guests who wanna buy hooch. Called it a 'finder's fee.' Too dangerous for him to come to the hotel, so I give the guest an address to go get the booze. I figured, well, that seemed okay. I don't see no victims."

He caught himself. Of course, the lady. So, one. At least.

"So when the football player and the lady checked in, I took the lady's bag to her room, and she tells me straight out she's looking for some drinky. I write out an address over in Allapattah. She slips me ten. Never got a tip like that in my life. On top of what Mosley gave me for hooking her up, it was a really good night."

"You got off at midnight. How'd you find out what happened to the lady?"

"My maw woke me up at six. She says I still had her nice lighter that Pa had gave her before he died. She had let me borrow it. I'd left it in my cubbyhole at the hotel during my shift and forgot it. I asked could I get it that afternoon when I went in, and she said no, remember she was taking a morning train to see my aunt in Sebring for a couple days and she wanted to have the lighter. I said I just wanted to go back to sleep, but she told me to get my—to get over to the hotel and get the lighter, and then I could go back to bed. I threw on some clothes and took the bus over.

"In the lobby, one of the other bellhops grabs me. He's all whispering. He says, 'Holy cow, Andy. You missed it.' Then he tells me about the lady bein' dead. I felt like someone dropped a bowling ball on my head. The lady. Dead! I knew I had to get away. I scribbled a note to the boss, 'I quit,' and grabbed mom's lighter and the rest of the stuff in my cubby. And I scrammed."

The patrol guy appeared at the door again. I held up two closed fingers to my lips like I was drawing on a smoke and motioned toward the kid. The officer reached into his pocket and took a step in with a cig. The kid took it and accepted the officer's lit match. His hands shook. I stuck a candy cig in my mouth. The kid looked at it and realized what it was. I said, "Missus made me quit." He just took another drag.

The cop walked back down the hall to his desk. I leaned in. "You didn't know the hooch was bad?"

He shook his head hotly. "Hell, no. On the soul of my dad. I, uh—well. I guess it don' matter now. I sold hooch to probably two dozen guests. No one ever had a problem."

"Did you say anything to the Mosleys?"

A drag on the smoke. "I took a bus back home and tried to sleep for a few hours. Didn't work. After lunch, the other guy you caught with me—that's Artie Middleton—come by my place. Tells me the Mosleys are fixin' to crap their britches 'cause this lady died. He says they been adding wood alcohol a little at a time, and they musta been a little heavy-handed on this batch. They done thrown it out, but they worried other customers'll croak.

"Middleton says Mosley told him to let me know I'm in it right up to the neck, too. 'Cause I'm the finder man. Says Mosley told him if we come out that night and help the Mosleys load some hooch on their boat, they give me extra money. Said they were gonna shut off the stills for now and head out of state and lay low for a while. Said we could go with them. Or I can stay and take the fall for the bad hooch. Not a lot of options for me."

I said, "Hudson, you might be able to help us. And then maybe we can help you. Understand, son?

"Officer, if the gang finds out I turned, made a deal, they'll feed me to the gators. Heck, they'd probably try to bust me out just so's they can kill me."

"Right, son. But we nearly killed you out there. And we did kill Mosley's dad. You said it yourself. Not a lot of options."

I let him finish the cig. Then I cuffed him and signed him out and walked him around the block to Chief Burke's office. Dirk came by, too. I figured the kid was getting up the nerve to cross a line that when you do, you don't go back. I sat him down, and the chief and Dirk and I waited. A while.

Then: "Lori Ritter."

Burke and Dirk looked at me. Name meant nothing.

"She, uh, been Mosley's moll since before I started hanging with these guys. I think they been lockin' lips a couple years. Her family settled a stretch of the Lake Okeechobee shore back at the end of the Great War. It's even named for them."

Now I did remember the name. I passed once through a spot along the lake that had a general store and a handful of cottages and a sign saying, "Ritter. Pop. 19." Funny. Nineteen people.

Burkie said, "Okay, son. What about the dame?"

"Middleton tol' me that lately he could see her and Claude were fighting a lot."

"What about?"

"Maybe about you, Chief."

***

The two-lane hugged the eastern shore of the lake. I looked out over that big water. That's what Okeechobee means in Seminole. Big Water. I thought about its power. Wasn't too long ago, a hurricane made it jump its banks, and it drowned thousands of people. It was ugly.

I saw the Ritter sign and pulled off in front of the general store. On with my fedora. A nice breeze came in off the lake. I looked around. Not a person to be found.

In the back corner, a newspaper hid a face. The sound of the screen door opening made the person peek around. She looked about thirty. She was pale and her eyes were sunken. Looked like she last brushed her hair a week ago. Wore a plain tan shift dress.

"Whaddya need?"

I pulled out my badge. "Miami PD."

Her face turned even more pale. She said, "Put it away."

I dropped to a stool. She put down the paper. Her chest started to heave, and her eyes filled. Her head dropped to the counter. I counted to thirty in my head.

"Umm, Miss Ritter, we know about you and Claude Mosley. Don't make no never mind how we know. Good old-fashioned police work."

She sobbed some more.

"Ma'am, you know he's just about public enemy number one right now. Left a lotta corpses. The Seminole. The jailkeeper. Officer Lummus."

She wouldn't look at me.

"You know about our ambushing Claude out in the Glades. Ended with Claude's pop dead, we're pretty sure, and put a Miami copper in the hospital, and me and my boss nearly got killed as well."

She was about to either open up or give me the back of her hand. I took a chance on the first.

"Look, Miss. No one saw me drive up here. No one saw me come in your store. And no one will see me leave. And even if they do, I'm just a businessman from Orlando stopping on the way to Miami for a Moon Pie and a soda pop."

The dame ran a hand up her forehead and through her scraggly hair. I waited.

Lori's shoulders dropped. She talked to the floor.

"Claude said it was getting too hot. The lady dying from the hooch. And you guys finding his place. And icing his pop." She looked up. "Which you did."

Settled that question.

"They shut down the stills and sold the rest of their moonshine to some Ybor City guys over to Tampa. Found a pal to stow their airboat. Then Claude's cousin hit that bank in Davie. When they saw it was five thou, it was like Christmas Day. Claude said it was time to scram up north somewhere, like Georgia or Tennessee. Wait for the heat to go down. Then, he said, he'd come back down. And—"

I waited.

"And kill the Miami police chief."

Hudson, the bellhop turned moonshine goon, was sharp.

Wait a minute. Wait just a minute. Something clicked.

"Claude wanted to take his vacation in the Smokies without you."

No expression. Click.

"And you got sore."

She looked like I'd stolen her wallet.

"That ain't why I'm snitchin.'" Which of course meant it was. I leaned.

"How about this, Lori. You're snitching because you know how this could end up."

A tic.

"Believe me, young lady, you want me to be the one who finds your boyfriend. I follow the law. So long as he don't take a shot at me, I take him in, alive and in one piece. And he at least gets his day in court. But he's a cop killer. Some other cops don't do the straight and narrow. They find him, they won't wait to put the bracelets on him. Or his pals. And you love him too much to be there when he gets shot down like a dog."

She looked at me for a long time.

"How'd I do, Lori?"

A mumble.

"They, uh, they pulling out of Miami probably an hour from now. They were gonna go up the highway to Jacksonville and then head over to Atlanta."

I stood.

"You did the right thing. For yourself as well. Sooner or later, Claude would have pulled you down with him."

I reached into a basket on the counter and grabbed a Moon Pie. I thrust my hand into a barrel next to my stool that was packed with chopped ice, then pulled it out, fingers wrapped around a cold bottle of pop. I slid it in the opener on the side of the barrel and popped the top. I laid the two items on the counter and pulled some coins from my trouser pocket and dropped them on the counter.

Lori Ritter didn't say a word.

I tipped my fedora and picked up the Moon Pie and pop. On my way out, I caught the screen door so it wouldn't slam.

If the road from Miami to the big lake was rough going, the road east to the coast was pure hell. Every ten minutes, the wheel went over a rock the size of my fist. The rock would go flying, and the car would shudder. It took an hour to make my way to a police station. Where? We'll leave that unspoken for now.

The guys got me on the horn with my chief down in Miami. We did some math about miles and timing. The chief called the sheriff over in the next town. The sheriff called the station where I was.

"We have a warrant for Mosley as well. Did one of our banks a while back. On the way out, he shot at the bank manager. He was in a hurry and just winged him. Otherwise, we'd have Claude up on murder."

I said, "We already do."

"Your chief told us about the jailer and the officer. Said it was your department's first. Wish I could say the same. Two nigger rumrunners shot down two of my boys on the beach about five years ago. We put them down right there."

I don't like that word. Don't like it. But I held my tongue.

He said, "But the Mosleys, they're still on the lam, detective. They're a menace. Let's go get 'em."

The sheriff said the best place to set up along the highway was on a small wooden bridge that crossed a creek.

An hour later, I was on the bridge with the sheriff and two deputies. The sun was dropping. We had a box with some ice, and some sandwiches, and a jug of water, and some soda pop. Each of us packed a shotgun.

Just after it got dark, the deputies strung a thick rope across the road from one rail of the bridge across to the other rail. They hung a kerosene lantern with a red filter.

We couldn't narrow down when the Mosleys would arrive. Or if they hadn't already come through. Or if they were taking this route at all. All we had was the word of Lori Ritter. But a pinch this big was worth taking a chance.

We went through the sandwiches and pop. The other guys right away went for smokes. I took out a candy cig. In the dark, no one noticed.

An hour went by. It was a little cool. Glad I had my suit coat. That didn't stop the mosquitoes who came up from the creek. I heard the other deputies slap their necks and curse. I've said the things mostly leave me alone, for some reason. This night, the magic word was "mostly."

Two hours. We'd finished off the water. Three hours. I'd gone through my pack of candy cigs, and the deputies were out of their real ones. I was worn out from all that driving I'd done that day. My eyes were heavy. I pulled out my watch. It was way past my bedtime.

Lights appeared around the corner. We tensed, the shotguns across our chests. Headlights caught the lantern. A car stopped at the rope. The sheriff stepped out toward the driver's side. He shone a flashlight.

Two kids. Couldn't have been eighteen. I remembered the two who'd been working with Mosley at the still. But something told me these two weren't part of the gang.

The driver stuck his two hands out the window. His eyes were as big as hubcaps. He looked like a gator was about to take off his head.

"Sir. Sir. Please. Please. Don't shoot. Don't shoot. Don't shoot!"

The sheriff leaned in. "What you boys doin' out here at this hour?" Then, "Why, you're the Dunlop boys."

"Yessir. Just doin' some late-night giggin' for frogs."

The sheriff moved his flashlight around the inside of the car. We could see fishnets and bottles of soda pop.

"Might be some trouble here in a couple minutes. You boys best move on. Don't stop until you're a couple miles from here. You unnerstand?"

The driver said, "Yessir. Yessir."

The sheriff waved his flashlight. The kid driving was so nervous he nearly stripped the gears. We watched the car vanish in the darkness. Then we stepped back into the shadows.

It wasn't even a minute. Another set of headlights.

The car rolled to a stop at the rope. From the passenger side, I saw the sheriff's flashlight on the driver's side. And the silhouettes of four heads.

I leaned into the passenger's side and shined my own flashlight. Between the men's legs, I saw satchels, picnic baskets, and water jugs. I turned my light to the driver.

"Hello, Claude."

I could tell Claude Mosley recognized me. His face filled with hate. Gave me a chill. Mosley turned and looked straight ahead. He did not speak.

Any guilt I felt from showing him his rotting brother had gone up in a poof when Mosley killed the jailer and the cop. My friends.

I stood and called across the car's roof. "It's him."

The sheriff said, "The four of you are under arrest. Now, please step out of the car."

All four did. Nobody spoke.

I stuck my head into the back seat and felt around on the floor. My hand closed around a paper bag. I lifted it and peeked in. I saw bills with "100."

I stood and showed it to the other cops. "The haul from the Davie

Cattleman's Bank. I'll take this back with me."

I said, loud enough for everyone on the bridge to hear: "Claude Mosley, on behalf of the Miami police department, I arrest you for escape, and for the murders of Karl Scheerer and Officer Paul Lummus, and complicity in the attempted murder of Officer Raulerson."

And, just loud enough for Claude's ears: "You son of a bitch."

Our eyes locked for several seconds. The silence was a roar.

Behind me, I heard the sheriff say, "We'll go through the rest of charges, including from Davie, and ours, when we get you boys back to town. It's a long list."

I looked up at the sheriff. "I'd like to run back to town and call my chief, let him know we got Claude and these other guys. I'll also alert your people that you're on your way in."

I walked to my car and turned it around and drove off. About a minute later, I was jolted. Those were gunshots.

I did a three-point turn on the dirt road and sped back. I jumped out in the dark, my shotgun pointed in front of me. "It's Nate Moran. Everyone okay?"

No one answered.

I ran up. In the light of the lantern, the sheriff and the two deputies stood, shotguns pointed straight down.

Claude Mosley lay, face up, a red splotch on his chest. His three pals sprawled near him.

"What happened?"

The sheriff looked at his two deputies. He cleared his throat.

"When we pulled out our cuffs, Mosley must have seen 'em glint in the light from his headlights. He dropped his hands and yelled, 'Shoot, boys. I'll never wear those again.' We had no choice but to fire."

I looked down at the four. Then at the coppers. A long time.

"Sheriff, I didn't see what happened, and this is not my jurisdiction. I have no power here. I'll make my stop in town. But after that, I don't want to have anything to do with you fellows." I straightened my fedora. "I'll make my report to my chief."

I found a hotel in town and called Chief Burke. The next morning, I washed up as best as I could. I found a diner and had some flapjacks. Then I made the long ride down the highway to Miami. I pulled into the motor pool and turned in the car. I walked across the street and grabbed a sandwich and coffee. I stopped at my desk just long enough to drop off my lunch. Then I walked to Burkie's office.

"Just got off the phone," he said. "A county judge up there ruled the shootings justifiable." He sighed. "Shut the door, please." I did.

"The rest of our conversation is unofficial, and none of it ever will end up on paper. Are we agreed?" I nodded.

"So, Nate. What do you think?"

"I will tell you, Chief."

"You always do, Nate. One of the things I like about you."

I laid my fedora on the corner of the desk. I didn't sit.

"I think this sheriff decided a guy who already robbed who knows how many banks, and shot up a bank manager up there, and shot at us in the Glades, and killed a jailer and a cop, that no jail or prison ever was going to hold him for good. I think maybe Mosley or one of the other guys did make a wrong move in the dark, and one of the bulls, or maybe all of them, just panicked and opened up, and then they all did. But I think maybe they just executed them."

I looked out the window into the motor pool.

"I think nobody is going to weep for these guys. But I also think the girl out at Lake Okeechobee will believe I betrayed her. And that my betrayal led to the death of the man she loved. They very thing she was trying to avoid. And maybe all of this will get her killed if the Ashley family ever finds out she snitched."

The chief could see I was done. He said, "Now here's what I think." His look could knock over a lamp.

"I think that if I ever find one of my cops used his gun when he shouldn't have, he's out on his ass. Or maybe even in the lockup. Period. I train you guys, and you take an oath to uphold the law. It ain't easy. God knows. Things happen in a split-second. And then people take their time second-guessing. But you make that deal when you sign up for this job. And if you can't handle that rule, I don't want you."

He sighed. "We're a city police force. With two newspapers down the street. Hard to get away with anything. Out in the boondocks, like where you were last night, those boys know no one is looking over their shoulder." He put out his palms. "Nothing I can do about it. Like you said, no one will weep for these guys. Especially me."

He looked down at his hands.

"But it don't make it okay."

Chapter Eleven: A Hanging

On a Sunday, right before dinner, the phone rang. It was Garrison, the Bureau of Investigation guy.

"Need to borrow you again."

Henry Ward, the rumrunner and killer of Feds on the high seas, finally was set for trial in the morning. Garrison said he'd gotten a tipoff that someone would try to spring Ward before that. Wanted someone in plainclothes in the last row in Miami Federal Court.

Since the carnage on the Atlantic, an amazing but not unexpected thing had happened. This punk had become a celebrity.

Some people just want their giggle water. Some believe the government shouldn't be busting into their kitchen. And some, apparently, fell for this weasel. I've seen his kind many times. When the heat is on, they wrap themselves in the Stars and Stripes. Or the Lord.

The first thing I noticed in court was the dames. Must have been two dozen of them. You don't usually see one here unless she's a mope's mom or his squeeze. These were Ward's cheerleaders. They came in with Bibles in one hand and big, lacy hankies in the other. They lined the back row, politely stepping over me into the pews.

One turned to me. "Are you a friend of Henry?" I said, "Just an observer, Ma'am." She said, "He's innocent, you know." I smiled politely. She said, "Those evil men attacked him on the ocean. He's a man of God, and God will show the way." I nodded.

The low hum in the courtroom rose. Beside me, the woman gasped. I followed her eyes to the side door.

Henry Ward wore a white suit with a red rose. Really. He had the smile I'd seen on many a snake oil salesman. Around me, I heard low cries of "Henry!" and quiet sobs. As Ward sat, I saw in his right hand what clearly was a Bible. I looked at the women. None seemed a threat. I kept an eye on them just the same.

"This isn't about whether you like or dislike the Eighteenth Amendment," the federal prosecutor began, "or what the proper conduct of officers should be. This was cold-blooded murder."

When Wiegel took the stand, we locked eyes. I looked to see if Ward was giving his former henchman the dead eye. Ward just had that grin, like everything was hotsy-totsy and the angels would be along any minute.

On the fourth day, I watched the jurors shuffle in. The foreman stood. "Guilty."

Women around me screamed and gasped.

Well, we didn't get justice for Monk. Not yet. But at least we did for those poor Feds on the boat.

When the judge said, "Hang by the neck until you are dead," I felt dead weight on my shoulder. The woman beside me had fainted on me.

Ward's right hand lay on his Bible. His eyes aimed heavenward. He neither smiled nor frowned. He seemed…at peace.

Two days later, I met Garrison at the Columbus Hotel. I already had breakfasted with the Missus and the kids, so it was just coffee.

Garrison took a long sip and lit a smoke. I leaned back and out of the way. The Fed didn't notice.

"We've got a problem."

"Yeah?"

"The problem is who's gonna hang Ward."

"It's a Fed case, Garrison. Your rope."

He shook his head. "We got no scaffold. We'd have to build one. And figure out where. And—" he took a long pull—"We don't need the headache."

"You mean you're already the bad guys, and if you put the noose to this folk hero—"

"Exactly. Eleven of the twelve jurymen, not to mention a long list of supporters, even some preachers, wrote the governor, members of Congress, even the president. That they wanted leniency. Which"—he took another drag—"cannot happen."

I said, "Hmm. You are in a fix." Then, "Anything new on the rumors that someone's gonna try to spring him?"

"That's why I need to borrow you again, Nate. Your bosses are providing uniform guys around the clock. I need you to supervise. Ward swears he's found God. But he still has a lot of friends."

The next day, my phone rang. "Nate Moran. Detectives."

"Problem fixed." It was Garrison.

"How so?"

"The federal judge found something buried in the old maritime laws. Going all the way back to the buccaneers. Anyone committing piracy on the high seas is hanged at the first port of call."

"The closest port of call to where the crime occurred? But that would be…"

Later that day, at the Miami jail, a bull led Garrison and me to Ward's cell. He sat, Bible in hand.

"You ran out of appeals," Garrison said.

Ward smiled. "The big man in the White House let me down. But Jesus is with me still."

I couldn't decide if he really believed it, or was bluffing, or had gone loco. Or all three.

Garrison said, "Your execution is set."

Ward smiled. "And?"

"The hangar at the Fort Lauderdale Coast Guard station. The one the guys left that morning. And the place they came back dead. And you came back a killer."

Ward opened his Bible and ran his fingers along a line. He looked up. "It's my hanging. I want to invite my friends to it."

Garrison shook his head. Ward stared him down. Then he sat back on his cot and returned to his book. Garrison motioned me out. In the hall, he said, "If someone's going to try anything, it will be on the drive to Fort Lauderdale.

We'll have a bunch of guys up there. And me. And Fort Lauderdale coppers. You lead the parade from here."

The next morning, I was at the jail before sunrise. About a dozen patrol guys stood by their cars. I walked to the cell.

"Time to go."

Ward closed his Bible and laid it on the cot. He lifted something from the bed and handed it to me.

"This is for the *Miami Herald*. Please don't open it. It says I made a mistake going down the path of crime. It led me to the devil. All the money I made doesn't do me any good now. And I leave my family broken-hearted." He looked me in the eye. "But I am at peace now with my Lord."

Maybe Ward had done the right thing after all. Instead of making himself a martyr, and encouraging more of his kind, he'd gone the route that just maybe will discourage others. Except I doubted any would be swayed. There's something about the energy radiating from a dollar bill.

The jailer cuffed Ward, then led him out. The man squinted in the sunlight. My hand was on my gun. I looked all around. This is one of the times when a cop is really scared.

We loaded Ward in the back of a roadster. The patrol guy got in next to him, then lifted a chain bolted to the floor and snapped it to Ward's handcuffs. I hopped in the front and nodded to the driver.

The day was cool, but I sweated the next hour. Every tree might hide someone. Every glint might be a gun. Every loud noise might be someone hammering a roof, or it might be something else. In back, Ward had his eyes closed. His lips moved, but I couldn't make out anything.

My stomach began to settle as we came around a corner and I saw the Coast Guard hangar. Our car drove right inside the giant opening. In the back of the hangar, I saw a structure I knew well. A gallows.

Some police cars followed us inside. The rest parked out front, forming a barricade. Big Coast Guardsmen pushed the giant hangar doors closed.

I stepped out of the car and stuck my head in. "Let's go." The guard unlocked the chain from the floor bolt. Ward stepped out, his hands and ankles shackled. He stood for a second and looked up at the scaffold. The cop took his elbow, and Ward began to shuffle toward the thing.

Garrison came alongside. "How'd it go, Nate?"

"So far, so good."

"We're probably okay here. But we'll stay on guard."

Most of the cavernous hangar was in shadows. My stomach tightened all over again.

I saw a black car off to the side. Garrison shrugged. "The hearse."

I said, "Did you check it?" He hadn't.

I walked over. Sure would have liked a smoke.

I tapped the window with my wedding ring. It rolled down. My hand instinctively moved toward my gun. Then I said, "That's a really bad beard, Renault."

The man exhaled in defeat. "Hi Nate."

"I give you newshounds credit. Don't know how you pulled it off. Just be glad you weren't taken for one of Ward's pals, here to spring him. I nearly shot you."

Barry Renault pulled the fake beard down below his chin. "You gonna expose me?"

I looked over to Garrison. The Fed's eyes asked was there a problem. I paused a half second. Then I waved. All clear.

"This isn't my show, Renault. Later on, if the Feds put the elbow on your editors to put the kibosh on your story, I can't do anything about that. I won't be your fall guy. But anyone asks me, I never recognized you. Your disguise was too good. My mistake."

"Deal. I owe you."

About halfway back to the scaffold, I stole a glance over my shoulder. The car's window was about a third of the way down, and a pair of eyes peeked out.

Ward already was at the bottom step. He was…singing. Garrison took him by the elbow and guided him up to the platform. I saw a preacher and a man dressed in Coast Guard whites. I guess they hadn't been able to find a proper executioner's hood, so the guy wore an upside-down flour sack that came to his nose and had two eyeholes cut in it. He looked so stupid I'd have laughed if we weren't about to hang a guy.

The preacher leaned in. Ward just kept humming. The preacher turned away, and the Coast Guardsman pulled a similar flour sack over Ward. This one didn't have eyeholes. The hangman slid the noose down and cinched it tight around Ward's throat. I still heard him hum.

Garrison nodded.

The executioner pulled the lever. The trap door dropped.

I have a confession. This was my first hanging. I expected to hear a sickening snap and then see the body hang limp. That's not how it happened.

The hinge working the drop jammed. The body sort of bounced around off the sides and dangled. I heard Ward gasp and gurgle and choke. Bile rose into my throat, and I grew faint. Garrison had pulled his hanky and wiped his forehead.

It probably was all of five minutes. It seemed like days.

The noises stopped. The executioner turned a crank and pulled up the hanging body, then lowered it onto the platform. The doctor knelt. Ward was dead.

I didn't get out of Fort Lauderdale until after lunch. Which I didn't get any. Got back to Miami and told Chief Burke I was taking the rest of the day off. He saw my face. He didn't argue.

The Missus and the kids were on the sofa. She was reading to Zach. I dropped into my easy chair. My head fell into my hands. The room was oppressive in its silence.

I lifted my head and wiped my nose. I walked to the sofa and held out my hand. The Missus handed me Zach's book. I squeezed in between her and the tyke and started reading.

Chapter Twelve: Porto Rico

"Why do we spell it wrong?"

"Huh?" Detective Harvey Comeau looked up.

I held up the front page of the *Miami Daily News* and touched my index finger to a headline.

"Puerto Rico. It's Spanish for 'rich port.' But after we got it from Spain, everywhere I read, we're now spelling it P-O-R-T-O. Like they do in Brazil."

Comeau looked at me for a second. Then he said, "Gimme that."

I shrugged and handed over the paper. Harvey rifled to the sports section and laid it on his desk. He turned to the back page. His pencil stabbed the paper. "Thanks, Nate!"

He grabbed the phone and dialed. He said, "It's Harvey. Five on Porto Bello Gold. Seventh race at Havana. Okay. Bye."

He put the earpiece back on the candlestick and caught me eying him.

"Harvey. Do me a favor. Next time you call your bookie, would you at least do it from a payphone, so I don't have to say my fellow detective was breaking the law in the police station? Right in front of me?

Harvey gave a goofy smile. "Cut me some slack, Nate. The old lady took a powder and cleaned me out. Left me just enough money for groceries. I put something down on a nag every once in a while. Hope for the best."

I said, "How've you been doing?"

A shrug. "Not great." A pause. "Not great at all."

I started to say, "Well, how are you affording bread and milk?" But the phone rang, and then I forgot about it.

I came in Monday morning with doughnuts for the detective team. Two for Harvey, of course.

"How'd you do with that tip I gave you Friday? For your activity that might or not be illegal? Porto something?"

He shrugged. "She also ran."

I shook my head. "Good old 'also ran.' Harvey, Harvey, Harvey. Lemme see. That fin coulda bought twenty doughnuts. Or a tank of gas." Harvey said, "I don't need—" and then didn't finish. He stuffed one of the pastries in his puss.

I wanted to ask what that all meant. But the door to Dirk Monroe's office opened, and he stuck out his head. "Nate. Coconut Grove." He handed me a slip of paper.

When Dirk gives me just an address, I know what that means.

It was a bungalow on a side street off Bayshore Drive, just north of Dinner Key. A uniform guy at the door waved me in. Just inside, another officer aimed a Kodak Hawkeye at a stiff lying on his side next to a small table.

I said, "Hogan, right?"

"Didn't touch him yet, Detective. Waiting for you."

I kneeled. The back of the guy's neck sported a ragged hole inside an ugly black ring. I steeled myself and turned him over. The hole over his left eye was a lot bigger and even more ugly. Big bullet from behind. Real close. Nasty on the way out. Sad to say, this wasn't my first.

But my attention turned further south on the guy. His mouth gaped in a funny way. It threw me for a loop. Then I realized. The guy had no teeth. Wait. He had teeth on the bottom. Just not on the top. What in blazes?

I looked up at the patrol guy and pointed. He scratched his cheek. "I'll be damned."

I looked the corpse up and down. His pockets had been turned out. Someone wanted to make it really hard for us to make this poor chump.

"Hogan: You call the meat wagon boys yet?"

"Sure did, detective. Should be—oh, here they are."

The morgue guys lugged a stretcher, turned sideways, through the doorway. I was used to seeing Marshall. But the coroner's office had so much business, it now needed two teams. I recognized one of these guys.

Seen him at too many of these parties.

"Samuels, right? Can you lean down here?"

Samuels kneeled. I wrapped my hanky around my index finger and slid it in the stiff's mouth. "Ever seen anything like this?"

Samuels's hands were inside bulky rubber gloves. He pushed in two fingers, and the mope's maw opened wider. I was able to see the roof of his mouth.

"I'll be damned."

"That's what Hogan said," I said, nodding at the patrol guy.

"Look here." Samuels pointed. "This guy got set up for dentures."

"Dentures? He can't be more than thirty years old."

The man shook his head. "I've done a little dental. Someone pulled all this guy's uppers. Look in the back. They left only the molars so they could clip the dental plate. Then the plate slides over the upper ridge."

My forehead scrunched. "Why would a young guy get dentures if he didn't have to?'

Samuels shrugged. "Moran, I think that's your turf."

I slid up my fedora. "Dentures, huh? Well. Where are they?" I looked on the floor around the body. Then into the black hole where his top teeth should be. Whoever emptied his pockets took the choppers as well. Why?

"Hey, Moran." It was the patrol guy from outside. He leaned back out of the doorway, revealing a short, middle-aged man with maybe ten strands of hair on his head and a suit that might have fit him once.

"Detective, I'm—I'm—"

I stood. "It's okay, sir. Take your time."

Hogan, the uniform, said, "Harold Hoster. He owns the place. He found the guy."

The man had pulled a hanky and was wiping his chrome dome. He looked like he'd faint. I motioned to a chair in the kitchenette, and Hoster fell into it.

"This has never. Ever. I mean, we've had some drunks. Cops had to pick up a fellow knocked his lady around. But we keep a clean place. No whores. No punks. Now this. Wait 'til the Pan Am guys hear about it. Once the word gets out, I won't get anyone."

"Pan Am?"

He looked up. "The airline refers us for folks who need a place, come into town the night before they're flying out on a seaplane. That's what this guy…"

I said, "Name?"

"Signed the ledger as Juan Garcia."

Juan Garcia? That's like John Doe.

"Did he give you any identification, sir? Anything that showed his name?"

Hoster shook his head.

"The guy checked in late. About ten. Asked could I have a cab here at 8:15 this morning. It's just five minutes over to Dinner Key. There's a 9:30 to Havana, so I figured that was it. This morning, the cabbie pulled up, and I knocked. Got no answer. I know the guy had to meet the plane, so I used my passkey in case he already took another cab or maybe walked over. And I found—I found—"

He waved his hanky in front of his face.

I wiped my palms on my trousers. "Thanks, Mister—"

"Hoster."

"Mister Hoster. You can go. Okay boys. You can take the guy."

The Pan American terminal at Dinner Key is one of the prettiest buildings you'll see. I drove the block from the hotel and parked in the circular drive in front. I stepped into a gorgeous lobby. Right in the middle: A giant globe, slowly spinning on some motor. Like how Earth spins. This was one of those relief-map things. The mountains were like bumps on it. What a beauty.

I stepped to the counter and asked for a supervisor. I got a Latin-looking guy in a pencil-thin mustache and perfectly combed hair, wearing a uniform with a pin showing a globe and a pair of wings and "PAA." His name was Sanchez. I flashed my badge. "You had a 9:30 Clipper to Havana this morning?"

"Yes, sir."

"Could you show me the manifest?"

"Certainly."

He walked me around the counter and opened a portfolio. He pulled out a typewritten list and handed it to me.

No Juan Garcia. No surprise.

Each of the names had a penciled check mark next to it. Except one. Someone had scribbled, "NS."

I pointed to it. Sanchez said, "No-show."

Sometimes the best clue is something that didn't happen.

Carlos Baez.

I said, "You don't have to worry about him taking a later flight. Someone iced him."

Sanchez blanched.

"Do you have any information on him?"

Sanchez shook his head.

"Could it be a fake name?"

"Not if he intended to get on the Clipper this morning. He didn't have to show anything when he bought the ticket, but he would have had to show his passport here at the terminal before he boarded. Leaving the country, and all."

"But you don't know where he lives or anything like that."

"Sorry, no. But I can tell you his destination."

I was confused. "The plane went to Havana."

"That's the first stop. It flies to Camaguey after lunch and overnights in Santiago. Then over the water to Hispaniola. First Port-au-Prince. Then Santo Domingo. Then it makes its last stop."

"Where's that?"

Sanchez pointed at Baez's name on the list. To the right were three letters: "SAN."

San Juan.

"Moran!"

It was Bruce Keyes. The Prohibition agent. He smiled. "Saw you at the trial." Then his smile vanished. "That was bad."

I said, "What brings the Feds here?"

"You first, Nate."

I told him about Carlos Baez, including the hole in the guy's head and his missing uppers.

Keyes said, "We have a guy comes over here every morning, Nate. Before the plane leaves for Havana. Checks everyone's luggage. Then we pat them down."

I said, "Why on earth for? It's not like someone'd hide a bottle of hooch in his sock. And you're worried just about stuff coming in. Not going out."

He shook his head. "Not hooch. The other commodity."

I'm a dope. A dope. A dope. I rubbed two fingers. Keyes nodded.

"The big guys have to pay their suppliers. Wiring money out of the country is too obvious. Banks let us know right away. Putting big wads of cash on a fast boat and heading out on the ocean is too chancy. Would you do it? So, here's a nice way to have mules deliver moolah. Flying is not cheap. So, they make each delivery count. Lots of dough. Since there's just a few flights, we've been checking every passenger on the way out. We've found bills hidden in the lining of suits. Taped to ankles. Even inside socks. Seems every day they find a new hiding place."

Oh no.

"Dentures."

"Huh?"

"These guys got too smart for you, Keyes. They found a guy willing to lose his choppers if the price was right. Then they fitted him with dentures. Special dentures with spaces to hide…hide…hide what?"

Keyes was thinking. "Not bills. Maybe you could fit two or three folded C-notes up there. That's chump change."

Now I was thinking. Something that would be worth a lot in a small package.

Behind us, Sanchez snapped his fingers. He surprised both of us. "Diamonds?"

Keyes smiled. "I think you hit it, pal."

He shrugged. "Sorry. I was eavesdropping. But what made me think of it is, I like to read a lot of the crime pulp magazines."

I asked when was the next flight to San Juan. Sanchez said the next morning. I said, "Save me a seat."

Then wheels turned in my head.

"Put me on the manifest as Carlos Baez."

Sanchez's eyebrows went up.

"I'm guessing you wire the passenger list to all the stops. When you do, just say Baez missed this morning's flight, and he'll be on tomorrow's."

Keyes said, "Don't get insulted or nothin', but Nate, you could pass for a guy named Baez."

I tipped my fedora. "Grandson of a Cuban beauty. Comes in handy."

I asked Sanchez could I use his phone. I called over to Purdy, the coroner. He said sure, he could get a photo of the mope to me this afternoon. "It won't be pretty." I said that was jake.

I called Dirk Monroe and filled him in. He okayed the plane ticket. Not cheap.

"This better pay off, Nate, or Chief Burke will have my keister." I appreciate that he said his butt, not mine.

If it did pay off, I told Dirk, Keyes and his guys would end up being part of it, and he'd already told me maybe they could pick up some of the cost.

I drove back to headquarters. Purdy already had come through. He was right. It wasn't pretty. But he had one shot of the guy with his mouth shut and one with the puss open, showing that black hole where the teeth should be.

I stopped in the business office and grabbed the check written to Pan American. I wrote up what I knew and had copies made up; one for Dirk and two for me. I went home and had a good dinner with the Missus and the boys, and packed a bag and got out my passport. Dirk had made sure all his detectives had 'em. This is South Florida. Gateway to the world.

In the morning, I drove myself over to Dinner Key. Sanchez found me a parking spot in the back. I handed him the police department's check, and he wrote up my ticket. I boarded the small boat that ran passengers about fifty yards to the floating dock where the seaplane bobbed. Keyes rode out with me.

"Got a confession, Keyes. This is my first aeroplane ride."

"You're one up on me." He looked at the plane. "Uh, Nate. Do you get sick?"

I gulped. I had been so focused, I hadn't given a thought to my tendency to motion sickness. Always embarrassing for a guy who lives in South Florida. Nothing to do now but tough it out.

I stepped onto the floating dock. Keyes waved, and the shuttle boat backed away. I stepped in and dropped to a seat. The plane's doors shut, and the engines fired up. We started moving. The Clipper picked up speed and lurched off the water. My stomach jumped, too. My knuckles gripped my armrest. The world fell away from us. I pressed my face to the open window and gulped air. What to do? What to do?

After a few minutes, I realized I was all right. Not great. But all right.

I never want to relive those twenty-four hours. We were on the ground in Havana for ninety minutes. Then two other stops in Cuba, the second overnight. At least I got some authentic Cuban grub. And coffee. Better than the café con leche in Miami, if that was possible. But even as I lay in my hotel bed, the room still was moving. The next morning, stops in Haiti and the Dominican Republic. Then back over water.

Late in the afternoon, I saw land in the distance. We circled and dropped into the harbor with a splash. The plane slowed, then stopped, and the engines cut off. A few minutes later, a shuttle boat pulled alongside. Twenty minutes later, I was on solid ground in the capital of Puerto Rico. That's how I spell it.

I was one of ten passengers who stepped up to U.S. Customs. I did not show my police badge. Just another businessman here for an important meeting.

I stepped past the guard and onto the street. I pretended to look around for someone.

It was like fish in a barrel. A young man in light trousers and a T-shirt approached.

"Taxi? Taxi?" he said loudly. As he drew close, he said, "Señor Baez?"

Behind him, a large man in a suit took three steps and pinned the young man's arms. He rattled off something. My lousy Spanish picked up most of it. The guy was under arrest.

Twenty minutes later, we were in a bare room in the federal building. The man who'd collared my contact stood against the wall. I sat in a hard chair. Again, I still felt like I was moving. The young man sat in his own chair, his hands cuffed in front of him. He rocked like someone with a lot on his mind. And how.

The man against the wall was Pedro Cuellar. He's Keyes' federal counterpart in Puerto Rico. Wouldn't want that job.

I said to the man in the chair, "¿Hablas inglés?"|

He scowled. "Yeah."

"What's your name?"

Silence.

"Okay. Who's your boss?"

Silence.

Cuellar said in English, I guess for my benefit, "Son, here's what we're going to do. We're going to let you go."

The man looked up in surprise. He started to smile. Then it hit him. His eyes bugged out.

I said, "Exactamente. Your bosses will want to know why you didn't pick up the diamonds." I smiled. "Or they might decide you *did* pick up the diamonds."

Cuellar leaned down. "Estas en un buen lio." I knew that one. This kid was in deep doo-doo.

I looked at my fingernails and picked at a cuticle. Cuellar lit a cig. In the corner of my vision, I watched the punk. The tobacco smell hit his nostrils, and he licked his lips. He looked up at the second hand on the wall clock. I saw wet beads on his forehead.

I do love sweating out mopes. We don't have to do anything. Just wait. Cops do this so often that Cuellar and I hadn't had to rehearse.

At what seemed the appropriate time, the Fed peeled off the wall and straightened. "OK, amigo. Time is up." He started to walk to the door. I counted down. Cuellar reached for the doorknob.

"¡Esperar!"

I knew that word, too. Wait.

Cuellar's hand dropped. He turned and crossed his arms. He looked at me.

Time for the money play.

I said, "Son: You came up to me at the plane, tells me you knew your mule only by name."

A nod.

"Have you been wondering why me instead of him? Tell you. We found him face down in a Miami hotel room."

The kid actually gasped. I locked eyes with Cuellar. Then I pulled out the photo the coroner had given me. "Here's your contact. Someone put an extra opening in his head."

The man's face turned white, and I thought he'd lose his breakfast. I turned back to my pesky cuticle.

Now the kid mumbled something. We leaned in. He spoke louder.

"José Paseo."

You could have knocked me over.

"Paseo? As in Antonio Paseo?"

El Gordo. From Puerto Rico. The guy I saw sprawled in the back room they called Hypocrite's Row.

"His cousin. He's got a nickname, too. El Caballo. The horse. It's about the ladies."

I didn't need to hear any more details about that. I said to Cuellar, "My chief said El Gordo never touched the hooch business. Just had a good stable of suppliers."

Cuellar said, "Let me catch you up. After the big man got iced in that hotel in Palm Beach—"

I said, "I was there."

"Right. After that, some of our snitches here started jawing. Just the other day, we got a tip that El Gordo's supplier had been his cousin. El Caballo."

Paseo, Mosley. Gregg. Booze bosses keep showing up. Like a door-to-door salesman. Except potential customers don't slam doors on 'em.

Cuellar looked like he didn't care that the kid was listening. Actually, he just was pretending he'd forgotten the kid was there.

"When Antonio got it, El Caballo was going to go up to Miami and take over the family business. Gambling, girls, the works. Plus, combine it with his hooch operation."

I said, "But diamonds?"

Cuellar shrugged, "We may be a U.S. territory, but the rules are different here. The local police pretend to work with us. But half of them are in the bag to guys like El Caballo. They run shiploads of rum from the port at Mayaguez, over on the west side of the island. Put them on British ships. Unless we catch them in the act, nothing we can do. The Brits run the stuff to the Bahamas. Then, on the dock in Freeport, along with the royal Scotch, there's Puerto Rican rum, best in the world, for the smugglers to bring in to South Florida."

I said, "Why don't they use the Brits to move the money?"

"Would you? Nope. They got it down to a science. It's a big triangle. The rum goes from Mayaguez to Freeport. From Freeport to Florida. Mules ferry the payments on Pan Am from Miami to San Juan. To El Caballo. He's got fences here who sell the diamonds to local retailers. Rich American tourists on a cruise buy their wives an anniversary ring at an amazing price. Everyone's happy."

I looked over to the kid. He wasn't saying anything. He probably didn't know all of this. I said, "You know how the mules hid the diamonds. Don't you?"

He said flatly, "Fake teeth."

"Good boy. Here's another little item for you. When we found the guy, he was missing the fake teeth."

If the punk wasn't sweating before, he was now.

"That means someone double-crossed El Caballo. Made off with the diamonds. Sounds like it wasn't you. But you're the first guy they'll look at."

The kid was thinking.

I said, "Clock's ticking, son. You can tell El Caballo what we told you about the mule in Miami. He might believe you. Might not. Might give you the same hole someone gave the mule."

I almost felt sorry for him.

Another few minutes. Then the kid surprised me.

"Reed."

Who?

"Charlie Reed. I heard El Caballo tell one of his partners that if something went wrong, it would be Reed. He wants to take over El Gordo's business in South Florida."

Who the heck is Charlie Reed?

Cuellar said, "We've heard of him, Nate. Keyes will fill you in back in Miami."

I stood. Fingers clutched my elbow, and I turned back. The terror in the kid's face shook even me.

Cuellar leaned in. He still was talking English, for my benefit.

"Son, you ever been to Venezuela? They found oil there. Big business. Need a lot of workers. The accent's a lot different than here. But I suspect you can fit in just fine. El Caballo never find you. We'll get you transportation over there." He stood and put out his hands. "Or you can stay here and take your chances."

More silence. I pulled my pack of candy cigs from my jacket and started sucking on one. Cuellar spotted it and smiled. The punk—I still didn't know his name—was too busy trying not to pee his pants.

"Okay."

Cuellar: "Okay?"

"Okay."

My two-day ordeal in the air back to Miami was about as miserable as the journey over had been. When I got back, I asked for the rest of the day off and spent it on the couch, hoping the world would stop spinning. I told the Missus I never wanted to be in an aeroplane ever again. That night, I was out cold by nine.

The phone rang a little after seven the next morning. It was Dirk Monroe.

"Sorry, Nate. Crime never sleeps."

Then he gave me an address. Just an address. I've told you what that means.

Bass Diamond Exchange is in the Halcyon Arcade, on Flagler Street, a few blocks from the police station. I asked Dirk would a few minutes make a difference. He said no. I was stale from my journey through the tropics. I did a shave and washed up and was at the arcade within a half hour of the phone call. I pulled up out front and held my badge out the driver's window. A patrol guy waved me to a loading zone parking space.

Usually, the arcade would be full of guests from the hotel next door, scoping out souvenirs or a nice piece of jewelry to take home. This morning, the only people inside the arcade were in front of the Diamond Exchange. Two patrol guys. And inside, the owner. Oh. And a stiff.

Nope. Dirk Monroe had sandbagged me. Two stiffs.

A man stood in front of his counter. Short. Round. Bald. He wore a suit and vest. He was wiping his face. Looked like he was about to throw up. Turned out he already had. Sure was a lot of that going around.

I showed my badge. "Nate Moran."

"Richard Bass. My shop. I figured this would happen one day. But not like this."

A patrol guy held out a gun lying on a hanky. "Browning .25."

Bass said, "Picked it up in Belgium on my way home after the war." He shook his head. "Had the same six bullets in all these years. Used them all today."

I said, "Tell me from the top."

The other patrol guy had turned both corpses on their backs. Bass pointed to the one closest to the door.

"Caught me up at first, being a colored and all. Came in right when I opened. He pulled out a tobacco tin and scattered these on the counter."

Bass pointed to a piece of felt on the countertop. I counted six diamonds. Hello, girls.

"May I?"

"I guess so. You're the cop."

I leaned in. Some of the diamonds were covered in sticky stuff.

"What's this?"

He said, "I think it's denture adhesive."

It's a small world.

"I recognize the smell." Bass tapped his teeth on the right side with his index finger. "Lost three uppers in the war."

The second stiff looked Latin. I nodded at Bass to go on.

"When the coon brought in the diamonds, he was as nervous as a mouse. Looking around. I took one look at these rocks and knew in an instant they were the real deal. Thousands. Each. Right away, I was thinking, 'What's a colored doing with these?'" Had to be hot. But I never got the chance to ask the guy.

"I look up, and the spic is in the doorway. I was so scared, my mind just shut down. He could have dropped me on the spot. But he clearly wanted the colored first. The colored got a gun halfway out before the spic put three slugs in him. That broke the spell. In that split-second, I just knew the spic wanted no witnesses. I reached under my counter just as he was turning toward me. I emptied the Browning into him. He dropped like a sack of flour. I laid the gun on the counter, grabbed the wastebasket, and threw up in it. I had to sit on the floor behind the counter, I was shaking so much. Killing a guy in combat is one thing. I was catching my breath when I heard Nolan calling for me from the doorway."

That would be the cop who'd shown me the gun. He said, "The arcade is on my beat, detective. Because it's the busiest spot along Flagler, I make sure I'm here at opening time. I heard the shots. I'd just relieved Maxwell, who'd just finished his night shift. He was heading to the diner, and he heard the shots, too. We both come running to find these two guys on the floor. The colored already had checked out. The spic gave up the ghost before we could do anything. We heard Mr. Bass coughing on the floor behind the counter."

I leaned and used a pencil to poke the colored guy's piece. A Colt .38. I looked over to the Latin guy's gun. "This is an Astra. From Spain."

The cop shrugged. "Never seen one."

"Check the stiffs for ID?"

Nolan shook his head. "Not even a matchbook."

I called Keyes and filled him in. He came by police headquarters around lunchtime. We didn't want eavesdroppers in a diner, so Dirk Monroe ordered in sandwiches.

"Wish you'd given us more of a heads-up on this Reed guy, Keyes," Dirk said.

"That was a mistake. We just caught on to him, and we were gonna fill you in, but then the mule with the fake teeth bought it in the Grove."

Dirk sighed. "Well, no harm done. We're all caught up now. I'd say we're all in agreement that the colored was a goon for Reed, who had sent someone to kill the mule and take the diamonds. Reed must not be very smart. Or he's new at this. If you are trying to fence hot diamonds worth thousands of dollars, you don't want to draw attention. Don't have a colored walk them in."

I shrugged. "He coulda been discreet all he wanted. El Caballo must be plugged in with his dead cousin's operations. Once he learned the mule never got on the plane, he had no trouble tracking down Reed and putting a tail on the colored with the diamonds. If it hadn't been for Mr. Bass, Jose Paseo woulda gotten his diamonds after all."

The diamonds sat on a piece of cardboard on Dirk's desk. Keyes leaned in and used a pencil to poke them around. He reached into his jacket pocket and laid a folded paper on the table.

"This is a receipt for the rocks. I'm taking them over to the morgue and have Purdy compare the denture paste on 'em with the mouth of the stiff from the bungalow. I'm sure they'll match."

The door cracked open. It was Harvey Comeau. He said, "When it rains, it pours, Chief."

* * *

The New Congress Building was just two blocks north of the Halcyon Arcade. I got off the elevator, and a patrol guy waved me through the glass office door. Inside, a lady in a nurse's outfit bawled into a hanky. I'd deal with her later.

James Gittes, DDS, sprawled next to one of his chairs.

The patrol guy said, "The dentist closed down the office yesterday morning, just before opening time. Gave his girl no notice. Usually, she's the first

181

one in, but he already was here. Told the assistant he'd gotten some new equipment in and wanted to set it up. Told her to clear the calendar and take the rest of the day off. She came back this morning to open the shop and found him."

The dentist been popped once, right in the face. Ugly. The dried blood told me he'd been dead a while. Like a whole day.

I looked at the hole. A .38, my guess. Like maybe the Colt .38 the colored was carrying. Might be coincidence. But probably not.

About a half dozen denture plates lay scattered on the counter. I put a hanky around my hand and lifted one by the corner.

It looked like someone had sloppily gouged three or four holes in each plate. Or gouged something out.

I stepped back into the front office. The assistant had calmed down, but she still was gulping and blowing her nose.

"Ma'am. I know this is a tough time. A few questions. Please. Did anyone ever come in for dentures who seemed, well, too young for them?"

She shook her head.

"Okay. Did, umm, the dentist have other days when he had the office to himself?"

"A couple other times, he said he had new equipment. Like today. And when I got engaged, he cleared about five Fridays in a row and gave me those days off."

"Did that seem odd? A dentist having so many days with the place to himself? And always Friday?"

She shrugged. "He gave me the days off with pay. Said it was his wedding gift to me. I wasn't gonna argue."

"Did you ever hear him speak Spanish?"

"Sure. He was really good with it. Sometimes someone would call with really bad English, and the doc would take the phone and talk to him. I know some numbers and days from my high school Spanish, so it sounded like he was making appointments. He'd write stuff down in his notepad, but when I asked him if he'd scheduled stuff and should I put it in the calendar, he said no, these were family friends. Like I said, none of my business."

"His name doesn't sound Spanish."

"His dad was a Jewish guy from the Bronx. But his mom was from Puerto Rico."

Again.

Late in the day, I was back in Dirk Monroe's office. With Keyes. And another guest: Garrison, my FBI friend. The gang's all here.

Dirk lit a cig with his artillery lighter. He blew out smoke.

"Gents," he said, "it's official. We've got an old-fashioned turf war. This Charlie Reed is trying to keep El Gordo's cousin, the Horse, out of Miami. I don't think there's any question of that anymore.

"I think Reed got one of the late El Gordo's goons, or maybe one of his girls, to spill about the diamonds-in-the-dentures scheme. He tracks down our mule in the bungalow, who's getting ready to fly to San Juan the next day. Sends a hit man who encourages the mope to give up the good tooth doctor. Then the guy gives the mule the business. He scoops up the dentures, rocks and all, from the poor stiff's mouth. He, or some other Reed henchman, goes to the dentist and takes him out. And picks up some more diamonds. Which the colored guy takes down to our jeweler friend for a big payday."

Keyes said, "I still don't understand how he'd be so stupid to send a colored. Draw attention."

Garrison shrugged. "He was gonna ice the jeweler anyhow."

I said, "But El Caballo catches on to Reed. Or gets a tip. He starts having his guys tail Reed, and his associates. He sends a trigger man to the jeweler to intercept the colored and get back his diamonds, the loss of which has set back his accounts receivable something fierce, as my wife the bookkeeper would say. But the hit man doesn't count on the jeweler having his Belgian friend in his pocket."

Garrison sighed. "Now what?"

I said, "These dead guys might as well be department store dummies. We probably won't never make 'em."

Dirk Monroe said, "Let's try anyway. And you two guys–" he motioned to Keyes and Garrison– "work your Fed folks. Especially the ones down in San Juan. Someone's gonna slip up."

I said, "We know El Gordo distanced himself from all the other Florida booze operations. But I don't know enough about this Reed character. Is there a chance he's working with…"

Dirk flicked the end of his cig.

"Mark Gregg."

Chapter Thirteen: The Cigarette Girl

The Missus and I count our pennies. Three tykes on one paycheck, the money's gone quick. But we have a rule. On our anniversary, we go first cabin.

Nancy Monk came over to watch the kids. We fought with her mom for twenty minutes before Sandra let us pay her. We walked to the Royal Palm. I know the manager, Barney Wilde, from when he was assistant to Ted Forman. He took over here when Forman moved to the Columbus. Department policy, and the way my momma raised me, forbid me from taking any freebies from Wilde. But he did give us the best table in the place.

A lot of these joints, after midnight, they break out the hooch. Figure they're safe. We'd be in bed by then. We just had ordered some lemonades, and I saw the band setting up. Hoped to do some hoofing with the Missus before the night was through. Not good hoofing. But we don't care who looks.

"Hey," the Missus said. "There's a cigarette girl. I need a pack of gum."

I waved to a girl snaking through tables, a tray out in front of her, and held by a strap that went behind her neck. It held cigarette packs, matchbooks, playing cards, tins of mints, and packs of gum. The girl came close and let out a giant smile. My eyes widened.

"Hi, Mr. Moran."

"Lara. As I live and breathe. Charlotte, Lara here was—was involved in one of my cases."

I'd told the Missus about Lara and her demons. The Missus played dumb. "Nice to meet you, Lara. How about a Juicy Fruit?"

Lara took the coins and handed over the pack of gum. I said, "Don't happen to have any candy cigarettes?" She shook her head. "Sorry."

The Missus said, "Nate, I need to run to the powder room. Be right back."

What a shrewd dame. I waited for her to move off.

"How are you doing?"

Lara let out a big sigh. "I know this sounds dramatic, sir. I think you saved my life. I woulda ended up as dead as El Gordo."

I waved her off. "Just gave you a little push. You did the rest yourself."

"I been clean since the last time you saw me. It wasn't easy."

"I know that, Lara. I see it on the streets every day. It's like a monster living inside someone. You're very brave."

Her eyes welled. Her voice came out raspy. "Sometimes I don' feel so brave."

"Well, you are, young lady. Umm, what happened to your pal the carhop?"

Another smile. "You were right, sir. Danny stuck with me. We came down together from Palm Beach to, well, start over. He's another person saved my life."

I shrugged. "Tried to tell you. Glad you listened."

She looked across the room. "Gotta go. Boss giving me a dirty look."

I slipped a dollar bill on her tray. "Good luck."

She smiled and moved off.

The food was great. The portions were just a bit bigger than I remember. That Barney.

The Missus puts up with my two left feet, and she's a gazelle, so we worked up a good sweat on the dance floor. We were home by nine.

Looks like I picked the right Saturday night to take the wife to the Royal Palm. Folks who went there two weeks later had a different dining experience.

My telephone rang about half past one in the morning. It was a cool night, and I briskly walked the few blocks to the hotel.

The restaurant looked like someone had set off a bomb. In a corner, the bandstand was deserted, instruments flung down, and microphone stands scattered like broomsticks. Across the room, broken plates and glasses littered the floor. Tables were overturned, or held unfinished plates of food and open wine bottles. The wine was the least of my worries right now.

Back in Palm Beach, at that back room, Hypocrite's Row, I'd found El Gordo on his back, red splotches staining his bright white tux shirt. This time, his cousin, El Caballo, was on his side, under a chair, behind an overturned table. His cheek pressed against the uneaten portion of his ribeye.

And there was my pal, Sergeant Ginze. Funny how we keep meeting like this.

"Gotta tell you, Ginze, I'd rather be sleeping in bed with my wife than standing here with you."

"Same to you, Nate."

I said, "Jose Paseo. Now Antonio Paseo. This is getting ugly. What did the diners tell you?"

He flipped his notepad. "El Caballo came in about 11:30, each arm around a flapper. He tells the waiter, 'Me and the dames are ready for some steaks. We been exercising.'"

I shook my head. "Classy guy. The dames weren't embarrassed?"

Ginze smiled. "Not these girls. I seen them with El Caballo before. Dripping with jewelry, I'd say it's them taking El Caballo for a ride."

He looked back at his notes.

"The steaks come out, and since it's late, some vino as well. You can take that up with your friend Barney later. The Horse and his girls are chowing and laughing, and the band's jazzin' it up, and the girls are pulling on the guy to hit the dance floor, but he wants to finish his steak. Except he never does."

That Ginze. Loves the drama.

"The place is packed. Diners and waiters and busboys are snaking between the tables. No one's paying attention to anyone. One of the dames says El Caballo looked up, and in a split second, a rod comes out and the man gets the pop-pop. The girls scream, and the table goes over."

"Anyone see the guy before he opened up? Was he at a table? Dance floor? Bar?

Ginze pointed to the bar.

"He'd just had a lemonade. And bought a pack of cigarettes from a girl."

Not that girl.

Lara sat in the coat room, a waitress's arm around her. She jumped up and threw her arms around me. She sobbed for a long while. She coughed. A croak. "Why is God doing this?"

I pulled her arms away and looked her down. "This is not divine. This is bad men." Then, quietly, "You just have really bad luck."

She wiped her streaking eye makeup. "I need a hit so bad. So bad."

I gripped her wrists. "You don't. You're done with that. You're strong. Got it?"

I led her back to the chair, and she fell into it. The waitress still was there. Lara used a cloth napkin to wipe her smeared face and then blew her nose into it.

"I–I saw El Caballo come in. I seen him a couple times with Antonio. But even if I didn't, anyone can see from their faces they're cousins. Guess he didn't recognize me. Dames like me are forgettable."

She honked into the napkin again.

"Then I'm busy working the people up and down the bar. I get to this one guy. He's sitting, but I can see he's tall. Good looking. Dark. But not my type." A little smile. "He asks me do I have any of these such-and-such cigarettes, and he gives a name I never heard. When I tell him no, he says never mind. I move on down the bar, and thirty seconds later, I hear the pops. I turn and see that same guy lowering the gun. Around him, people are screaming and tables tipping over. I see him run out the back service door."

"Good, Lara. Umm, do you remember the name of the cigarettes he asked about?"

"Umm, Gallo or Galway or somethin' like that. He said they were French."

Gauloises.

"Did the guy have an accent?"

"Yeah, but I'm lousy with accents."

"Spanish?"

"No. I've heard enough of that."

I thought about the cigarettes. "Maybe French?"

"Maybe."

"How are you getting home?"

She told me Danny, the valet, was downstairs. I asked if she was sure she was all right. She said she was. I nodded a thanks to the waitress who'd stayed with her.

Downstairs, I spotted Danny. He must have been parking someone when I'd come up.

"Hi, Mr. Moran. Good to see you again. Sorry it's like this."

"Danny, you're a good man."

He shrugged. "Naah. Just in love."

"She's a wreck. Wanted the smack real bad."

Danny's lips were set tight. "She's had a lot of these moments. She's fought every one. She's my hero."

"Funny, Danny. She says that about you."

I got home about five and slept nearly to noon. The kids had friends over in the morning, but I was so bushed I slept right through the noise. I was dopey all afternoon, and I dragged in to work Monday morning. Dirk Monroe was off for the day and had left a message that he planned to meet with Ginze and me on Tuesday. I called Keyes.

"I heard about the hit. Can't say I'm boo-hooing for El Caballo."

"Right, Keyes. But it would've been nice for them to kill each other somewhere private, instead of the guy popping him in a jammed restaurant. Some innocent could have gotten it. These guys don't care. Turf wars never are neat."

"I'm with you, Nate."

I called the Royal Palm. The restaurant manager took a message for Lara. An hour later, she called.

"How are you feeling?"

A long sigh. "Danny took me home. I had the shakes all night. He held me through all of it."

"Sounds like you know how to pick 'em."

Then, "You said when you were with El Gordo, he didn't talk much about his cousin. Did he ever talk about a guy named Charlie Reed?"

"Umm. Yeah. Yeah. Remember the name. Antonio said it a few times. He'd talk to his goons about the guy. When he was drunk and didn't know I was listening. It was mostly in Spanish. But I heard him say in English that the guy was a pain in the butt."

"Did he ever mention Reed working with someone who was French?"

"Sorry. No."

Dead end. Maybe not.

Lara said she'd call me if she thought of anything else. She rang off.

"Hey, Harvey."

Harvey Comeau looked up.

"Where do you get your cigs?"

He motioned with his head. "Been laying off a while. It was Williams Sundries. It's in the Halcyon Arcade."

Of course it is.

Max Goldstein stood behind the counter. Even me seeing just the waist up, he looked like he'd played football in college. I flashed my badge.

"Arthur: Watch things," he said to a kid at the postcard kiosk, looked like he was in high school. Max motioned me to a back office.

"You missed all the excitement last week at the jewelry place at the other end of the arcade, detective."

"Actually, I was the investigating officer."

His eyebrows raised. "Is this about that? I was out that day with a sick kid."

"It's not, sir. But it might be related. Umm, do you sell foreign cigarettes?"

"Sure do. This is Miami. I got the best selection in town."

"How about Gauloises?"

His face scrunched up like a dog had squatted nearby.

"Nasty. The tobacco's from Syria and Turkey. No filter tip, of course. They're really strong. When someone in the room is smoking one, you know it. When people want to test one, I make them go into the cigar room."

"Do you sell a lot?"

"No. Maybe a few packs a week. But there's one guy buys a carton."

I love my job.

I said, "Really?"

"Yeah. He came by maybe a half dozen times in the last year. He'd tell me he was from out of town and was here for a few weeks and needed his smokes."

"Did he ever say where he was from?"

Max smiled. "No. But I'd spot that French accent a mile away. All my pals at Edison High were taking Spanish. Figured that was the language of the future for Miami. But my mom pushed me to French. Go figure."

"So this guy was from France."

"Actually, detective, he wasn't. My teacher was Parisienne. A real snob. Nothing worked her up like a bad French accent. She really hated the ones from the islands."

"This guy was from the Caribbean?"

Max smiled. "Absolument."

Nate, you idiot. You were looking for a Frenchman. France is a long way from here. But the Caribbean is dotted with a whole line of French-speaking islands. Martinique. Guadalupe. St. Martin. All working the U.S. hooch trade.

"Umm, Mr. Goldstein. Based on the accent, would you want to take a stab at which island?"

"My bet, detective? Haiti."

Back at my desk, I was on the phone with Keyes.

"Haiti isn't a French colony, Keyes. It's independent. And right now, occupied by Uncle Sam."

"Right, Nate. But if you thought Puerto Rico was a nest of snakes, Haiti's an acre of 'em. Not much of a government. And lots of rich white guys live up in the hills. A lot of them are French nationals. A lot aren't. Born in Haiti. But they still love their crepes. Oh, and their French cigarettes."

Ooh-la-la.

I told him about the guy with the Gauloises. He said, "I'll tell my guys at the seaplane terminal to keep an eye out. Let you know."

I said, "But you don't know who you're looking for. Unless he's smoking one of those stinky cigs."

My desk phone rang at 11:30 the next morning.

"Nate Moran. Detectives."

It was Max Goldstein. "The guy just left. He wanted just a couple packs. Said he was flying out this afternoon."

I called Sanchez, the Pan Am ticket agent. He said the next Clipper was leaving at ten after one. He had one man getting off in Port-Au-Prince. Gave me the name.

My next call was to Keyes. He said he'd alert his guys at the terminal, and he'd meet me there.

I beat Keyes to the terminal. I didn't want to approach Sanchez, the Pan Am clerk. I stayed in the shadows. I figured our guy with the smelly smokes was a pro, and he'd spot a dick from across the room.

Ten minutes later, I smelled it. I told you I've become a lot more sensitive to cigarette smoke since I quit. This stuff you couldn't miss. Like burning rope.

I scanned the room. A man was checking in at the ticket counter. Tall. Good looking. Dark. Lara nailed it. He looked like a sophisticated European businessman. Smoke curled from his palm. He was talking to Sanchez, who didn't dare break eye contact with him.

Keyes appeared in the front doorway. I'd told him which corner of the terminal to look, and he spotted me in the shadows. I motioned at the tall guy with the cig. Keyes jabbed a finger at me. To make the collar.

I slid my hand across my chest and felt the bulge of my piece. I took a deep breath.

The man turned from the counter and slid his tickets into his inside coat pocket. He mashed his cig in a standing ashtray and strode toward the door to the shuttle boat. I got in line behind him like I was boarding as well. Then I took three steps and placed my left hand on the man's tall left shoulder.

How long have I been doing this? I made a rookie mistake. I was in the wrong position. I should have known guys like him always are on guard. His right elbow shot out and caught me in the gut. My lungs locked. I dropped and curled up like a baby. I worked my jaw, but no air entered. I must have looked like a grouper gulping and flapping out his life on the deck of a fishing boat.

I heard noises and grunts, and screams. But they were muffled and seemed miles away. I was light-headed. This is how I die? On the filthy floor of a seaplane terminal?

My lungs unlocked, and I took in a giant breath. My head cleared. I rubbed my belly. Felt like someone had hit it with a ball peen hammer. I forced myself to sit. My brain cleared.

Keyes was on his knees astride the man. The tall guy's elbow was up around his shoulder blades, and I heard him cry out. A second man was alongside. Blond and rugged. Looked like an oil worker. A rod came out and went against the tall guy's temple.

I put out my palm and wrestled myself up. I limped over to where all three men now were on their feet. In a flash, the guy I didn't know had cuffs out and snapped.

Keyes nodded to me. I cleared my throat.

"Claude Petion: You are under arrest for the murder of Jose Paseo."

Keyes said, "Nate, for now, he's your prisoner. I'll call Garrison over at the FBI. This might turn federal. Him being a Haitian national and all."

"French." It was Sanchez, the gate agent. He'd seen the passport, natch.

I said, "Thanks for saving my keister, Keyes. And thank you, agent…"

"Mark Cone. Just transferred from Texas."

"Cone, welcome to Florida. Where nothing happens."

Chapter Fourteen: The Cotter Pin

I was catching up on paperwork just after lunch. My ribs still were sore from taking an elbow from Claude Petion at the Pan Am terminal. The doc said no ribs broke but to take it easy. I said that was unlikely. I reminded him what I did for a living.

Next to me, Harvey Comeau was putting together a stakeout. He'd got a tip someone was going to hit a car dealership up Miami Avenue.

The phone rang. It was Chief Burke.

"Run over to Brickell Avenue. Feds just pulled over a guy in a hot roadster. Lotta contraband in the trunk. They need us to book him for them. And also to store the seized hooch overnight."

I grabbed a patrol guy, and we rode over. I saw a familiar face. Bruce Keyes, the federal Prohibition agent. He walked me over to a man sitting sideways in the open driver's door of a Maxwell, his hands cuffed in front of him.

"Charlie Reed, this is Detective Moran, Miami PD. They'll be providing your accommodations for the night."

Charlie Reed. Finally.

He gave me that smile that makes me want to put my shoe in punks' faces.

"You guys do like running around in circles, dontcha? It's all jake. I'll be out on bail before you can do the paperwork. Just like Mark Gregg."

Keyes took a step. I grabbed his left forearm and felt incredible strength. Then he relaxed.

He said, "Gregg might have gotten off for blowing my colleague's face off. But he's still gotta stand for the other agent he killed." He leaned in. "And even if he survives all of that, well…I don't know if you're a religious man. But I am. And I believe with all my heart that one day Gregg will be in front of a different judge. And he won't have a lawyer in a ritzy suit standing next to him."

Charlie Reed shrugged. "That's between Gregg and you-know-who."

"I said, "Just curious, Reed. How do you know Mark Gregg?"

That grin again. A shrug. "Just what I read in the papers."

"Charlie, I wouldn't be mugging around if I was you. You've got your own problems."

A prowl car pulled up and braked hard. Comeau jumped out with a patrolman. "Just heard from another snitch. Boat coming into Baker's Haulover in the next half hour."

I pointed to Reed. "Harvey: Can your guy take this mope in and book him?" Comeau nodded. Keyes fired up his car, and we worked our way up to the Haulover. When we pulled up, the sun was setting. The inlet was empty.

Sumbitch Charlie Reed had set us up to waste our time. And if it wasn't him, it was someone else. Maybe Gregg. I didn't know if he and Reed were partners, or they just did each other favors, or were rivals. Seems like Baker's Haulover is the locale of choice for bum steers. Gregg had tried to bribe my friend Monk to make sure everyone was away from here. Maybe that got Monk killed. Now this. I said out loud, "Sumbitch."

Keyes looked out over the darkening ocean. He was smiling. "It's all jake. Reed. Gregg. Whichever. Or both. Or neither. All these guys are smart. And they have a lot of friends. But their luck won't hold out forever."

He turned to me. "Thanks for stopping me back there on Brickell. All I need is a police brutality beef for breaking Reed's schnozz."

"Couldn't happen to a nicer guy."

"And I didn't get a chance to say it was nice of your chief to send you to Arlington for Bailey Monk's funeral. You guys are good partners with the Feds."

He lit a cigarette and faced west and watched the sun drop into the Everglades. His back was to me.

"I'm gonna tell you something, Moran. You tell anyone, I'll call you a liar."

"Okay."

"After that sumbitch Gregg got off, I went home that night and bawled like a baby. I told my wife I was done. Washed out. I asked her why we're out there risking our lives, and sometimes getting killed, for a stupid law. Hell, Nate, Monk thought it was a stupid law too."

"He told me that too, Keyes."

The Fed, still with his back to me, let out a little laugh and took another draw on his cig. "You'll never believe this. It was my bride talked me out of quitting. Said she thought it was a stupid law. And the idea of burying me made her spend her nights staring at the ceiling. But then she said, 'Bruce, it don't matter it's a bad law. These mongrels are gettin' rich breaking it. You've sworn to stop those bastards. You walk away, they win. You'll never live with yourself.'"

Keyes turned around. "And then she said, 'And you defile the memory of your friend Bailey Monk.'" He smiled. "'Defile.' That's what you get when you're married to an English teacher. But that was it."

I said, "Bruce, my chief has loaned me out to Miami Springs PD. Gregg's haunt. You know Franks, their chief. Used to be with us. My chief said for me to help them for as long as it takes for him to put the kibosh on Mark Gregg." I put a hand on his shoulder. "That's my obligation to Monk."

* * *

Mark Franks walked me up Main Street to the Old South diner. The street was only about two blocks long. I was able to see both ends. They looked odd. Then I realized. At each end was a half-finished two-story building.

"Can't build 'em fast enough," Franks said.

"Gotta be honest with you, Chief. I figure what's the use of living in Florida if you're not near the water. Might as well be in Kansas. That's me."

Franks said, "Yeah, I do miss it. But it's just down the road. And this was too good an opportunity."

I heard a buzzing. It got louder. I looked up toward the noise. The sun blinded me. The buzz got really loud, and I saw an aeroplane pass overhead.

It was so low I could read the writing on the wing. It said, "Curtiss School."

I said, "That Curtiss guy again."

"He's the biggest man in town," Franks said. "Heck, he created the town. Got famous in upstate New York, building and racing motorcycles. Then he flew aeroplanes just five years after Kitty Hawk. Came down here and hooked up with a rancher. They bought up a bunch of land. At the height of the boom, they sold a million dollars of lots in ten days. A million dollars! That became Hialeah. When some not-so-savory guys started getting influence in Hialeah, Curtiss got out. Part of the land him and the rancher had bought was over this way, and he started thinking about homes. And then golf courses. And then a country club. And when he was digging, he found all sorts of freshwater springs."

I said, "Why the name."

"Curtiss was full-time on the land business. But he did build his flying school."

I said, "Is it a public airstrip?"

"Yes and no. This whole aviation thing is new. The federal government has decided airstrips would be like roads. The public can use them free, anytime, anywhere. The airfield's owner can't charge for use. What he can do is sell fuel and repairs and oil changes and storage. That's where the money is. Curtiss built a bunch of aeroplane sheds and a fuel pump. He's hands-off now on the flying school and the crop-dusting, and he has a manager runs the sheds and the pumps."

In the afternoon glare, the descending aeroplane had vanished.

* * *

A week later, Chief Burke called just as I was packing up for the day.

"Some kind of robbery and shootout in Colored Town."

I called the Missus to say not to hold dinner. I rode out with a patrol guy. It was close to six, but the sun still was above the horizon and the day still was toasty. I left my jacket on the front seat.

Two patrol guys standing by a roadster parted. Window glass was scattered

197

on the road. Inside, a man lay back in the driver seat. The side of his face was blown out. More ugly red splotches just below his left armpit.

I leaned in. The face was a mess. But I recognized it.

I pointed to a general store about a hundred yards away. I asked the patrol guy at the car door, "You know if there's a phone in there?"

"That's where we called it in."

"Don't touch anything." Like I had to tell these guys.

Inside the general store, a man stood behind the counter. His eyes followed me. He was so tense he looked like he might snap in two.

I showed my badge. He blurted out. "I din' see nothin, suh.' Din' see nothin'!"

I put up a hand. "Talk to you later. For now, I just need your phone."

He pointed to a back wall. I rang Dirk Monroe. "You need to get Bruce Keyes over here pronto. It's Charlie Reed. Sure looks like an execution."

Keyes made it in twenty minutes. I stepped aside so he could see the driver's side.

"Charlie Reed, as I leave and breathe."

I got the joke. Live and breathe. Which Charlie was neither.

We had no love for this guy. He was a piece of trash who mocked us. He very likely was in league with Mark Gregg. He might have had some kind of role in Monk's death. And many others. But a murder victim is a murder victim, and we had to do our jobs.

Keyes said, "We'd heard he was working Colored Town. I suspect he dumps rotgut. Probably picks it up cheap on the dock at Freeport. Big guys like Gregg don't even bother with that stuff. But around here, he can make it up with volume."

I said, "Maybe Charlie and one of his colored customers had a falling out."

Keyes shook his head. "Look at the spray of bullets. This was a professional ambush."

I walked a big circle around the car. I stopped. I swiveled back about a quarter circle. Out of the corner of my eye, a kid sat on his porch. He looked about thirteen. He wasn't playing with a ball or eating ice cream. Just sat there. Watching us.

I called out to Keyes, "Be right back."

I walked up the sidewalk. As I passed the kid, I looked straight ahead, but said, just loud enough for him to hear, "I'm a police detective. Meet me behind the general store, son. Look natural."

I kept walking like I was going to the general store. I stopped and looked back at Reed's car like I was thinking about something. I got out my notepad and made like I was looking over my scribbles. Then I looked around me and walked back to the back of the store. Anyone who saw me would think I had to take a leak.

I stood about five minutes. A dog barked in the distance. I smelled the garbage at the back door. A black alley cat sniffed around me, then slinked off. No, I don't believe in that stuff.

I heard a noise. The kid stood at the edge of a stand of trees.

"You saw it."

He didn't say anything for a beat. Then, "I scared, suh."

"Try like hell to keep you out of this, kid."

The shadows were lengthening. The humidity still was as thick as soup. The kid looked at the ground and spoke nearly in a whisper.

"Ofay came by around five. I seen him before. He sell rotgut to Carl."

Ofay. Don't hear that word too much. Strange to hear colored slang used about white folks.

I motioned. "This is Carl's store? That was him just now behind the counter?"

"Uh-huh. Usually, the rotgut man pull around the back here, toot three times, pop the trunk, and Carl come out."

"How you know this?"

"I plays sometimes in the woods. Plays cowboys and Indians by myself. I likes to pretend I'm the Indian."

It seemed right. Coloreds know that point of view.

"This time, I was on my porch when the guy pull up front. He turn off the car and he make like he gonna have a smoke before he drives around back. He put the cig in his mouth and...and..."

The kid had frozen. I waited him out. And waited.

"What's your name, son?"

He gulped and wiped his mouth. "Jackie."

I said, calmly, "Listen, Jackie. Take your time."

He stood another few minutes.

He said quietly, "Another car pull up alongside. Two white fellas in it. The one on the passenger side, he shooting and shooting. Glass going everywhere, and the man in the other car was jumping like—like—"

The boy's eyes filled. No kid should have to see something like that.

"The two men. Ever seen 'em before?"

He shook his head.

"Can you describe them at all?"

"Just they white."

He looked around. "I gotta go." He melted into the saw palmettos.

I stood for a couple more minutes. I heard a door open behind me. Carl's head stuck out. Just as quickly, he shut the door. I'd deal with Carl later.

The sky was nearly black now. I walked back to our patrol car and reached in for a flashlight. Bruce Keyes was circling Reed's roadster with his own light. The morgue guys had shown and were tapping their feet.

I looked in at Charlie. The smirk he'd had when we'd pulled him over on Brickell was gone.

"Well, Agent Keyes, this is beginner's detective school. Let me know how I am doing. I don't suspect he was iced at random. Or by accident. Talked to a kid just now. Told me it was two white guys. So that means…"

"Turf war."

"Agent, I know we're supposed to keep an open mind. But we know who probably has been having dealings with Charlie."

"I'm thinking the same thing, Nate. Mark Gregg."

"But if he's behind this, something happened to their friendship. And recently. But what?"

"Nate, you've been around the block. For the people we're dealing with, life is cheap. It wouldn't have taken much for Gregg to turn on Charlie. Could have been anything. Maybe Gregg regretted giving Charlie the commerce with the coloreds. Maybe that got too lucrative."

"'Lucrative.' There's your English teacher wife again." Keyes laughed.

I said, "But I don't think so. This rotgut is pennies compared to the good stuff. No. It's something else."

Keyes motioned to the car. "Can the boys have him now?"

I nodded. A minute later, the morgue guys slid Reed out. He'd mostly bled out. It wasn't pretty.

Keyes walked with the stretcher to the morgue car. I leaned into Charlie's front seat. Blood soaked the cloth. I also smelled beer. I don't touch the stuff, but I know it. This was strong. Like ale or malt liquor. I turned my flashlight to the passenger side floorboard. Two bottles lay smashed in a pool of brownish liquid. On the passenger seat, a wad of bills. It was thick. Also splotched with Reed's blood. Blood covered the cracked windshield. The overhead fabric was dotted with blood and other stuff that I didn't wanna know.

I was about to lean back out when my flashlight caught something shiny sticking out from the crease between the chair's seat and back. I used my hanky to slide it out.

It was shaped like one of those things the Missus used in her hair. It was a dull-edged, U-shaped pin that had a little bump at the top. The ladies called it a bobby pin. But this was a lot bigger, about five inches long, and many times more solid and heavy. Looked like it was made of brass.

I walked to Keyes. I opened the hanky and used my other hand to shine my flashlight on the thing.

"This must have slid out of Charlie's pocket. I'm clueless. Ever seen one of these?"

Keyes leaned in. He looked hard at it. He said, "Remember our rumrunner friend Henry Wade, who swung in Fort Lauderdale?"

"How could I forget. I watched."

"Right, Nate. You did."

He turned the hanky in the light from his flashlight. "I was with a group that scoured the bad guy's boat from bow to stern. We went through it with tweezers and toothbrushes. We even took apart the motor. You know, the one that wouldn't start, how the shootout got going."

He held the thing out to me. "This is a cotter pin."

"What's that?"

Keyes: "It slides through holes and holds a propeller in place."

"A propeller?"

He said, "Yeah. A propeller for a boat."

Wait a minute. I looked at Keyes. "Or an aeroplane."

Keyes had to go, and I had a mind to do the same thing. But Dirk Monroe had taught me any time I finished a crime scene, I should take one more look before I left. He called it "an insurance walk."

I shone the flashlight on the floorboards in front of the back seat. The light stopped on something.

It was half a doughnut.

* * *

I sat across from Miami Springs Chief Franks. "I want to go talk to Gregg."

Franks blew out air. "That's a real risk. He plays the dumb yahoo, but he's savvy as hell. I told you he smells us when we're tailing him."

"That's why I should go instead of you."

Franks said, "That what Chief Burke says?" I nodded. "Burkie's a smart man. Taught me everything I know." He leaned in. "But we start asking Gregg about Charlie Reed, we'd be tipping our hand."

I shrugged. "Chief says so what? Gregg already must figure we suspect he was in with Charlie. And turned on him. Why not let him sweat? Maybe it'll make him slip up."

"OK, Nate. You go. I don't want to drive down his street again anyway. Too many bad memories. If Gregg asks, you are rogue. My department doesn't know you're in town. Neither do the Feds."

I felt bad I hadn't told Franks about the cotter pin and had led him to think Baker's Haulover was our only link between Gregg and Charlie. Something told me to hold back on that for now.

I parked about a block from Gregg's house. I walked up the sidewalk, through the gate, and onto the porch. My breathing came fast. I was standing where Monk fell.

The screen door and front door, blown out by Gregg's shotgun blast, had been replaced. I knocked once and stepped back. Just like Monk did.

"Who is it? What you want?"

Female.

"Mrs. Gregg. I'm Nate Moran. I'm a Miami police officer."

The door opened a crack. I saw a chain. Behind it, half a face.

"Ain't you off your turf? Can't you people just leave us the hell alone?"

"Ma'am, I know other agencies have been around here a lot. But not ours."

"Great," Shelley Gregg said. "The more the merrier."

"I can't speak about whatever Miami Springs police or the federal Prohibition agents have been doing out here. I'm here to talk to your husband about Charlie Reed."

Even seeing just half her face, I saw her expression change. "What about Charlie?" Her voice cracked just a little. She didn't know. And she called him Charlie. I let the wheels turn in her head.

The chain fell. The door creaked halfway open. Shelley Gregg stood in the shadows. She pulled a ratty housecoat tight, and her red hair was tangled.

"You stay where you are." She repeated, "What about Charlie?"

"He's dead."

I'm usually a little more diplomatic, but something had told me to slap Mrs. Gregg with it. Turned out to be a good call. She might have been married for years to a slick criminal, but as poker faces went, hers stunk out loud. She threw her hand to her mouth, and tears filled her eyes.

"Daid?"

"Yes, ma'am. He was shot last night in Colored Town."

She sure seemed broken up about a guy she barely knew. I kept playing dumb.

"This Reed person might have been connected to your husband. We're checking it out. Can you tell us anything?"

A shadow behind her emerged into the light, and I saw over her shoulder the face of a teenager. Same red hair and freckles. Mrs. Gregg didn't even turn around. She looked straight at me and said, "Mildred, go back to your room."

I've heard it said mothers have eyes in the back of their heads. I've seen the Missus pull that magic trick.

"You a cop?" the girl asked.

"Yes. Miami police."

Mrs. Gregg's voice was more forceful. "Mildred."

"Ma!"

"Now."

The face melted back into the shadows. Mrs. Gregg took one step onto the porch. I tensed. But her hands were empty.

"I don't need an earful from you, sir. I have nothing to say to you or any of your pals. You leave my husband alone."

"We're here about Charlie Reed."

"You git off my porch."

I'd gone as far as I could. But for someone who didn't say anything, this redhead had said a lot.

* * *

"Nate Moran. Detectives."

"Barry Renault, Nate." The reporter over at the *Miami Herald*. "Remember that favor I owe you? How about a café con leche? Tulipan."

Renault was at a back table. I got there just as the waiter set down two steaming cups, along with a plate with two pastries.

"Empanadas? Renault, you tell my wife, I'll get the mayor to yank your press pass."

The waiter said, "¿Algo más?" Anything else? I said, "Gracias. No." At least not right away.

Renault waited for the man to leave. He leaned in.

"So, Nate, you know the game. I start to tell you what I know about something. Then, if you know, you tell me a little. Then we go back and forth. Everything is off the record for now. But if it leads to something, maybe I help you solve a crime. And I get a scoop."

I took a sip. Aah. Love that coffee.

"So, last month, I got married."

"Congratulations."

"Yeah. Dani. She's a sweetheart. It's one of those strange deals where the dame makes more than the guy. She runs her dad's lumber yard. Fine with me."

I nodded as if to say, "Get to it." Renault didn't miss the signal.

"When we started getting serious, we decided it was jake for us to splurge sometimes. We'd go up over to the Columbus. Up to the Roof Garden."

The Roof Garden. The hairs stood up on the back of my neck.

"The restaurant manager—"

"Kopp."

"Right, Nate. How'd you know?"

I wanted him to c'mon already.

"Kopp knew I was a reporter, so he'd feed me little pieces of gossip. About celebrities and politicians. Also, about his competitors, natch."

"Natch."

"One day, he's talking about how all the hotels get their hooch. Not him, of course."

Of course.

I looked Renault in the eye. "Mark Gregg."

He took a big bite of his empanada. "These are really good." He took another sip of the café. I did the same. And took a bite. These things go right to my waistline. The Missus'll have my hide.

"One night, we go over to the Roof Garden, and there's some new manager. Says the other guy left on short notice. Kopp. It was right around the time Gregg killed your pal and the other Fed."

I already knew that. "That's not the end of your story, is it, Renault? I still have half an empanada."

Renault waved to the waiter and pointed to my cup, then his.

"So me and Dani get hitched. For our honeymoon, we take the train down to Key West and hop the steamship to Havana. The fourth night there, the wife had got too much sun, and ate too much arroz con pollo, and drank too much rum, so she sacks out early. I head down to the hotel casino. She said I could have ten bucks to gamble. That's it. But that's a lot for me! I walk past the bar, and, dang! You'll never guess who I see behind it.

I waited.

"It's Kopp, the old manager from the Roof Garden."

Hmmm.

"Says he's about to clock out, and it's great to see a familiar face, and can he buy me a drink? That ten-spot already has come and gone at the craps table, which took ten minutes, and I'm not tired, so I say sure.

"We do small talk for a while, and Kopp has a second drink, and a third. You know they keep 'em coming in the casino, especially for desperate Americans, but they're generous with the staff too. Now he's loopy. And the booze lubricates his jawbone but good. Well. I'm on vacation. But like detectives, reporters never go off the clock. I'm all ears.

"Kopp says yeah, it was Gregg supplying the Roof Garden. Said he told Gregg he had to dump him as a supplier. Didn't need Forman to find out the hotel was getting its hooch from a guy just killed two federal agents. Kopp said Gregg wasn't happy. Told him it would be a bad idea to close the account. Real bad idea. Now Kopp's thinking it's like no one finds your body bad. He decides it's a good time to relocate. Like to another country."

Just like Ted Forman had figured it. That guy'd make a great detective.

Renault says, "I ask him there at the bar in Havana, I say, 'One thing I always wondered, Kopp. All that hooch, how did you keep the coppers away from the Roof Garden?' Guess what he says."

Renault had a smile like instead of watching his tenner vanish at the craps table, he'd hit one of those yos. The eleven.

"Kopp says, 'Renault, we'd get tipped when they were on their way. We had a guy on the inside.'"

Just like that, the meat pie in my gut weighed about a hundred pounds. My face must have turned the color of the tablecloth.

"Inside?"

Renault nodded. Big grin.

"Inside?"

He nodded again.

I ran my finger through my hair. I started to reach for the cup but stopped. Didn't want Renault to see my hand shaking.

"Kopp said the dick was plainclothes and never used his name. It was all cash behind the bar. The guy always made sure Forman didn't see him coming around. But Kopp did tell me something funny. Said the guy loved the hotel's doughnuts."

Doughnuts.

For the next week, the Missus and the kids dined alone. Anybody at headquarters asked, I was working a tip about smugglers out in the Everglades. But I wasn't. Each night, I visited a different hotel on Biscayne Boulevard.

The fourth night, I was at the McAllister. Its high-end eatery was right on the first floor. I'd slipped into the lobby with the eight o'clock rush and stood against the wall, hiding behind a newspaper.

It was about ten when I saw him. I grew a little dizzy. A giant lump formed in my throat.

Nothing to do now but do it. I swore an oath.

I moved into the shadows but had a view of the bar. I saw him talk to the bar manager, then slide something off the bar and into his overcoat. It was the same one he'd loaned me to take the train to Washington.

He turned for the lobby, and I came up behind him.

"Harvey."

He stopped. I saw his shoulders sag. A long pause. His back to me, he said, in a monotone, "I needed the money, Nate. I told you the wife cleaned me out. I even had to sell my heap and walk to work. Why I dodged your questions about gas money."

He turned around and smiled weakly. "Can't you cut me a break? For a pal? A partner?"

My face was set. "Sorry, Harvey. I never would. You know that. But if I did, it wouldn't be for this. Gregg killed Monk."

Then my eyes widened.

"It wasn't Charlie Reed sent us on that bum steer out to Baker's Haulover.

It was you. You, Harvey. You and Charlie. Pals. Why I found your half-doughnut in his shot-up car. And that means Charlie Reed and Mark Gregg are partners after all. Or maybe were. Well, you just cracked one last case for us. Last of your career."

I shook my head. "Mark Gregg."

Harvey looked how a guy looks when his girl says she knows he's been stepping out on her. He gulped. "Look. I hate the guy. But I'd sold him my soul. I got in over my head, and I couldn't get out."

"Harvey. How many times some mope gave you that story?"

I turned my face.

"I can't look at you."

* * *

"You could knock me over with a feather," the Missus said later in bed. I'd woken her up when I got home. In the dark, I knew she was looking right at me.

"Father, grandfather, uncle. All were cops, Hon." I shook my head. "Said he got in over his head."

God, I needed a cigarette. You think you know people. Harvey. My friend.

I said, "I won't lie, Hon. I'm shook." We whispered so as not to wake the kids.

"I won't lie either, Nate. Right now, I'm being selfish. Gregg went after Harvey, and Harvey took the dive. He went after Monk, and Monk told him to go to hell, and that son of a bitch left Monk's wife a widow. Gregg will go after you. Try to turn you. If it ain't him, it'll be someone else. After Prohi's gone, maybe it'll be a gambler. Or a pimp. Or some other gangster."

I said, "That's the life of a cop. Don't worry. My momma raised me right."

"That is what worries me. I know you will tell them to get lost. Then someone's knocking on my door, like you knocked on Sandra Monk's door. That's why my heart goes to my throat every time I hear someone walking on the porch."

* * *

Pan American Field sits not far from Miami Springs, in what used to be a grove of orange and grapefruit trees. Pan Am had built a field house out here, working on the new single-wing aeroplanes. The building had big windows and a balcony so people could watch the things leave down two long airstrips. I walked toward two big sheds.

Inside, one of the planes stood in a corner, its cowling open.

"Rusty Houck?"

"Yeah?" A voice, muffled, from under the hood. A head popped out. A young man, his face caked with grease. Skinny. Blond hair specked with something. Likely something from under the hood.

Showed my badge. "Nate Moran. Miami police. Your office told you I was coming by?"

"Don't have a lot of time. I need to find the leak and get this baby back into the fleet. Whatever it is, make it fast."

I pulled out my hanky and opened it. Houck leaned in. "Where'd you get that?"

"I know you're doing me a favor, Houck, but I cannot tell you."

He shrugged. "That's okay. I've handled enough of them in my time. It's a cotter pin."

That Bruce Keyes is good.

"What else can you tell me?"

"Well, it's not for these single-wing babies I work on. Different size propellors. Different-sized pins. The post office and any private fliers can't afford 'em. Still use the biplanes."

I said, "And biplanes use these types of pins."

"Yeah. They're standard. But they're exact. You have to mail away for them. One guy in North Dakota. He tools them by hand."

"By hand?"

"Yep. I've used the guy for years. Give you his phone number."

Back at headquarters, I called Franks out in Miami Springs. The cotter pin still was a long shot, so I decided to still wait to say anything. I did fill him in on my visit with Gregg's wife. And about my friend Harvey Comeau.

"I'm so sorry, Nate. That's a gut punch."

I said, "Chief, now that we're sure Gregg and Reed are partners, or at least were, we were talking this might be a turf thing between them in Colored Town. But maybe…" My voice trailed.

"Maybe what?"

"Fill you in later."

Chief Burke had okayed the long-distance call to North Dakota.

"Chase Mandan." A voice on the other end of the country. I love living in these modern times.

"Mr. Mandan: I'm Nate Moran. I'm a police detective in Miami, Florida."

"Miami, huh? The Dakotas are God's country in the summer. But every February, I curse you guys down there."

Can't say I blamed him. North Dakota in February? I'd be dead in five minutes.

"Sir, I'm told that if a private biplane owner anywhere in the country bought a cotter pin, he bought it from you."

"Anywhere in the U.S. or Canada. Just shipped a pin to a mail pilot in Manitoba. He's got two hundred customers in an area the size of South Carolina."

"I know you're a busy man. Can I ask you to check your ledger for any sales to anyone down here?"

There was silence on the other end. Then, "I dunno. I have an obligation to my clients. Their privacy."

"Mr. Mandan, we're investigating a murder. Search warrants are a pain. Especially long-distance ones. You can save us the expense of another telephone call to North Dakota, and an unnecessary visit to you by your sheriff up there. I'm sure it wouldn't look good for your business. Get you in Dutch with the sheriff, too, I'd guess."

Another pause. I heard him exhale. "Hold on," he said, frustration in his voice.

More silence. Chief Burke was paying for this call. I tapped my fingers on the desk. It probably was about a minute and a half, but I was imagining dollar bills with little wings.

He was back. "Okay. I'm not real comfortable with this. But here you go. In the last year, I sold cotter pins to just one private biplane owner down your way. It's a company called 'Big Wings.' Care of the airfield in"—a pause while he looked again—"in some place called Miami Springs."

Chapter Fifteen: The Flying Machine

I had no trouble finding Carl's store in Colored Town again. I parked in front. He stood when the door opened, and his face went tight.

I showed my badge again. "Hi Carl."

"I din' see nothing."

I had my fedora off and slid onto a stool.

"Carl, you lost your supplier."

He was stone-faced.

"The way I look at it, that works out for you."

Now he looked confused.

"You might have seen another guy standing with me out at Charlie Reed's shot-up car. That guy's federal. I've waved him off. Told him we'd handle the hooch here. Do it locally."

I picked up a can of beans, eyed the label like it was a novel, and put it back down.

"Here's what I'm gonna do. Since you never got Charlie's delivery for this week, your inventory probably is getting low. I'm gonna work up a search warrant for whatever's left. But I gotta take care of some other things first, so I don't expect to get back over here with the search warrant until maybe Monday."

I looked him in the eye. "Not 'til Monday. By then, you'll probably be sold out."

It took about five seconds for things to click in Carl's head.

"Carl, anyone in this neighborhood asks, I came by today, and you told me to go to hell."

He smiled.

"Now I've done you a favor. So now you tell me about Charlie Reed."

He sat back on his stool. He let out a big breath.

"He, uhh, bring me a case once a week. The stuff ain't that good, tell you the truth. But in this neighborhood, we cain't come close to Charlie's price for good stuff. So, we drinks what we can get."

"Was that all the business you did with Charlie?"

Another pause.

"Carl: You might want to consider cutting out the illegal parts of your store's business from now on. They require a good poker face. You don't have one."

Charlie looked down at the counter.

"I gots a room upstairs. Rent it out sometimes. It ain't a dump or nothing. I keeps it clean. But I ain't licensed or nothin' for rentin', so I tries to be quiet about it."

"Carl, that's a minor thing between you and city code enforcement. I'm trying to solve a murder. Maybe more than one."

He said, "Okay. Umm, ever couple weeks, Charlie show up with this lady friend. They come aroun' lunchtime and they gone by about four."

"Did you give him the room as a favor?"

"No, suh. He paid. Charlie always had lots of cash."

I remembered the bloody wad of bills I'd seen on the front seat next to Charlie Reed's riddled body.

"Carl: Who's the skirt?"

Nothing.

"Carl."

Still nothing.

"Carl, Charlie Reed can't hurt you."

He put out his palms. "Don't know a name. She look about my age. Hard to tell age wif white folk. Tell you this. She had red hair."

Bingo.

This time, I had a bad poker face. Hope he didn't notice.

"Anything else, Carl?"

He paused again.

"Carl?"

He shifted on his stool.

"One day, Reed bring me some papers to sign. I say, 'What these?' He say, 'Don't need to read. Just sign 'em.' Thing is, Mister Detective, Reed an' I never traded no paperwork on the hooch, so maybe Reed don't know that I can read just fine. I make like to sign this thing, but I reads it real quick. It say at the top, 'Articles of Incorporation.' Reed points to the line for me to sign. It say 'President.' Next to it, someone typed my name.

"I say, 'Mister Charlie, I don't just sign my name on somethin', don't know what it is. I walkin' a line already buying your hooch.' Reed say, 'Someone come ask you did you sign this, you are a dumb coon. Unnerstand? You say some guy you don't know gave you twenty bucks to sign it.'"

"I'm shakin' my head. I say, 'Charlie, this is hinky. I don't wanna sign it.' He say, 'Carl, you don't sign this, you off my customer list. And maybe I drop a dime to the PD. Ya unnerstand?' I say, 'Charlie, I got a little on you. I can say what I know about the lady.' Charlie jes' laugh. He say, 'You don' know her name. And anyone ask, it my word against a dinge.'"

Carl looked right at me. "Mr. po-leese, you mean it when you say you won' tell anyone what we says here? You on the level?"

"I am, Carl. But you're done with the hooch."

He let out a big sigh.

"Carl, losing your hooch trade is a lot better than sleeping over in the jail for six months. Or endin' up like Charlie Reed."

Carl sighed. "I signed it. He give me the twenty."

"Any chance you saw the name of the company?"

Carl nodded. "Funny name. Caught my eye. 'Big Wings.'"

* * *

The last time I climbed up the steps of the Dade County Courthouse was to watch Mark Gregg get off for shotgunning my friend. This time, I was headed to the county's records office.

I flashed my badge. "How can I help?" the smiling clerk said.

"When someone creates a company, do they have to submit some sort of document to you?

"Yes. Articles of Incorporation."

Another bingo.

"Would it show the officers of the company?"

The clerk nodded.

"Do you check what people submit?"

She shrugged. "Mostly, we just take their word for it. They can list their dog as an officer. If no one calls them on it, it don't matter."

They can list their dog. Or someone like Carl.

"Ready for the name?"

"Go ahead." She had a pencil in her hand.

"Big Wings. Address would be in Miami Springs."

"Do you know when it might have been submitted?"

I said I didn't. But it would have been in the last three years, based on what Mark Franks said about when Miami Springs and that airfield got going.

She said, "Well, that helps. But without an exact date, it could take a little time. Have a seat."

A few minutes later, the clerk came back. "You're lucky. It was filed just in the last year." She slid a folder to me. "You gotta look at it here at the counter."

I saw the corporate name and the date. The hometown of Miami Springs. My eyes went down to the list of officers. I saw Carl's name. And his scrawled signature.

"How do you know if someone signs a fake name? Or someone else's name?"

"No clue." She smiled. "Maybe you call a cop." A smile.

I moved my finger down the list of officers. The vice president caught my eye. Michelle Hawkins.

Might be a coincidence. Might not be.

"Sorry, Hon. Gonna make more work for you."

She said, "What I'm here for."

"You keep marriage records. Do you have some sort of ledger? Cross-index? I can look up someone and see when they got married? Maybe to who? And maybe the bride's maiden name?"

"All that. But you gotta go year by year. And it's in date order. Not alphabetical. Maybe someday, some machine will make it easier. For now, that's the only way to do it."

I looked at the clock. The chief had given me the morning to chase down my hunches. But no more. I said, "Okay." Then I said, "Hold on a minute. Maybe I can narrow this." I did some math in my head. The daughter said in court she was fourteen. Figure up to three years before she was born. Take a chance.

After an hour, my head was pounding. I never knew that many people got married every year in Dade County. I was tempted to rush through the last few pages of the third book, but I kept my discipline. After I turned the last page, I pulled a hanky and wiped my face. Sure would be great they get some kind of cooling machine in this place. It gets toasty. Worse over in the courtrooms. I seen people pass out during trials.

The clerk was finishing up with someone farther down the counter. I caught her eye.

"Sorry—"

"Colby."

"Colby. I need three more years."

"Sit tight. Got a couple people ahead of you."

I pulled out my candy cigs. Fifteen minutes later, Colby plopped down three more heavy books. I hit the jackpot in the first one. And in January. Michelle Hawkins married Mark Gregg.

* * *

Mark Franks leaned forward at his desk and lifted the cotter pin out of my outstretched hanky. He turned it. It sparkled in the sun streaming in through his windows.

"The sumbitch has an aeroplane."

"Right, Chief. Gregg created a shell company. His patsy was Carl, the guy runs the convenience store in Colored Town. Listed him as president. Gregg had Charlie Reed take the papers over and make sure Carl signed 'em. Duck soup."

And then I said, "This musta been before Gregg found out Charlie was double-crossing him. And not about hooch or jack. With his bride."

I love making police chiefs' eyebrows go through their scalp

"Gregg did something stupid. Or maybe there was some method to it. Listed his wife Shelley as the president in the incorporation papers. Used her maiden name. Michelle Hawkins. I'm thinking he had Charlie Reed be his straw man. Come out and buy the plane. And rent the shed for it. Reed told whoever asked he was Carl, president of the company. Waved the incorporation documents at the airfield manager. Everything looked jake. Legit. Charlie paid cash. Wham, bam."

I motioned to my hanky. "I'd never have made the connection if I hadn't found the pin."

Franks looked at it again. "Sumbitch."

"Sorry I didn't tell you about it before today, Chief. Wanted to make sure I had something."

"That's fine." He sat back. "Now what? We can't charge him with murdering Reed just on this little piece of brass."

"We could go to the airfield manager. Make him tell us who owns which plane, and when he uses it and where it goes. Get a search warrant if we have to."

"That's exactly what I don't want to do."

"With all due respect, Chief, you're not worried about offending the city's founder, are you?"

Franks leaned in. "Nate, anyone else say that'd get a boot up his keister."

I put out my hands. "I'm not questioning your character. Just covering all the angles."

He broke a smile. "No offense taken, Nate. I'd have asked the same thing. And you can be sure that if I thought Glenn Curtiss was up to anything hinky, I'd run him in just like anyone else. But I happen to know he's hands off on the airfield. Turned over the complete operation to that manager."

Franks leaned back. "No, that's not what I was thinking. We go into that airstrip like a bull in a china shop; we lose any chance to nab Gregg in the act of whatever he's doing."

"And what do you think he's doing, Chief?"

I had an idea what Franks would say. And I was right.

"Nate, ever since I got here, I've been thinking about those aeroplanes. How a flyboy can come and go. You see 'em overhead, but you don't know where they're going or what they do when they get there. And at night, mostly no one sees 'em at all."

The room had cooled. I heard rain patter on the window.

* * *

The next day, Keyes and I met Chief Franks at the diner in Miami Springs, then walked back to his office. I had filled in the Fed a little over the phone. Now I walked Keyes through my corporate search and laid out what we were thinking.

"Even with Florida growing like crazy," Keyes said, "there's still a lot of back roads and country highways. But the law is watching. And they still have to smuggle it into the U.S. before they can haul it anywhere. I don't have to tell you about the dangers of the open ocean. But these flying machines can be in the Bahamas in less than an hour. And they can fly from South Florida to Orlando, Atlanta—well, you get the picture.

"The smugglers up north are trying to serve New York City. But we're working with the Mounties to cover the major roads into New York state from Ontario or Quebec. Garrison was doin' some of that when he was up there. So, goons up there are sneaking in hooch through Michigan's Upper Peninsula. Or down through Minnesota. Or over Niagara Falls. But then they're a long way from Times Square. Or any place that matters. So, they fly."

Franks explained why he doesn't want to show his hand just yet.

"I concur," Keyes said.

I turned to Franks. "His wife teaches English." The chief smiled. "No problem. I was on the dean's list."

Keyes said, "Don't we want to at least stake out the airfield?"

"You never been out there," the chief said. "The layout doesn't work for us. They'd see us. There's a fence around the whole place. The gate's locked. You go through it, then you drive about a hundred yards before you get to the sheds and the start of the airstrip. It's sort of around a bend and through some trees so, from the road, you can't see anything. The machines seem to shoot right out of the tree line."

Then he said, "I've had my overnight guys keep a special eye out toward the direction of the airfield. They said they've seen an aeroplane leave after midnight and then come back. Nothing we can do."

I said, "Any ideas where it's going?"

Franks said, "Once they're in the air, they can turn any direction on the compass. My guys said the flights are short. Only an hour. Two hours. Three every once in a while."

"So, either the Bahamas or inside Florida. And to just pick something up. Or drop something off."

Keyes said, "Sooner or later, he's going to use this aeroplane for something big. We do our job, he won't walk this time."

I said, "Chief, we can't just count on your overnight guys."

Franks smiled. "There's something Gregg doesn't know, Nate. Besides, maybe walking on the wild side with Charlie Reed, Mrs. Gregg is a bit of a gossip."

I looked at him. "You don't say."

"I do say. And she doesn't know who her neighbor's daughter works for."

I looked up. Marian, Franks' young aide, had brought in another file. I looked at her. Then Franks. He said, "Thank you, Marian. Enjoy your evening."

* * *

The next day, I had just come back with my afternoon coffee when my phone rang.

"Nate Moran. Detectives."

"Just got off the phone with Chief Franks in Miami Springs," Chief Burke said. "Head up there, pronto. Tell your wife to plan to turn in tonight without you."

I called the Missus and then checked out a jalopy. An hour later, Franks met me in his lobby. I said, "That was fast."

He walked me to his office. He stepped behind his desk to an icebox and poured us a couple glasses of cold water. I said, "Did you go to Miami for a search warrant?"

Franks smiled. "Didn't have to. Bruce Keyes came through for us. Walked it to the regional Prohibition commissioner."

"Same guy who got the warrant for Monk and Paxton." Then, "Is Keyes coming?"

"No. He fought me, but I want this to be local, Nate. The Feds don't always understand subtlety. Sometimes they come in like those bulls running down the street over in Spain. I'll be damned, I lose this guy."

Franks said he'd picked up a couple barbecue sandwiches. "Then we'll sack out for a while. Then we'll be out under the stars. Okay with you?"

After we ate, Franks walked home, and I caught a few hours on the sofa in his office. I took off my jacket and stretched out. Franks had a small desk fan. It helped move the hot air a little, and the quiet drone of its motor helped me to sleep. Mostly. The mooing quit around ten-thirty.

I was eating ice cream outside a sweets shop on Flagler. The cold ice cream in the summer heat made me sweat under my fedora. But the chocolate was heavenly. Until it wasn't, because Franks was shaking me out of my dream.

Must have been the cows that made me dream of ice cream. I jumped up, grabbed my fedora, and threw my coat over my elbow. Franks said, "It's just after midnight right now. I know it's hot, but we gotta wear our coats. The rain's done, and It's nearly a full moon. Reflect right off our white shirts. They might as well be lit lanterns."

We stepped into the night air. It still felt like it was in the eighties. I'd knocked back a big glass of ice water when Franks woke me up, and that helped. And I'd made a trip to the john. No telling how long this stakeout would take.

Mosquitoes flew in the open window of Franks' sedan and buzzed around our heads. Franks waved them away. I've said they mostly leave me alone. Tonight, they didn't. Maybe they were drawn by the candy cig I had in my mouth. One found the flesh on the back of my hand. Last thing he did. But he got a good bite before I rubbed him into paste.

We pulled into some trees near the gate of Curtiss Field and stepped out.

"It's just the two of us," Franks said. "You can see I wasn't kidding that there's not a lot of places to hide. I've got two nightshift guys back at headquarters watching the sky for the aeroplane."

We opened the big gate and then closed it behind us. On the left side of the long airstrip stood a long garage shed with about ten doors. To the right stood a smaller shed. Atop it, a long cloth cone fluttered weakly in the light breeze. Franks said, "It's called a windsock. Lets the flyers know the wind direction and strength."

The heat lay on us like a blanket. Franks motioned to me, and we walked behind the small shed. I looked out toward the airstrip, and then up at the full moon. I touched Franks' elbow and then pointed up. I said, "Why Gregg is going tonight. Needs the moonlight. Gotta be able to see the runway."

I guess we stood for close to an hour. More than once, I ran my finger across my coat and felt the outline of my rod in its holster under my armpit.

Behind the shed was a fence, and on the other side, we saw black shapes and heard snorting and heavy breathing and an occasional moo. Now and again, a tail would move in the half-darkness and swat a flank. Sorry, ladies. When it comes to skeeters, better you than me.

The sweat must have added two pounds to the weight of my suit. But the breeze had picked up a bit. Helped a little. Hoped we didn't get rained on.

We heard the whine of an approaching vehicle. Franks and I pressed against the side of the shed and peeked out.

Down at the far gate, a service truck, its lights out, had stopped about ten feet in front of the gate. A man in a cloth driving cap stepped out. He lifted the latch, then got back in and slowly drove forward. Right toward us.

I heard a whispered, "Damn." Franks pushed the both of us back farther into the shadows.

But the truck veered to the left and aimed at the long garage shed. It turned and backed up to one of the doors. The man got out. Even in the growing darkness, there was no question. It was Gregg, all right. The son of a bitch.

He couldn't see us on the side of the shed. We saw him finger a big ring of keys. We heard a big click and a door rolled up. In the moonlight, we could see a little bit inside the shed. We saw a propeller.

We heard the sound of a crank being turned. The truck moved forward. Out of the darkness of the shed, a contraption began to emerge. One big wing on top and another on the bottom. A line of rope attached it to the front of the truck. Soon, the aeroplane was lined up on the strip, and Gregg had moved the truck back.

The breeze had picked up even more. I looked up. The moonlight illuminated large clouds that slowly crossed the dark sky.

Gregg wrestled a large, cumbersome shape out of the truck. He loaded it into an opening on the side of the plane's body.

Something was happening. The guy was melting into the shadows. I looked up. A cloud had moved across the moon. The air strip was dark, and the end of it vanished into the night.

Gregg looked up at the clouds, too. He took off his cloth hat and slapped it against his thigh in frustration. He leaned against the plane.

Franks looked at me. Then, at the sky. That big cloud in front of the moon was already moving. It would be dark for just a few seconds. This was our window.

I reached into my coat. Franks took out his piece and pointed it in front of him.

"Gregg. Police."

Gregg already had some practice in shooting coppers. Almost before the chief finished the second of the two words, Gregg had his own piece out and had started blasting into the darkness.

The sumbitch got lucky. I heard a grunt. In the corner of my vision, I saw Franks go down. He'd never gotten off a shot.

I didn't have time to think. I was emptying my own revolver in Gregg's direction. Just like Gregg, in the darkness, I didn't know if I'd hit him. I was thinking probably not, because he had run around to the other side of the aeroplane and was climbing in. I started toward him, but he fired at me. My left shoulder exploded. My gun flew out of my hand, and I dropped to my knees.

Through the haze of pain, I heard the engine fire up. The cloud had slid away, and the strip again was bathed in bright moonlight. The aeroplane lurched forward, and the whine changed pitch as the thing headed down the airstrip. I saw it come off the ground. The engine noise began to fade.

Then, in the distance, I heard a sputter. Then silence. Then a loud thud. Then I don't remember.

* * *

Bright lights. Daytime. A face. Out of focus. Then in focus.

I pulled apart my dry lips. "I must be in heaven."

The Missus rolled her eyes. Okay, so I'm not very original.

She held out a coffee cup. Could it be? It was. "How'd you get Cuban out here in Miami Springs?"

She started to open her mouth, but I heard a male voice somewhere. "You're downtown at Jackson Memorial." It was Dirk Monroe.

"I made the biggest mistake of my career, letting you and Franks handle this yourself." That was a different voice. To my left, Bruce Keyes stood against a wall. He took a puff of his cigarette. I croaked, "It was Franks' call."

Dirk said, "I might have made the same call. But it probably was a bad one, in retrospect. Nearly cost Franks his life. And nearly cost us one of our best men." He sighed. "But some things you don't learn in a book. Franks is a better police chief for it."

"Franks is okay?"

Keyes said, "Lucky you and Franks didn't bleed out. The patrol guys Franks had watching the skies from their headquarters heard the shots, then they heard the aeroplane's engine conk out, and they heard a thud. They couldn't tell where the thing dropped, so they figured they'd start at the airstrip. They found you guys. Didn't wait for an ambulance. Loaded you up and one of 'em drove you two all the way here."

I instinctively started to reach for the coffee with my left hand. I couldn't move it. Most of my shoulder was wrapped tight in bandages.

"Gregg clipped your collarbone," Dirk said. "You'll ride the desk for a couple months. Franks got it in the leg."

I croaked, "How bad?"

Dirk said, "Bullet hit his fibula." I knew from my coroner friends that that was the bone in his shin that looked like a violin bow.

"Hits the other bone, the tibia, Franks maybe never walks again," Burke said. "Hit an artery, he'd have bled out right there on the airstrip. As it is, he's on his back for two weeks, and he'll use a cane for a while."

The Missus had worked the cup into my right hand. I'm a lefty. The next few weeks were going to be interesting. I clumsily brought the cup to my mouth. The sweet, nutty coffee was divine.

"What about Gregg?"

Dirk said, "He's off the board."

In my mind, I saw the face of Bailey Monk.

"Took them an hour to cut him out," Keyes said. "The thing dropped down about a mile past the runway. Flipped over. A lot of the bottles broke on impact, and the ground was soaked. Amazing it didn't blow up from the alcohol. I guess it's because there was no spark. The plane dropped into mud. And the engine already had quit anyway."

"Quit?"

Dirk Monroe smiled. "Don't know how you did it, Nate, but you maybe just made history. First policeman ever to shoot down an aeroplane."

"Shot it down?"

"Glenn Curtiss himself was out there at sunrise. Not happy about the way things happened. Said he'd be making sure his manager wasn't so trusting. He's smart enough to know this probably won't be the last guy tries to use the airfield to fly hooch somewhere. They don't need the headaches.

"You're the luckiest shooter in Florida. We know from Franks' gun that he never got off a shot. So had to be you, somehow put four holes in the fuel tank. Curtiss said the metal ripped just enough for the gas to pour out. Once Gregg took off, the tank probably emptied in a minute. Gregg never knew anything was wrong until the propeller quit. Gregg's widow said—"

"Shelley."

Keyes said, "The assistant Miami Springs chief went out to tell her. We agreed. We go out there, Feds, friends of Monk and Paxton, it's like rubbing a cigarette into her neck. We were happy to beg off." He smiled. "Damnedest thing, Nate. Whoops. Strangest thing. Sorry, Mrs. Moran. Uhh, the assistant chief allowed as how Mrs. Gregg didn't seem as broke up as you'd think a lady would, her husband lyin' dead in the mud."

I said, "Charlie Reed. That'll happen when your hubby puts a hit on your boyfriend."

Keyes said, "The widow said Gregg flew the plane just a few times. Curtiss said a seasoned pilot might still have brought her in on a glide. Said Gregg probably panicked when the engine quit and steered it right into the ground. You know it's been raining out there just about nonstop. Gregg was trapped upside down. Drowned in a foot of water. How's that for justice?"

Indeed.

"Where was he going?"

Dirk said, "Well, Nate, why you were out there in the middle of the night? Because—"

"I know. Crime never sleeps."

Dirk gave me a smile. I'd beaten him to it.

Keyes said, "Shelley said he was making a special late-night delivery for a preferred client. Rancher up toward Kissimmee. Not near anything. Owns half the county up there. Gregg figured it was easier to use his flying machine than take his chances on the roads. Rancher even had an airstrip."

I said, "Gregg did a lot of work, and went through a lot of danger, and then ended up doing the big sleep. All for some bottles of hooch?"

"Well, this was fifty bottles of King George the Fifth's best Scotch. You could spend three days in a downtown hotel for what one bottle costs. The rancher used to get it regular when it was legal, and he really missed it.

Didn't care what he paid for it now. We can't get the rancher on anything. But the guy paid Gregg in advance. So, he's out more than a few Simoleans. His problem."

Dirk said, "Chief Burke's heading over to Monk's house now. Give the news to his wife and kid."

Rest now, Bailey Monk. Rest.

A nurse was at the door. I said, "Any chance I can get some grub?"

"Nothing but soup today. Maybe somethin' solid tomorrow. I coulda lost my job just letting in the coffee."

I said, "Soup. Okay." I knew it wouldn't be okay. It's hospital food.

Dirk said, "Heck of a job, Nate. Heck of a job. You made the whole department proud."

I smiled weakly. "Just trying to do my job. And save my own keister."

The Missus spoke up. "Gentlemen. Can I have a moment with my husband?"

Everyone stepped out. The Missus took the coffee cup from my one good hand and laid it on the side tray. She leaned in, making sure to angle around my shoulder, and gave me a big smooch. A long one. It was better than the coffee. Heck. It's better than anything. I felt her wet tears on my cheek.

Her voice cracked, she whispered, "I ever lose you."

She lifted her head and, through the tears, let out a big smile. The one that makes her look like an angel.

A Note from the Author

Sources

(Unless otherwise credited, most of the material for these stories came from historical features written by the author for *The Palm Beach Post*.)

A Search Warrant/Monk

Inspired by the deaths of Robert Knox Moncure and Franklin R. Patterson, Jan. 18, 1930, West Palm Beach, Florida.

Palm Beach Post coverage, January-April 1930.

Adam Williams, Manager, Airport Policy, Aircraft Owners & Pilots Association.

Florida Archives, Florida Secretary of State

Robert Moncure III, Boca Raton, Fla.

Stuart McIver, *Dreamers, Schemers and Scalawags.* 1998, Pineapple Press, Sarasota.

City of Miami Springs

Miami Springs Historical Society

Glenn H. Curtiss Museum, Hammondsport, N.Y.

The Storm/The Cemetery

Based on the great 1926 Miami Hurricane.

L.F. Reardon, *Florida Hurricane and Disaster 1926.* Lion & Thorne Publishing, Tulsa, Oklahoma, 1926

Erika Lee, professor of History and Asian American studies, University of Minnesota

"I Had a Better Year"

Inspired by Babe Ruth's 1930 Florida visit.

The Roof Garden
Tangentially inspired by the film, "The Greatest Show on Earth."
"Sarasota's Circus Legacy Lives On!" May 22, 2017, Deborah Walk, Assistant Director of Legacy and Circus, John & Mable Ringling Museum of Art
Miami Herald coverage, opening of Columbus Hotel, 1926
Howard Kleinberg, "Holiday football has a storied Past in South Florida," *Miami Herald.* Dec. 29, 1998
Buddy Nevins, "The end of an Era," *South Florida Sun-Sentinel*, Jan. 6, 1988
Ca' D'Zan, the Ringling Museum and Home, Sarasota

Hypocrites' Row
Inspired by the many stories of Prohibition, and the inability to enforce it in South Florida, as well as the 1929 murder of gangster "Fatty" Walsh at the Biltmore Hotel in Coral Gables.
Sally Ling, *Run the Rum In: Rumrunners, Bootleggers and Stills.* 2007, History Press, Charleston, SC

The Gulf Stream Pirate/A Hanging
Based on the life, exploits and death of rumrummer James Horace Alderman, the "Gulf Stream Pirate."
Hal Caudle, *Hanging at Bahia Mar.* Wake-Brook House, Fort Lauderdale, Fla., 1976
Records of the U.S. Coast Guard Board of Inquiry, and U.S. District Court trial. National Archives, Southeast Region, Morrow, Ga. Visit by author, April 29, 2006
Audio interview of Jodie Hollinsgworth, 1962, Fort Lauderdale Historical Society
Joe Crankshaw, "Finding God on Death Row an Old Story," *Miami Herald*, Feb. 9, 1988
Attorney David A. Kleinberg

Tamiami Trail/The Mosley Gang

Loosely based on the life, exploits and death of John Ashley, Laura Upthegrove, and the Ashley Gang.

Hix C. Stuart, *The Notorious Ashley Gang.* St. Lucie Printing Company, Fort Pierce, 1928

Ada Coats Williams, *Florida's Ashley Gang.* Florida Classics Library, Hobe Sound, Fla., 1996,

Alice Luckhardt, *O. B. Padgett: A Florida Son.* Lulu Press, Morrisville, N.C., 2014

Porto Rico

Pan American Airlines advertisements and timetables, 1925-1930

Dr. Neil Stringer, DDS, Naples, Florida

The Cigarette Girl/The Flying Machine

Monte Chase, Vintage Propeller Collection, Mandan, N.D. (notplane-jane.com)

Dr. Jeffrey Torine, Sarasota, Fla.

Vintage plane pilot Brad Ammann, Manhattan, Calif.

Whiskey aficionado Howard Newmark, Boca Raton, Fla.

Epigraph courtesy Dr. Paul George.

The 1920s slang terms used in these adventures came from the following sources:

"How to Sound Like the Bee's Knees: A Dictionary of 1920s Slang," *The Atlantic/The Wire*, Oct. 19, 2012

"1920's Slang Dictionary," Al Capone's Dinner & Show, Kissimmee, Fla.

"59 Quick Slang Phrases From The 1920s We Should Start Using Again," thoughtcatalog.com

The "-30-" at the end of a Nate Moran adventure is a nod to the old-time practice in which reporters, when they typed up stories, put "XXX" at the bottom to indicate the end. Because "X" is the Roman numeral for ten, the practice later morphed to typing "30."

   -30-

Acknowledgments

The author hopes these tales will inspire you to learn more about Florida's amazing history, and not just the sordid parts.

Thanks

Howard Kleinberg (1932-2023)

Archives of *The Palm Beach Post, Miami News* and *Miami Herald*

Florida Historical Society, Historical Society of Palm Beach County, HistoryMiami

National Archives

Library of Congress

Arva Moore Parks (1939-2020)

Stuart McIver (1921-2008)

Ada Coats Williams (1920-2014)

Rodney Dillon

Debi Murray

Dr. Paul George

Sue Gillis

Patsy West

Louis Park

Scott Eyman

Lou Ann Frala

Alan Orloff

About the Author

Eliot Kleinberg is that rarest of Floridians: a native. Born in South Florida, he spent nearly four decades as a reporter, including more than 33 years at The Palm Beach Post in West Palm Beach. In addition to covering local news, he also wrote extensively about Florida and Florida history, producing two separate weekly columns. He has produced fourteen books—and co-wrote or contributed to several more—all focusing on Florida. He separately runs a blog on better writing called "Something Went Horribly Wrong." He is a frequent lecturer and is a member of several historical societies. The son of longtime prominent South Florida journalist Howard Kleinberg, he graduated from Miami-area public schools and the University of Florida. He and his wife are the parents of two adult sons and live in suburban Boca Raton, Florida.

AUTHOR WEBSITE:
www.ekfla.com

SOCIAL MEDIA HANDLES:

https://www.facebook.com/eliotkleinbergbooks

https://x.com/eliotkfla

https://bsky.app/profile/eliotkfla.bsky.social

Also by Eliot Kleinberg

Peace River

Palm Beach County at 100: Our History, Our Home (with *Palm Beach Post* staff and Historical Society of Palm Beach County) (2009)

Wicked Palm Beach: Lifestyles of the Rich and Heinous (2009). The History Press

Palm Beach Past: The Best of Post Time (2006). The History Press

Weird Florida II: In a State of Shock (1998, 2006). Florida Historical Society Press

Black Cloud, 2003 (paperback 2004). Carroll & Graf. Reissued 2016 by Florida Historical Society Press

Our Century, the Post's history of Palm Beach County and the Treasure Coast in the 20th Century (2000) (Primary writer)

War in Paradise, true stories about Florida in World War II (1999; reissued 2005). Florida Historical Society Press

Weird Florida (1998; reissued 2007). Longstreet Press/Florida Historical Society Press

Historical Traveler's Guide to Florida (1997; reissued 2006). Pineapple Press

Florida Fun Facts: 1,001 fun questions and answers about Florida (1995; reissued 2005). Pineapple Press

Pioneers in Paradise: West Palm Beach, The First Hundred Years, with Jan Tuckwood (1994; reissued 2004). Longstreet Press

235